FACE THE STORM

MATTHEW BECKER

AETHON THRILLS

aethonbooks.com

FACE THE STORM

Aethon Books
www.aethonbooks.com

Print and eBook formatting: Kevin G. Summers. Cover art: Steve Beaulieu.

Published by Aethon Books LLC.

ALSO BY MATTHEW BECKER

RUN

DON'T LOOK DOWN

FACE THE STORM

For Caroline & Marian

May you grow up to be women
the world writes stories about.

PROLOGUE

"I need to tell you both something," I said, wording it as carefully as I could. "There's going to be a big change ahead, and we're going to have to be brave."

Nico and Maria, recognizing the seriousness of my tone, stopped listening to their Toniebox and faced me. I came into their bedroom and squeezed myself down between them on Nico's bed, the mattress squeaking a vain protest.

"Mom!" Maria squealed, lunging to retrieve the Ghost Spider figurine that I accidentally dislodged.

I waited until she hopped back onto the bed. "Do you remember the night dad didn't come home?"

Of course they did.

They nodded apprehensively. These poor souls had already gone through more than any kindergarteners should have. They were strong and fierce and battle-hardened—all qualities I loved but wished they never had to learn. Parents are supposed to make life easier for their kids than they had had it. That's the entire point.

I never understood those complaints about how previous generations of eighteen-year-olds went to war and now current generations just did dances on TikTok. Wasn't that exactly the sign of society moving forward? We had all gotten too comfortable.

Things had gone so well for so many people that now they were pining for olden times when life was tricky because hard times provide opportunities to prove yourself.

As someone who had proven myself over and over, it wasn't worth it. It never is worth it.

I realized I was just procrastinating talking to the kids. Letting my mind wander to anything but the next discussion. Two pairs of expectant eyes looked up at me.

I took a deep breath and grasped one of each of their hands. They say kids grow up too quickly, but these little hands, they were still so small in mine.

"Look..."

CHAPTER 1
VERONICA

Night, March 13

"Ben, I'm home!" I slung my small bag over the coat rack and slipped off my high-viz fluorescent running shoes. They were caked in mud and sticky sap. Ben would be upset with me for not taking them off outside the house. He loved order and cleanliness. His darkest fits of anger—never physical, of course, and never directed at the children—were reserved for when a family member intentionally made a mess.

Not great when living with two young kids and, well, me. I never cared about mess. I always felt like I had more important things to think about. You want to leave your shoes out? Sure, go for it. Don't clean up your room? Doesn't affect my life.

Anyway, I had a pretty good reason for the mess tonight.

I couldn't believe that I was so naive that six months ago I blissfully thought I was done with violence forever. I could remember the night clearly. The kids had gone to bed and Ben was 'resting his eyes', to use his euphemism for falling asleep before he'd fully accepted bedtime, so I had gotten up out of bed and snuck downstairs, avoiding the creaky spots in our 1940's Old Town Alexandria townhouse.

I'd plopped down on our couch, a nightcap glass of milk in my right hand. This wasn't unusual. I often snuck back downstairs for a bit of me time. Time to yourself, just simple quiet time, was hard to find as a parent, so I enjoyed spending an hour in the dark on my own, listening to a podcast or reading a book on my e-reader.

But that night I noticed I hadn't locked the deadbolt. We had a code lock as our main, but anyone could steal that information, so I always made sure the deadbolt was set before we began the kids' bedtime routine.

The bolt was unlocked. A jolt of adrenaline had surged through me but faded as quickly as it had emerged. The memory had popped into my head: I'd triggered the code-lock and then turned away, distracted because Nico was laughing uproariously at Gobby's antics on their favorite TV show, *Spidey and His Amazing Friends*.

I had forgotten a security measure. Never before in my life had that happened.

I sank myself further into the couch and considered why. How could I have forgotten?

Easy. Because I didn't need to remember. No one had ever found me. The sense of relief that flooded through me was like nothing I had ever experienced. For the first time I allowed myself to accept that my future did not have to include my past. I could just be myself. I wasn't going to abandon all security measures—the gloves were staying on—but maybe I could breathe a little easier.

I didn't read or listen to anything that night. I just sat in silence, fully appreciative of what I had, and what I made it out of. I was Veronica Walsh, well-respected mathematics professor at Georgetown University, married to the love of my life, mother of my beautiful twins, and with a lifestyle that afforded me time for my own interests beyond work and motherhood.

I had a genuine life of my own and no one was lurking in the shadows waiting to take it from me.

Or so I thought.

I never knew how close the shadows really were, or that sometimes it's not what hides in the shadows at all. Sometimes the danger stares straight at you and smiles.

I had to run after confronting Jeremy Wiles at Pierce Mill went wrong. Did I know that disappearing likely meant my entire past would come out? I probably did. Not surface level, in-the-moment, knowledge. But deep down, I knew anything that brought attention to myself could bring all of my past out. The thing is that I'd do it again because it meant Ben and Nico and Maria were safe from Jeremy. That Francisco was so close to finding me was a shock, but nothing compared to my own birth father showing up in the hospital after I'd almost been killed. The best was saved for last, though, when my own husband was the one to wear a wire and get Jeremy Wiles to confess and finally end the threat.

Even after all of that, I thought life would return to some semblance of normalcy. I could do the private eye thing, and national interest in me would eventually run its course. There would always be something else shiny enough to distract the public.

Then Mikaela Alonso came along and changed everything. A widow, a friend, a sister-in-law. When she arrived for the first time on our doorstep all I thought was that she had an interesting story and maybe I could help. Her husband being part of a group of college students involved in the cover-up of a deadly accident ten years ago and that she sought me out because she was Ben's half-sister was not on my bingo card. But now that we had stopped Jacob Jordan, albeit only after he killed a United States Senator and several others, it was time to look forward. Mikaela was going to be fine, she'd stay in the hospital a day longer but would be released with no lasting damage.

Stella appeared at the top of the stairs, peering down toward me. "Oh, Stella, I didn't realize you were still here," I said, waving up to our babysitter. She was a slight woman who should have used a cane but steadfastly refused. Whip-smart and endearingly earnest, she had become our favorite go-to for babysitting ever since the death of our good friend Miranda.

"The kids are up here. They're watching their shows." She pointed her head backward, indicating Nico and Maria's shared bedroom. Soon enough they'd be asking for their own rooms to go along with their own tablets—I still couldn't believe we gave in on that one.

"Hi mom!" Two voices in unison called down.

"Where is your father?" I called back.

Stella shrugged and shook her head as neither Nico nor Maria responded.

"Did he not come back at all since earlier?" I glanced down at my phone. Nine o'clock. Six hours since I left the house, heading off toward World's Edge and our showdown with Jacob Jordan.

With Jacob Jordan headed to jail, and my newly discovered sister-in-law Mikaela safe and under supervision overnight at the hospital, I could exhale the deep breath I realized I had been holding in for weeks.

What Jacob said of this shadowy cabal that Senator Billingsley and the Belles were involved in, well, that could just wait for another day. A familiar, lingering sadness took the place of the exhaled carbon dioxide in my chest. Jacob Jordan really had thrown his life away.

When he was arrested after the botched assassination attempt on President Leishear, I was distraught. But after we uncovered the truth that he was an unwilling patsy, I'd felt such a surge of relief.

Turned out to be even worse. That poor kid.

Was it slightly problematic that I still felt bad for him? I considered it just being human. Not that those out there who only saw me through a black and white lens would agree. Another notch in their "she's a psychopath!" screeds on YouTube. I knew I was consuming more of that content than was healthy, but I wanted to know what people who didn't like me were saying. It was easy enough to hear from fans, see my name dropped as an inspirational figure who escaped the clutches of a violent upbringing, yada yada yada. But I knew that while the groundswell of positive public opinion still held, there was a significant minority who hated me. The memorable lines stuck with me: *She murdered people in cold blood on the orders of a crime lord. There's a reason there is no age restriction on murder convictions here. Once a killer, always a killer. Death follows you wherever you go.*

Did it matter that I hadn't perpetrated any such wanton violence in decades? Nope. Redemption arcs are like nicknames. They don't get to be autobiographical. They exist only in the minds of others. I wasn't about to lose sleep over it, but it still hurt. Only an actual sociopath wouldn't care.

"No, I haven't heard from him," Stella said, bringing me back to the present.

My mind started to race. Where had he said he was going? He hadn't, had he? I remembered him saying he had an idea. What was it about?

We'd been talking about Senator Billingsley, and exactly why he was at World's Edge in the first place. I racked my brain. He said he thought he knew who could help. I pulled out my phone and called him. His smiling face stared up at me as I willed him to pick up. Come on, Ben.

Nothing.

"He didn't answer? That's not like him."

I took a deep breath and let it out slowly. "No luck. I'm sure it's fine—he lost track of time and assumed I was still here." I ushered Stella down the stairs and helped her get her things and depart. She looked like she wanted to say more, but I needed her out

I wasn't sure it was fine. But I wasn't going to say that out loud. We Walshes always dealt with issues internally. Well, until the last few months, when our lives were turned upside down.

I tidied up downstairs before heading up to see the twins.

There was a time when they would have come running to the door, pushing and shoving to be the first one to give me a hug.

But that part of their childhood had come and gone. Earlier than most, since they were only just six, but I didn't mind. I was never one of those parents who agonized over their kids growing up. Watching your kids grow is a blessing, and every day they get more interesting. Why would I want them to revert back to something they were before?

Nico paused his tablet as I walked in. After a raised eyebrow from me, Maria followed.

"It's way past bedtime, isn't it?" I said, forcing my tone to be steady. "You've had a big night, haven't you?"

"We had mac and cheese for dinner! You never let us have mac and cheese," Maria scolded.

"Who do you think told Stella to give you mac and cheese?" I laughed. "Times up, though. Jammies and brush your teeth." I clapped my hands twice and they jumped up.

We were blessed with the twins. Older parents loved telling us about how they'd become terrors once they were teenagers. But isn't that just part of parenting? Telling younger ones that they're unprepared for the next stage. *Just wait until she walks. Watch out, the 'threenager' stage is coming. You won't be ready for…*

It was all a bore. This was why it was hard being friends as adults. Fellow adults without kids, however well-meaning, couldn't understand. But those with kids, well, they were almost worse. You end up with a small, close-knit group.

I sat with the two of them as they fell asleep, keeping my phone hidden but on high, my entire body—*and mind*—tensed and ready for Ben to call. When they were down, I went into the kitchen and made myself a steaming mug of hot chocolate and took it out into the living room and finally surrendered to my exhaustion and collapsed onto the couch.

I hadn't allowed myself to think all the intrusive thoughts that had been running through my head ever since I stepped through the door. But two hours had passed since I put the kids to bed. Two hours of lying on the couch waiting for the door to open, or my phone to ring.

There was no more time to wait. I dialed a number I'd become far too familiar with. Detective Brown picked up after a single ring. "Hi Veronica, is Mikaela doing okay?" she asked.

"This isn't about her." I took a deep breath. "Detective, we have a problem."

CHAPTER 2
ELAINE

Evening, March 16

"What's going on with Georgetown? How much shit can possibly go on here?" Elaine Iverson hustled behind her senior partner up one of the neighborhood's iconic brick-paved sidewalks.

Detective Brown replied with a scowl and a quick shake of her head.

The pair walked along a small street east of Tudor House, with the sun just barely peeking through the clouds. An idyllic location, if you could discount what they were about to see.

Elaine pulled the metal gate open in front of the house where Detective Brown stopped. A single officer stood at the top of the concrete stairs between a pair of blindingly white columns, signaling they had the correct location. Elaine didn't know much about houses, but the home in front of her, its bricks speckled white, bleached by the sun over decades, screamed wealth. A giant evergreen hugged the front corner of the house, with perfectly manicured branches all trimmed to be the exact same size.

All Elaine knew was that someone, presumably this officer, had called in to report a deceased individual found during a wellness check. There must be some reason that homicide detectives were coming, but Detective Brown hadn't shared that with her. She had been short-tempered and on edge for three days, ever since they learned that Ben Walsh was missing. "You can't even enjoy a win for five damn seconds," she had lamented to Elaine. "Hope to God he's just out blowing off steam."

Seventy-two hours had passed, and he was clearly not just out blowing off steam.

"Detectives." The officer nodded to them as they approached. "Come this way." He opened the door and stepped inside the house.

"Watch your step," Brown said, leaning down to pick up a pair of plastic booties. Elaine followed suit, trying her best to focus on what was ahead, instead of the gorgeous foyer. They walked down the entryway hall and turned into the living room. Elaine had always thought the fact that blood smells like copper was just one of those things exaggerated for effect—that there really was no good description, so copper was just the best they could do.

But now she recognized again that smell that had become too familiar this past week.

It was hard to think it was exactly a week ago that Chief Branaman had informed her she was now working with Detective Brown. She'd grown up ten years in the last week. Not every detective can say they took down a serial killer—*is that technically what he was?* —in their first week. She didn't embarrass herself, she showed she belonged. She could do this job, all the naysayers —many inside her own head—be damned.

Elaine looked around the space, taking it in. The living room was almost entirely covered by a white speckled rug, with a matching white armchair and ottoman opposite a brick fireplace, next to a small tv stand and accompanying television. The anachronistic juxtaposition of the sprawling size of the room and the tiny TV made Elaine start to chuckle before swallowing it down. The large east-facing bay window looked perfect for letting light stream into the house each morning.

What caught Elaine's eye, though, was an elderly man sprawled out across the rug, lying face down in a pool of blood centered under his torso that almost reached the far wall. A long smear of blood tracked from the body toward the front door. He had thin white hair that blended in with the rug. A loose dark flannel robe covered most of his torso and matching pants completed the outfit. His feet were bare.

"Who…" Elaine's voice came out only a whisper. "Who kills an old man like this?"

He looked like he woke up in the morning and decided to dress as the perfect stereotype of a grandfather. Wiry tufts of hair rose out of his skull at odd angles. Cracked spectacles lay inches from his head.

"Take a breath. Look at it dispassionately. His name was Daniel Flint. He was a professor at Georgetown. What can you tell me?"

Elaine took a deep breath. She studied the placement of the body, looking for any clue she could grasp. Clearly Brown had spotted something already. Her tone told Elaine as much. *What does she see?* "Gunshot to the back. Excuse me, gunshots. Two. He fell forward and bled out…" Elaine let her voice trail off, waiting for Brown's validation.

"Yes, and?"

Damn. And what? What was he doing?

"Was he defenseless?" Brown prodded.

Of course he was. Wait. His right hand was partially open, but empty. Elaine looked again and finally realized "What's under his arm?"

The corner of Brown's mouth flicked upward in an ephemeral smile. "Very good. You can't see it at a glance, but his right hand and arm are covering up something, aren't they, officer?" She glanced over at the officer who had let them in.

"You're right. There's a fireplace poker perfectly hidden underneath his arm."

Elaine scanned the room. "No evidence of a fire."

"Exactly. But notice where it likely came from." Brown pointed next to the fireplace.

Well, yes, obviously. What point is she making?

"Within arm's reach of where he was shot." Elaine realized. "He knew he was in danger, and reached out for it, but the shooter was too fast."

"We'll need Zeke to help us with the minutiae, but yes, that seems likely," Brown said. Pointing at the blood on the floor, she added. "I'm a little concerned here."

"Concerned, how?" Elaine asked.

"That's a lot of blood. And what's the other big problem here?"

"That streak of blood." This time Elaine knew the answer immediately.

"What does it look like?"

Elaine nodded. "That looks like he was dragged."

"I agree, but from where? The blood stops by the door. And there's too large a pool underneath him to think he was shot anywhere but right where he fell."

Elaine felt her stomach begin to sink. "Are you saying…?"

"Yes." Brown read her thoughts. "I think that's from someone else, who was dragged out of here. I bet we'll find a few drops outside. This blood is not only from Dr. Flint."

CHAPTER 3
ELAINE

Evening, March 16

"What was so important that we had to push our dinner back?" Belinda Leishear asked, as she carefully cut a piece of medium-rare steak and lifted it to her mouth.

"You know I'm not supposed to talk specifics of my cases, mom," Elaine said. She picked up her wine glass, swished the liquid around, then thought better of it and put it back down. No matter how many times she told her parents she didn't like wine, they still insisted on ordering it and making sure there was a glass for her. They loved presenting opportunities for their daughter to disappoint them. Why else would they insist on weekly dinners at fancy restaurants that were always *accidentally* scheduled right after she got off work, so she wouldn't have time to change into something more appropriate?

This is our daughter. Yes, she's a police detective. No, she's not interested in politics. I know, right, but you can't choose family.

"I heard there was quite a to-do over by Dumbarton Oaks in Georgetown," Curtis Leishear tutted.

Elaine sighed. "Okay, look, dad, since you obviously already know, a Georgetown professor was killed in his home and we only just found him. Happy?" She shot respective pointed looks at each of her parents.

"Dr. Flint was a pillar of the community. An icon of his field. His loss will have devastating effects on that campus."

Elaine stared at her father. She knew she shouldn't have been surprised. They were Leishears after all. A political super-family. The next dynasty, if the media were right. Nothing happened in this town without them hearing about it. But it had been barely an hour since she left the crime scene, only a few hours more since it had been called in. How did he already know who the victim was?

She knew what he was doing. Asserting once again, that he could have full control over her job and career if he wanted to. Because she'd chosen a small career. A measly one, with little influence. Not befitting of her family's good name. She knew she couldn't hide her background, but using her mother's maiden name at least kept it off the lips of anyone she met. Not that mom ever used it. She knew what marrying into this family would mean and jumped in with two feet. Elaine wasn't given any such option. When your father is governor of the state of Maryland and your uncle is the president of the United States, you are expected to behave a certain way.

It hadn't always been this way. Her father had been a loving parent during her childhood. It was only after he was elected to his first public office that everything changed. She became an afterthought, an unwanted clinger-on who could potentially ruin his career. He catastrophized every action she took, panicking that it would be the start of his downfall. She believed that the only reason they had any relationship at all was only because he wanted to keep her close.

Elaine had only just learned more about the victim while riding in her Uber to dinner. Dr. Daniel Flint, professor emeritus of mathematics at Georgetown University. An expert in the field of mathematical analysis, a term that meant very little to Elaine. Isn't it all analysis?

He was something of an icon on campus, where he was infamous for his single patched-up sweater vest he wore to every class. Over the course of many years, it had turned into more patch than vest.

Then, the elephant that had been in the corner of the room ever since she realized it. Mathematics at Georgetown. He was a former colleague of Veronica Walsh. What might DC's favorite femme fatale have to do with his death?

"Crime just gets worse and worse here, doesn't it? No matter what you do to stop it, evil will always be out there," her mother said, sagely.

Thanks mom, very deep. Very insightful.

But they didn't raise a shy, retiring type. "Nationwide, the murder rate fell precipitously last year, actually," Elaine said. "And I just played a major role in stopping a multiple murderer here in the district, so I'd say there are some things you can do."

"Poor Andrew." Her father shook his head ruefully. "You never think it could happen to someone like him."

"What do you mean by 'someone like him'?" Elaine asked. "Uncle Dennis—I'm sorry, *President Leishear*—was shot at just last year and a congressman was badly wounded. Political violence is always a present danger. Plus, didn't you hear about all that shady sh—stuff that went down at the Belles' mansion?"

"A bit of playful roughhousing that went too far." Her dad waved his hand dismissively. "Nothing more to that."

Nothing more.

As if a Senator drunkenly driving a golf cart over a cliff, killing two college students and permanently disfiguring a third was *nothing*. A horrifying accident that would have captured the imagination and become a trite and exploitative eight-part docuseries in the years following. But instead, Ulrich and Yvonne Belle and Senator Billingsley covered it all up. No accident, no deaths, no news. None the wiser, except for grieving parents paid handsomely for their silence.

"Oh, come on, dad." Elaine groaned. "We discovered a huge

cover-up, to the extent that college student deaths were hidden, as if they just disappeared. And the one thing that Jacob Jordan did have right despite his actions: that could not have just been the acts of the Belles. They didn't have the money or pull to do that. There's something way deeper at play."

"What do you think was happening, then?" Her mom leaned in, suddenly very interested. She was never one to miss any gossip and took no care to hide her glee at the topic.

"We think—Detective Brown and I—that the key to all this is why Senator Billingsley was there in the first place," Elaine said.

"What do you mean?"

"Well, how did he end up in the middle of a gathering of college students? I don't think it's reasonable to assume he was invited over for the same event, do you?"

Her mom steepled her fingers and wiggled them gleefully, like a villainous cartoon boss. "Ooh, okay, so you need to see what he was doing there and then you think you'll crack the whole thing? What fun!"

Her mom was born to be a socialite. Gossip was her currency, and she could never have enough. "That is the idea."

"Is this why that Congresswoman has been making statements?"

"What statements?" Elaine did her best to avoid the Beltway media, save for news she absolutely had to know.

"Didn't you hear? Moore, that… lady from Boston. She went all over the networks talking about how Senator Billingsley deserved to die."

"Mom, there's no way she said that." Elaine shook her head.

"She really did. She said it was *'indicative of Congressional corruption'* or something like that." Her mom huffed, as if the notion was far-fetched. "She's the one who's always on television angry at Senator Thresh."

"Do you think you actually can?" her dad asked.

"Can what?" Elaine responded.

"Solve it. Unearth the conspiracy."

"Of course. Do you think I can't?"

"I'm just asking." Her dad raised an arm and shrugged.

Elaine could feel her father's judgment bearing down on her. Of course he didn't believe she was going to solve the case. He never believed in her. Why he even helped get her this job in the first place was beyond her.

CHAPTER 4
ARCHON

Night, March 16

Archon picked up his mobile phone, touching the number in the bottom of his contact list. He waited as the phone rang. He didn't appreciate being made to wait, even just for a phone call. He wasn't a man who waited.

He knew all the stats, that if you read in the dark it would make your eyesight worse, the strain eventually wearing them out over time. But he liked his setup, his quiet nook with the little lamp, bookcases filled with books flanking his chair, where he could sit peacefully each night and read. Or, in this case, take care of some business.

Three rings before a voice finally answered. "Sir."

"Talk to me. I need an update."

Archon heard a long sigh.

"It's not great, sir. We're as exposed as we've ever been." The newest member of the organization talked with a certainty that he had not yet earned. "This shit with Billingsley, we should have dealt with all of that long ago—"

"Don't tell me what we should have done," Archon growled. Who did this guy think he was, lecturing Archon on something he knew nothing about?

"Sorry, sir." The man paused. "Well, Jacob Jordan turned out to be more of a problem than we thought he would be. We believed he just wanted simple revenge. We were wrong. When he was arrested, he said far more to the police than we would have liked, although he still knows very little, of course."

"I'm aware of this, and you know the pains that I have taken to make sure no one can see the full picture."

"Yes, sir. I'm sure you've heard about Flint over in Georgetown by now?"

"I have."

"What should we do?"

"What we always do. We stay in the shadows, and we minimize any risks. I had our friend take care of that McDowell, the Belles' neighbor. They'll never find him."

"I don't like that those detectives are going to sniff around us."

Archon rolled his eyes. It wasn't just him. Cowards, all of them, each in their own way. Not one had the stones to be him. "We'll watch closely. And if we need to strike, we strike."

"Would you really? Those detectives? Even—"

"We do what needs to be done. No questions asked. You know this. If they have to go, they have to go."

CHAPTER 5
VERONICA

Night, March 16

Three days. Three full days since Ben didn't come home. Seventy-two hours of agonizing, paralyzing fear.

When I disappeared last year, I understood intellectually that Ben and the rest of my family would be worried about me. Same as when I ran away from home as a teenager. Someone goes missing, family members worry. It's a time-honored formula. Cause and effect.

But there really is no way to describe the truth of it. The every-minute-of-your-life fear that encompasses everything.

I kept my emotions in check that first night when he didn't come back. There could be some reason. It would be okay.

When he wasn't there in the morning, the fear set in, churning and hardening in my stomach like cement. If I go missing, there's a reason. If he goes missing, something bad has happened.

The kids went off to school and I scoured the area. I went everywhere he would go. Capitol Hill, Old Town Alexandria, Rock Creek Park. His favorite winery in Clifton. The escape room he liked so much in Georgetown. No stones left unturned. I did everything but call in the National Guard.

But no sign of him. Phone off. No credit card purchases. Nothing.

He was here and then he wasn't.

The doorbell rang and I rushed over to open it.

"I..." Mikaela took a deep breath and didn't finish her sentence. Sometimes there were no words.

"I'm so scared," I whispered, ushering her in.

"We'll get through this," she responded, a steely determination in her voice. If anyone understood me right now, it was her. She had been to Hell and back in the past two weeks.

She approached me ten days ago because her husband, Tony, was missing and she had heard of my fledgling private eye business. At least, that was what she had told me originally. It turned out she had a very different reason for seeking my family out, which she divulged to Ben after Tony's body was found. Ben was her biological half-brother, the product of an affair between Ben's father and her mother.

Tony had last been seen by his car on the Woodrow Wilson Bridge and the police believed he jumped, and it was only a matter of time until they found his body. Mikaela had been devastated, believing that their fights over infertility issues had driven him to suicide, and pleaded with me to help her find the truth. I had wondered how much her clinging to manufactured hope was an attempt to keep the guilt from overwhelming her. When we found out he was a victim of Jacob Jordan, she at least had felt some comfort in knowing it wasn't her fault, although all that came apart again when he explained that he *hadn't* actually killed Tony. Tony did jump off the bridge on his own, but only because of the demons that had haunted him for a decade, ever since he wasn't able to help save Jacob's sister Janet, along with two other Georgetown students, from toppling over the side of the cliff at The Belles' mansion, World's Edge.

We hadn't had a chance to talk about how that news had left her, because after I dropped her off at the hospital for a concussion check—*all clear!* —Ben didn't come home.

I pointed at her stomach as we both sat down on the couch. "How are you doing?"

She placed her hand down gently. "Everything looks good. The doctors did an ultrasound just to make sure, and they said it looked normal." She smiled, but her eyes flashed with pain.

After everything, I still couldn't tell if it was karmic justice or just a nasty quirk of fate that Mikaela discovered she was pregnant only days after losing Tony. That was what prompted her to go to Ben and tell him the truth. She wanted him, and us as a family, in her life.

A week and a half later and the roles had been reversed. Now it was my turn to need her.

"What's the latest?" Mikaela asked.

"Nothing." I shrugged and shook my head. "No clues as of yet. No leads of any sort."

"What do the police say?"

"Detective Brown says she can't get involved because it's not her case. She does homicides, not missing persons. Some detectives came by, did their little song and dance about how adult men going missing often was benign, but that they'd follow up as best they could."

"He drove, didn't he?"

"Yes, but they haven't found the car either. No GPS. I just keep going over what he said. We were talking about this conspiracy, cabal, whatever you want to call it. He said he had a thought about who might know something and got excited and ran out the door. Why didn't he just tell me where he was going?"

"You know why, though," Mikaela said.

I leaned my head back and sunk into the couch. "Because he wanted to impress me with his detective skills," I said.

"Men and their boneheaded plans."

"The only thing I can think of is that photographer." I sighed.

"Which one?"

"The one who took the picture of you and Ben outside the hotel room."

"Oh, sorry, of course. What do you think they might know?"

"Well, if this was someone sniffing around Ben, then maybe they were watching him? Although I feel like I'd have seen if he or she were watching this house. The other thing is that Francisco said he'd found something out and wanted me to know as soon as possible."

Mikaela sat up straighter. "What was it?"

"That's the thing. He wanted to tell me right after he helped us catch Jacob, but I didn't have the time or wherewithal for it. Then I got a message from him later that night saying he had to go away for a couple of days to check on something, and that he wanted to talk in person so we could talk when he got back. I think he was going back to San Salvador, and I have absolutely no idea what he is doing there. I don't even know if it's related. I do know that he should have arrived back here today, or maybe tomorrow."

"You have to talk to him as soon as possible, then."

Francisco and Ben. My childhood best friend and my husband. The two men upon whom I had relied most in life. Francisco would know what to do. He always had before.

CHAPTER 6
ELAINE

Morning, March 17

"Come on Ivy, let's move." Detective Brown's voice carried a level of urgency that Elaine had rarely heard before.

"What is it? I literally just got here," Elaine said. She dumped her backpack down onto her desk chair. She had complained the first few times her senior partner had called her Ivy, but the nickname was growing on her. Not unlike ivy might, as Detective Brown had gleefully pointed out when Elaine said so out loud.

"Zeke." Brown nodded toward the hallway. "We've got answers already."

"Oh, shit."

Dzikamai Jackson, Zeke to his friends and co-workers, was a young crime scene technician who had garnered immense respect from everyone in the department for his professionalism and keen intellect at such a tender age. His boyish mid-twenties looks combined with his humorous mannerisms had made him an infamous member of the police community. While he did not run the crime scene unit, he had risen fast and was now trusted to handle the most important cases.

He must have something big to have called them so early.

Elaine had learned that Zeke was meticulous in his work, and, unless absolutely necessary, would wait until he could confirm every last detail before passing information on.

Zeke looked up as they entered the lab and strode over to greet them. Two other techs that Elaine didn't recognize milled around, trying to make themselves look busy but failing badly.

Detective Brown peered around. "Where's Wills?" she asked, looking for Zeke's supervisor.

"Out this morning. A Saint Patrick's Day event at his kids' school, I think," Zeke said. "But here, this is what you came for." He ushered them over to a small side table.

"What, no witty remarks this morning?" Elaine asked. "No comments about your own greatness? How we all should bow down at the altar of Zeke Jackson because of how impressive you are?"

Elaine had immediately gravitated toward Zeke when she started working here. Besides the fact they were of similar age, he was the only person she'd met so far who she felt like she could be real with. Behind the joking cockiness was a trusted friend she could go to when she was overwhelmed.

Zeke sighed. "Didn't feel right after this."

Elaine felt her blood run cold.

"What is it, Zeke?" Detective Brown asked.

"I've got a lot more to get through, but I fast-tracked this part. You were right on your hunch, Emilia," he said.

Elaine noted that he called her senior partner by her first name. She wondered how that relationship had grown to such a level.

"More than one victim," Brown said, nodding along.

"Obviously, most of the blood belonged to Dan Flint, but there was also some blood that wasn't his—the blood by the door. We can't test every single drop for which DNA is present, so I don't have an answer to your follow-up question of how much blood, but we do know who the other blood belonged to. We got a sample of his DNA on record to use for elimination purposes during the case last year." His heavy eyes met Detective Brown's as Elaine watched on.

"Damnit. No."

"Yes," Zeke replied. "Ben Walsh."

Detective Brown's phone rang as they left the lab. Elaine glanced at her screen and saw the caller ID. The chief calling? Something else must have happened. She watched silently as Brown answered.

"Sir? Okay, yes, sir. Coming immediately." She abruptly hung up the phone.

"What was that about?" Elaine asked, wondering if she wanted to know the answer. News in this line of work was rarely positive.

"They have an ID for a man at the scene."

"Wow. Hope the witness' memory is good."

Detective Brown glanced over. "No, there's a video. That's what we need to see immediately."

Elaine followed two steps behind as they rushed back to their office. By the time they reached the chief, she was struggling to hide her panting. She didn't want either of them knowing just how little physical exercise she did.

"Come on in," Chief Andrew Branaman said. He closed the door behind him as the two detectives sat down, and he walked around his desk and took his own seat. He swiveled his monitor so they could see it. A video was set up, full-screen, ready to play. "Ready?" he asked.

Elaine nodded as Detective Brown did the same.

Branaman pressed play. The screen was black for a second, then a grainy picture filled the space.

"Is that from a Ring camera?" Elaine asked.

"I think so, or some lower-tech version of it, considering the quality."

"What are we looking at?" Detective Brown asked.

The chief held a hand up. "Wait one second."

When the video ended, Branaman clicked back to the start and replayed it once more in full. "Tell me what you see," he said, sitting back.

"A tall man walking down the sidewalk holding a gun, his face partially obscured," Detective Brown said.

"That's 31st Street, the street Dr. Flint lived on, just a few minutes before the time of death," Branaman said. "But tell me what else you see."

"What are we meant to be looking for, sir?" Elaine never liked the I-know-it-but-want-to-test-you leadership. If he wanted them to notice something, he should tell them, not sit around waiting as if he was a teacher staring at a pupil struggling with a tricky problem at the chalkboard.

"Ethnicity."

"A tall Hispanic man holding a gun." Elaine realized what he was getting at. "Walking toward a house that had Ben Walsh in it."

Branaman made reassuring eye contact just as Elaine wondered if she had spoken out of turn. But, no, he clearly already knew about Ben Walsh. Zeke must have told him first. "It looks like Veronica Walsh's friend. He's our guy."

"He was with us later that day. He showed up at World's Edge," Elaine said.

"Oh, I'm well aware."

"I'm sorry, sir," Detective Brown said, contrition heavy in her voice. "We shouldn't have let him slip away."

"You all were distracted with Jacob Jordan. I get it. But there will be no more mistakes. Bring him in. Now."

CHAPTER 7
VERONICA

Morning, March 17

Dan Flint, dead.

Not just dead. Murdered.

I could not make the notion make sense in my mind. Of all the people in my life that I ever, ever, feared for, he had to be at the bottom of the list. A kindly old gentleman. A mathematician. Who hates someone like that enough to kill them? What could he have possibly done to warrant such violence?

He wasn't mega-rich. He didn't have flashy material wealth. He had a Georgetown townhouse, sure, and that alone made him more well-off than most. But, despite its outward appearance, it was a shabby old place, full of knick-knacks and trinkets.

I sat at the dining room table, enjoying the rising sun beaming in from the eastward window. If we had a cat, he or she would be resting luxuriously on the square of light on the tile floor. But alas, despite my fondness for those little beasts, Ben had no interest in pets.

I read the email from the Georgetown University president's office probably a dozen times. When they fired me, someone had clearly forgotten my personal email had been added to all the listservs and no one got around to checking.

Shot and killed by an intruder. An intruder doing what?

Death follows you wherever you go.

Maybe the online posters were right. I'd kept death at arm's length for so long. Not anymore.

Miranda Belle. I couldn't keep her out of my mind recently. Even though I hadn't been there when she was killed, it was a direct reaction to something I started. Could I have left it alone? Let Jeremy Wiles win the Presidency? Sure, but that wasn't me. And because of who I was, the deepest core of what I was as a human being, Miranda was dead.

There were too many names, too many faces from my adolescence to remember them all individually. The people I killed all blended together in my mind now. But they all were supposed to be dead. The rules of engagement, set up by my own father, said I was acting righteously. Not Miranda, though. Miranda should be alive.

Now it was Dan Flint's turn. A friend who was never privy to my previous life. A person who should not have fallen victim to wanton violence. Could it also have been because of me?

The photographer could wait. I needed to find out what happened to Dan Flint. I needed to rule out anything to do with Ben. They wouldn't let me in on all the details, but I would be able to ascertain pretty quickly if it was a viable lead or not.

I could call Detective Brown, but she'd likely shut that down quickly. What I needed was to go over to the scene. Do my sweet talking, badger the right officers, and get info that way. Give Francisco a call if that didn't work.

I grabbed my coat and pulled the door open.

CHAPTER 8
ELAINE

Midday, March 17

"What the—"

Elaine was just raising her fist to knock on the door when it swung open, and Veronica Walsh almost barged right into her and Detective Brown.

"Why are you here?" Veronica asked, her voice wary as her eyes flitted over to Detective Brown.

"Can we come inside?" Detective Brown pointed behind Veronica towards the still open door.

"Did you find my husband?"

"No."

"Then I don't think we have much to talk about, do we?"

Detective Brown lowered her voice. "We found something," she said, her tone conciliatory.

Veronica huffed and she turned around and waved for them to enter. Elaine followed her partner's lead, slipping her shoes off as she entered. She shut the door and looked at Veronica, standing in the middle of her living room, making no motion to sit.

"Talk to me," Veronica said.

To Elaine, this was the hardest part of the job. Searching for clues, examining evidence, all of that didn't require emotion. That was easy enough. But talking to victims and their relatives? She would rather face a firing squad. How could she understand Veronica right now? Elaine figured it must be like parents who don't know how to explain their bond to their children to those without. The last meaningful relationship she had ended junior year of college, when she walked in on her girlfriend tangled under the covers with her roommate, their clothes piled in a heap on the floor.

Only her closest friends even knew about her sexuality. "Gay marriage is old news," her childhood friend Aimee had told her last year over mojitos. "Literally no one cares who you date, I mean it."

She wasn't wrong. But she also wasn't a member of the most public-facing family in the country. It wasn't that Elaine was worried about anyone's reaction, it was that she didn't want a reaction at all. She didn't want anyone looking at her, no matter the reason. Don't give her father another opportunity to wonder if he'd have been better off childless.

Maybe one day. In the future. But for now, as she tried to read the emotion in Veronica's face, she might as well have been reading a foreign language.

Detective Brown explained the blood they found at Dan Flint's house. Elaine watched Veronica's eyes as she listened. Veronica had an incredible poker face, but every so often her eyes would flash.

"How much blood?" Veronica asked.

"We can't tell," Elaine answered.

Veronica leaned against the dark wood banister. "Okay, but what does this mean?"

"Well, we know your husband was there," Elaine started.

"Yes, I pretty well figured that out. And don't even think about telling me not to investigate, because you know how that will go." Her eyes dared either detective to say otherwise. "So, what is it? He was there, was hurt—we don't know how bad—and then what? You didn't find him in the house, you don't know if he was physically capable of movement. You've got nothing to go on right now."

"That last part isn't exactly true," Elaine said.

"What do you mean?"

"We do have something to go on," Detective Brown answered. "We have a suspect in custody. We arrested him this morning, just before coming here. We're letting him sit a bit before we see if he wants to talk."

"Okay, then by all means, go. Leave me here and go do your jobs," Veronica said.

"Don't you want to know who we arrested?" Elaine asked. How could she not want to know?

Veronica paused, looking back and forth between the pair of detectives. "Ah. That's what this is really about. You want to tell me who you arrested. Go on, then."

"He's not going by his real name right now," Detective Brown said. "But we've arrested your friend. I believe the name he's going by here is David Rodriguez?"

CHAPTER 9
VERONICA

Afternoon, March 17

I didn't have time to be angry with Francisco. What was he even doing near there, and how could he be so reckless to be caught on a household security camera holding a gun?

But those questions would have to wait. Of course he didn't kill Dan Flint and hurt Ben. Someone framed him. And whoever did it also knew what happened to Ben.

I did consider for a second if I was wrong. Could Francisco have killed Dan Flint? If it weren't for Ben's blood there, I might have believed it. If I had to pit my surety of Dan Flint's lack of enemies against my trust of Francisco, Francisco would win every single time. Anyway, all Dan had to have was one enemy, right? There isn't a quota of enemies you have to reach before one is allowed to kill you.

Beyond that, though, Francisco killing Ben? It beggared belief. He wouldn't do that, not even for my birth father. Right?

Yancey Portillo. The thought did make me pause. How much of our recent marital strife did he know about?

I grew up under his thumb. The only difference between myself and the rest of the organization was that my last name was also Portillo. Growing up in a criminal enterprise warps your view of the world. That's not exactly groundbreaking to say. Hierarchies, both spoken and unspoken, ruled the roost. Whether internal or external, who held power over whom was all that mattered.

In a way, it's not much different to the rest of the world.

More violence, though.

I got my start early. But what do you do when your home is attacked? You stand your ground. If deadly force is brought upon you and yours then it's entirely reasonable to fight back. But escalation only leads one way. Violence begets violence.

So, in hindsight, when an ambush killed my brother Kelvin, we should have been prepared.

It wasn't that there was an open role afterward that needed filling. I didn't step into somebody's shoes and make their role my own. I created a role.

I became a monster. A demon. Our enemies' worst nightmare. The epithets expanded as quickly as the bodies dropped. Every time I struck, leaving a severed pinky as my calling card, my legend grew. My *anonymous* legend. Because, aside from a handful of my father's most trusted lieutenants, no one knew who the mysterious assassin who did Yancey Portillo's bidding was. There was talk. Oh, there was plenty of talk. I soaked it all in, savoring every snippet of conversation, all done within my earshot because they felt sure that it couldn't be me.

But I had to admit that it grated that I couldn't enjoy my notoriety. I wanted to be known. The only satisfaction I truly found was the moment when some poor soul who had fallen foul of our organization realized I was the one they had been fearing all along. Of course, they couldn't tell their story after I was done, so that didn't help.

I didn't become more lackadaisical; it was a deliberate deviance in pattern. I *wanted* to get noticed. But, being a young teenager, I didn't exactly think through the plan. I thought I could get noticed, have word get passed around, and then everyone would know I was the assassin. I'd get the fame, and then we'd see what happened next.

It didn't turn out exactly that way. That all our rivals were pooling their resources, putting aside differences to work to try to find out who I was, was exactly what I wanted. If I hadn't been kidnapped in a ham-fisted attempt at retribution, maybe I could have enjoyed that fact. But instead, my own pinky was chopped off, my father threw me to the wolves and wouldn't negotiate for my release, and I escaped, ran, and never looked back.

Until my past caught up to me last year, when my father's decades-long search for me collided with Jeremy Wiles' presidential ambitions.

That was when Francisco re-entered my life, and he had been a constant source of support ever since.

He should not have been so reckless. What was he even doing? Was he still following Ben even though we'd agreed he didn't need to? No. The last thing he said to me before we parted ways near World's Edge was that he had to tell me about this photographer who took those pictures of Ben.

Why didn't he tell me immediately after?

That's who he must have been following. But how to find out that information now? If he wanted to call me from wherever he was being held, he could ask for that. But he hadn't, and all communication would be monitored anyway. That was probably why. Plus, clearly the detectives knew who he really was.

He was one of my problems on an ever-growing list of things I needed to fix. But he was lower down the list. He would be fine. Now I needed the photographer. He leapt back up to the number one spot.

Which meant I needed the man who wrote that story. The reporter who used the photo.

I'm coming for you, Gary Tiller.

CHAPTER 10
ELAINE

Afternoon, March 17

Elaine kicked off her shoes and stretched her feet out onto the ottoman. She leaned her recliner as far as it could go. Laying her head back, she breathed out a deep sigh. She glanced at her phone, checking that the timer was running, before setting it down on the small circular table next to her.

After spending all night at the scene, then the morning with Zeke before finding and arresting David Rodriguez, Detective Brown had told Elaine to go home for two hours. Elaine wanted to argue, but she could feel herself just about ready to fall asleep standing up. Safe in the knowledge that her timer wouldn't let her sleep too long, she closed her eyes.

She couldn't believe their luck in actually finding David Rodriguez, who Detective Brown kept calling Francisco. Despite briefly meeting at World's Edge, Elaine didn't know much about the man they were charging with murder. Her partner didn't know much more but filled her in on what she did.

Francisco had been in Yancey Portillo's organization and grew up in the shadow of Veronica. They were close friends and then he had risen through the ranks after she disappeared. By the time they heard whispers of her being alive and having made a life in

Washington, DC, he was Yancey's go-to for making enemies disappear. He was entrusted to find out if she really was his long-lost friend and then report back.

But after Veronica was shot, he stayed in Washington, a sure violation of immigration law, not that he'd likely come in legally to start with. The problem was that they had no proof that he was Francisco Orellana. His documents claimed he was David Rodriguez. So, to the legal system, they had arrested David Rodriguez, a US citizen. The Salvadoran authorities possibly had more, but they weren't forthcoming.

The phone rang right as she was dozing off. She leaned over with a groan and grabbed it. "Detective Iverson."

"Hi, Elaine, how are you?"

She pulled the phone away from her ear and looked at the caller ID. *Of course.* "I'm doing fine. How are things, Senator?"

"Just peachy, I'd say, and bless your heart for asking." Elaine rolled her eyes. Gary Thresh was the senior senator from Maryland, for goodness' sake. He didn't need to pretend to be a good old boy from the South.

He's going to make me ask. "So, what can I do for you?"

"You know, now that I've got you on the line, I do have a small request—if you wouldn't mind, of course."

"Of course," she replied through gritted teeth. Just because her dad was the governor of the state and her uncle the president of this whole damn country didn't mean that she was a middle-woman, just as a backdoor way of getting a message to the more important men in the family.

"Look now, you were the one who arrested that sick son of a bitch who shot Andrew, right?" As if he couldn't remember that it was her, with a little help from Detective Brown, Veronica Walsh, and, well, Veronica's friend that they just arrested. As if her uncle hadn't been telling everyone who would listen that his niece captured Senator Andrew Billingsley's killer.

So much for the partial anonymity using her mother's name gave her.

"That's right, sir. Myself and a few others."

"I've been hearing that this deranged individual has been saying some pretty crazy things."

"What kind of things?"

"Oh, all sorts of baloney about how he was trying to uncover some underground network of blah, blah, blahhhh." He held the final note for emphasis.

Elaine knew all about this so-called baloney.

When Jacob Jordan's sister, Janet, fell off the cliff down to the Potomac at the Belle family's aptly named World's Edge mansion, the Belles and their conspirators initiated a cover-up almost instantaneously. Two Georgetown University students were dead, and Janet sustained injuries she would never recover from. Surely that would have been front-page news?

You'd think so.

Janet Jordan was whisked home after she was released from the hospital. Diagnosed with akinetic mutism, she was kept hidden away, as if she had never existed.

Someone, presumably the Belles, had been paying the family continuously for their silence. Elaine knew that it wasn't just them, but the other families as well.

Jacob wanted revenge on everyone who had ruined his sister's life. He killed Senator Billingsley, after having forced him to flee in a terrifying cat and mouse chase around Roosevelt Island. He killed Bridget Lowe, one of Janet's friends who had cajoled her into getting onto that fateful golf cart before the Senator drove it over the edge—before saving himself, of course. Even before all of that, he had killed the Belle family—Ulrich and Yvonne, along with their daughter Tracy in a car accident. That it was seen by none other than Jeremy Wiles, who then blackmailed Jacob into becoming a part of his own murderous plan, still boggled her mind.

What odds could you get that Jeremy would have been there in Potomac Yard, coming out of the now long-gone movie theater at the exact time Jacob veered into the Belles and forced them off the road and down into that pond? And that he immediately saw the possibility of blackmail rather than just turning him in? The tiniest coincidence, and maybe none of this would have happened otherwise.

"What does this have to do with me?" Elaine asked, with no interest in the forthcoming answer.

"My constituents are concerned about allegations of impropriety."

What a meaningless word salad. "I can understand that, and my partner and I are looking into this. If there was an orchestrated cover-up, we're going to uncover it."

"No, no. You misunderstand me." He sighed deeply, a long, exasperated sound like he was explaining physics to a toddler. "If word leaks of an investigation like this, it will undermine faith in our elected officials. It's hard enough with damned Representative Moore running her mouth all the time, trying to whip up her base. Baselessly, I might add."

Elaine couldn't believe her ears. "Hold on a second, are you telling me to *stop* investigating?"

"What's the benefit in getting everyone jumpy only to come up with nothing at the end? No one will believe you—they'll think the big scary cabal got to you too. All this does is hurt the country."

"And instead, we let people who do this sort of thing off scot-free? That's not what this country is supposed to be about."

"God, you sound like Chamique Moore. The things I could tell you about that firecracker. Spouting off left and right. But, little lady," he chuckled. "That's what this country has always been about."

Elaine could feel the heat emanating off her forehead. "Little lady?" she repeated. "Senator Thresh, let me remind you of something. You called me because my father is the governor of your state, and my uncle is the president, and because of this connection you think I owe you my ear. But what you fail to comprehend is that this is a two-way street. You don't think the *president of the*

United States will hesitate to kick your sorry ass to the curb? All he has to do is say one word in Maryland, endorse one opponent of yours, and you'll never be in Congress again."

She ended the call and slammed her phone down. It bounced on the cushioned armrest and settled on the floor, face up. So much for a nice relaxing couple of hours. She probably shouldn't have hung up on a Senator. But then, he shouldn't have been an asshole.

One thing was certain, Senator Thresh had just catapulted himself to the top of her suspect list.

CHAPTER 11
VERONICA

Afternoon, March 17

What was Ben doing at Dan Flint's house?

I racked my brain, trying to think of what he said when I last saw him. He'd run out the door so quickly, and not long after the detectives arrived. What were we talking about?

I always prided myself on my memory. I could keep strings of digits in my head easily, constructing uncrackable passwords without ever having to write them down. Why couldn't I come up with what he said? I was just talking to Mikaela about it last night, what was going on?

My mind felt fuzzy, the normally crisp visions in my memory coming out blurry. I could feel myself starting to wallow, a behavior I was unfamiliar with. I paced around the downstairs, stopping in the kitchen, then the dining room, but with no real direction.

I had to snap out of it. I had a lead. This reporter.

It wasn't hard to remember his name, what with his *"What will vindictive Veronica's vendetta be this time?"* line burned into my mind. Does that sort of juvenile attempt at being clever actually draw readers in?

Like any good reporter, he helpfully had links online to all of his various social media accounts. A quick message, worded the same to each account and leaving my phone number, and I had no doubt he'd respond. I had that kind of draw.

Six minutes. I snatched up my phone as soon as it lit up. "Hello, who is this?"

"This is Gary Tiller, responding to a request by someone claiming to be Veronica Walsh," he said with an inflection in his voice I could only describe as pompous.

"Hi, Gary, this is Veronica Walsh. I—"

All pomposity vanished quickly. "Jesus Christ. It really is you. I was sure this was a hoax. Umm, what's up?"

"I need to know how to find Jamie Simon."

"Who?"

As if he didn't know exactly who I was talking about.

"Don't play with me."

He snorted. "Oh, I know all about you. I wouldn't dare. Who knows what you'd do to me?"

I did not appreciate the sneering tone, as if he didn't believe what he was saying. I was more of a celebrity than a threat to him, clearly. "You know that my husband is missing, right? And you're taking time out of my day dicking around just for the fun of it."

"Wait, he's what?"

"Are you not a reporter?" I thought it was a safe assumption that he knew what he was doing.

"I've been… busy. I don't have to explain myself. What happened?"

"He's missing. That's what happened."

"But…" he sputtered. "Why aren't the police out there trying to find him?"

"They are, you dimwit. If your spouse was missing, would you just sit back and twiddle your thumbs? Look, my husband's disappearance might have something to do with the man who took the photo of him in that hotel. Tell me how I can find him."

"How is he involved?"

"That is neither your business, nor your concern."

He produced a protracted sigh. "I can't just give up my sources. That's journalism 101."

"You're not giving up a source. We both know who this person is. I just want a way to contact him."

"Even if I wanted to, I couldn't, okay? All I have is an email address. I met up with him and he gave me the photos."

"Why didn't he just email you the photos?"

"I don't know!"

"What did he look like, then? Give me the email, tell me what he looks like, I'll go find him myself, and you can go back to your mediocre existence."

"You really know how to make friends."

I didn't respond. Let him think again about who he was speaking to and fill in his own blanks.

"Okay, look, fine," he finally said, before reading off a string of letters and digits belonging to a clear burner email address.

"And what does he look like?"

"Hmm, tall, thin guy. Wore a big cross necklace that looked like he always had it on. Definitely some sort of Hispanic origin."

CHAPTER 12
JAMIE

Night, March 17

Luck and clever improvisation. That's how most of life worked.

He hadn't meant to get caught on camera by Dan Flint's house, but as soon as he realized he must have, he knew it was only a partial image. He wasn't looking directly at that home security camera of the house a few doors down. He only realized it was there after he'd already passed it, when a crow cawed from high in a nearby tree and he'd been startled enough to look around.

No one would look closely for him. Not when his build was just similar enough, especially to the untrained American eye, to a much better-known criminal in the area. One who had a direct tie to one of the men in that Georgetown townhouse.

Luck and improvisation. But also, readiness. Knowing how to remedy a situation and understanding that anything can go wrong. And boy did that go differently than planned.

The police don't look gift horses in the mouth. Time is always against them. They solve the crime in front of them. So why would they look any further when he so conveniently dropped a few strands of Francisco's hair on the floor when he broke back in later that night before the police showed up?

It was key that no one looked further. Francisco Orellana would be charged, certainly be found guilty, and that would be that. A criminal killing a respected man. Outrage, and likely a spirited and entirely bad-faith debate about immigration, but no more.

Luck. It might just all be pointing his way.

CHAPTER 13
FRANCISCO

Night, March 17

Despite the trajectory of his life up to this point, Francisco had never been inside a jail cell. It looked exactly like he expected it would. A cot, four walls, a drab and soul-sucking gray color. All the hits.

It wasn't great, but he didn't mind. When your life was in constant danger for as long as you can remember, you grow to appreciate any situation in which you're still breathing.

But he needed to get out, and fast. He didn't trust the phones, so he couldn't use his phone call to tell Veronica what he needed to say. She needed to know the threat she faced.

He mentally kicked himself for allowing Veronica to take Mikaela to the hospital alone after World's Edge. He should have pulled her aside and told her right there. But he didn't want to make a scene in front of the detectives, and he assumed there would be time to do it later.

The plan was to call her the next day, but after coming so close to divulging his news, he realized he needed to check again and be one hundred percent sure. He left her a quick note, saying he'd be gone for a few days. No harm done, what he'd discovered was urgent but not frantically so. He would confirm, and then they would discuss together what to do next.

Coming back from his little fact-finding trip only to be arrested for the murder of Veronica's former colleague was not part of the plan.

He knew having a legitimate ID in the United States could cause him as many problems as solutions. But it was a risk he knew he had to take, and the documents, along with a little bit of hacking from a contact, allowed him to live here 'legally' as David Rodriguez as far as the government was concerned.

What that meant, though, was that his name was on his rental agreement, and he could be easily tracked if anyone knew his alias. How they knew his alias, he was unclear. Veronica would have never told anyone, but he couldn't rule Ben out. Not wittingly, since Ben was loyal to a fault, even during their recent marital issues. He wasn't built for a life of secrets, though, so it was possible it slipped out at some point.

But when no fewer than eight police officers burst through his door at ten in the morning, just as he was trying to sleep off the travel, he knew better than to put up a fight. Could he have taken them all down? Quite possibly. But was it more likely that one of them would kill him? Yes.

Plus, what would happen if he did get away? He'd not only be wanted for whatever they were there to arrest him for, but also the assaults—or murders—of eight officers. That wouldn't go away lightly.

He used his one phone call to dial long distance. Yancey should know what had happened. Despite all his history with Veronica, her father was the one he reported to. That always had to come first.

Whether a judge or court would find him guilty was one thing, but what caused him the most worry was what this photographer's plan was. Why did he go after Ben? What was he trying to achieve?

Veronica had to be the target. She was always the target. Ben and Dan Flint's involvement made no sense at all to Francisco.

She needed to know why, but he had to be the one to tell her. In person, with no one listening. The information he now had was highly sensitive and it was better if she didn't know than if she learned but others did as well. How to get to her?

The answer was clear. He had to break out of prison.

CHAPTER 14
VERONICA

Night, March 17

"Hey, um, did you see this?" Mikaela didn't bother with pleasantries when I picked up the phone.

"See what?"

"There's a news story. It's on TV right now. It's talking about your friend who got arrested." I set my fork down on my plate of takeout jambalaya and put my phone on speaker as I looked around for the remote.

"What is it saying?"

"That his real name is Francisco and he's a violent member of the gang you grew up in."

"Oh, fuck."

All of a sudden, I had no interest in turning on the news, but I grabbed my computer to see if it had taken hold on social media yet.

It sure had.

My mentions—muted since last year—were a dumpster fire.

Why I even stayed on social media, I couldn't quite articulate when asked. But internally I understood: I was unwilling to ever look weak or like I backed down. You want to hurl abuse at me from behind your stupid little anonymous screen names? Go right ahead, I'll even spread my arms wide and make myself an easy target. See those insults? They bounce off me like nothing.

But normal people wouldn't understand that, so I just said I hadn't gotten around to deleting them.

"What I don't get is who did this. Who would have leaked it?"

"Did the police know?" Mikaela asked.

"I think Detective Brown knew, so, yes I'm guessing they all do." Realization dawned on me as soon as I said it. "It must be a cop. I bet all of his documentation says he's David Rodriguez, a legal citizen here. But they know that's not the case."

I had no idea how that actually worked. If the cops knew but couldn't prove that someone was operating under a fake name, but the documents were so good they couldn't make their case, what happens? Could the documents even be that good? I hadn't exactly kept up with the state of the art when it came to forgeries. I made a mental note to go check on my go-bag and my own aliases.

This was what happened, I guess.

"He'll be deported, won't he?" Mikaela asked.

"Oh, yes, definitely." For a second my heart jumped at the thought of Francisco getting to go back home, finally being free of his assignment to watch over me for my father. Getting to see his family again.

Except he wouldn't be free. He'd just be in a different prison.

Not many people from my childhood ever went to jail. We didn't get arrested, even for the most minor of crimes. When Yancey Portillo threatens you and your loved ones, no one wants to test his mettle.

Once a young, foolhardy cop decided he wanted to rise above his station and make his mark. Francisco and I had been out together and came home to find the Landaverde twins huddled together by the swings, streaks of salty tears trickling down their cheeks.

"What's going on?" I asked.

"They arrested dad," Karla said.

It made so little sense in my mind I had to ask again. Same answer from her brother, Walter. Tomas Landaverde was pulled over and they found just under a kilo of cocaine in the trunk. I knew from experience that when this happened my father would simply chuckle, stare the cop in the eye, and wait. The silence killed them, as they filled in all the unspoken threats. Then we'd just drive off and everyone moved on with their day.

"But, how?" Francisco asked. "What does jail even look like?"

"It's just a room they put you in with no way out. There's nothing magical about it," I said.

"Every room has a way out," Francisco scoffed.

"Maybe you should be the one locked up then!" I joked, winking at the twins in an attempt to elicit a smile.

"Sure, why not? It's all in your head anyway." He turned to the Landaverdes. "I mean it, don't worry at all about your dad. He'll be out soon, and everything will be fine."

"Do you know that?" I whispered out of the side of my mouth.

"No, but do you know he for sure won't? I'm being positive here, that's what they need," he mouthed back.

After that conversation, I always wondered when Francisco's positivity was true or whether it was for my benefit.

Anyway, he had been right. Tomas Landaverde didn't even spend a single night in jail before they released him.

"Are you going to be okay? I mean, legally?" Mikaela sounded like she wanted to ask anything but that question.

I hadn't yet begun to consider that. I didn't think they could prove anything about me and Francisco, but simply his presence here would bring questions down upon me. They could probably find surveillance footage at the Irish pub where we liked to meet.

The court of public opinion would keep me safe. What an irony. No one would support deporting me right now while my husband was missing.

I never planned on doing any of this without Francisco. Being a private investigator without him to lean on felt hollow. Searching for my husband without Francisco's help was unfathomable. I was on a precipice, and despite my own strength it felt like I was just one gust of wind away from my entire world toppling down.

CHAPTER 15
ARCHON

Night, March 17

He knew he had to up the ante. Things were not going as hoped. The death of one of their own was to be taken seriously, of course, but barring anything unforeseen nothing would shed any light on him or their organization. Nothing would put their next move in jeopardy. They were laying that groundwork nicely, and he had no doubt that they would reap the benefits soon enough.

The culprit was arrested quickly, no doubt thanks to the fact that he was already known to them. But Archon could not understand why they were keeping his real name quiet, why they didn't shout from the rafters immediately that they had arrested Francisco Orellana. The name plus the backstory would drive all of the public interest. The identity of the victim would become secondary.

That's what his entire organization was about. There was no value to being publicly known. Everything they did worked best because of their secrecy. None but him even knew the number of members they had, let alone the identities.

The Princemakers worked best that way. Archon loathed the

name that a member had once dubbed them, but he couldn't argue that it did fit. Ulrich Belle had leaned in on it, and during a trip to Paris, he'd met with the Paris Saint Germain soccer team president. Their stadium was named the Parc de Princes, so Ulrich asked for a sign that he could put up in their meeting room. That sign now hung in Archon's house. He knew groups of shadowy figures working in secret weren't new, especially not in Washington, DC, but what kept them under the radar for so long was their outward ambition. They had the scope and breadth to make bigger splashes, but that wasn't their want.

The tallest blades of grass get cut first, or whichever aphorism you prefer. Why focus on world domination when you can home in on key issues? Ulrich originally formed the Princemakers as a means of keeping—and expanding—his wealth. He filled the pockets of important individuals, brought a select few into the fold, and made sure that his taxes remained unpaid.

Everyone understood that Ulrich drove the policy. But now he was gone, and Archon was in charge. He had his own agenda to set.

Veronica Walsh was going to be a problem. Archon didn't know what happened at Dan Flint's house. That Ben Walsh appeared to have been there troubled him deeply. He feared no one, but he was a pragmatist. Veronica Walsh was not someone to tangle with unless absolutely necessary.

Better to give her some reason to watch her back, just to tip the playing field.

The next step was obvious. She was beloved by the public and he understood the impulse. Deep down, we all wish that we could mete out swift retributive justice to our enemies. She got to do so, and people loved her for it.

He sat down in front of his computer. He still had a bulky desktop sitting in his study. It was simple enough. If someone ever made it this far, a heavy desktop was harder to steal. You can't slip one of those into a laptop sleeve and race away.

He typed out a quick email. It was nice to have a reporter with a friendly ear who spread his word with unfailing loyalty.

Once he clicked "send," he pushed his chair back and smiled. That would set the ball rolling. Veronica had the public on her side.

No longer.

CHAPTER 16
VERONICA

Night, March 17

So Francisco was tied to me publicly? So what? I could weather the dumb talk on the internet. That's what modern life was. Ignoring stupid stuff online.

Some people were taking his presence here to mean I was still involved in illicit dealings. Let them think that. I was more concerned about Francisco. The more everyone knew his story, the more they'd find proof of crimes perpetrated.

Best case scenario, he was deported. Worst case, he spent his life in a maximum-security prison for a crime he didn't commit.

I mindlessly scrolled through the tweets as I lay in bed with the lights out, listening to the pitter patter of rain on our window. Each night my mind and my heart staged a wrestling match. How could I possibly stay home when Ben was out there, somewhere?

But Nico and Maria were here. I owed them a fully present mother. If Ben could do that for them when I disappeared, the least I could do was be his equal.

Crash.

I launched myself out of the bed, immediately crouching down low so as not to present a target.

That wasn't thunder. *Someone is in the house.*

The kids.

I shuffled toward the door, slowly pulling it open, one hand clutching the small pocketknife—*not my go-to*—I kept in my nightstand. I paused, straining to hear anything in the silence. No point getting yourself killed rushing to protect your kids. Every mom voice inside my head was screaming at me, "Run to your children! Nothing else matters!"

But how could I know that wasn't exactly the intruder's plan?

I stretched my arm out first, presenting the most expendable target if there were someone waiting to strike. After a deep breath, I leaned my head out, peering down the hallway, the dim, obscured nightlight from the bathroom the only source of light.

A silhouette flashed in front of me. I reached an arm out, grabbed a handful of fabric, and pulled hard.

It was a child's frame. "Nico!" I cried as I pulled him close.

"Did you hear that sound?" His chin quivered as his wide eyes searched for comfort in mine.

"I did, baby. It's okay. I got you." I held onto him as I ushered him out into the hall, scanning through the dark. We hustled back into the kids' bedroom, where Maria met us as soon as we were inside.

I looked them both in the eyes, clasping one hand each. "I know I've tried to keep everything from you, but how much do you know about me when I was a kid?" I asked.

"Joey says you like to kill people, and that makes you a bad person," Maria said, her tone almost too nonchalant, like she was trying her hardest not to show how much it hurt her.

I made a mental note to find out who Joey's parents were after this was over and go have a talk with them.

"When I was a kid, I had to hurt some people who were threatening my family," I said as calmly as I could. "I am very good at protecting my family. So, you two don't have to worry, I will protect you no matter what. No one will ever harm you because I will stop them. Now, listen carefully. We're going to stay right here in the bathroom, out of sight. Remember, I've got you.

After five minutes, we're going to swing the door open and peek outside."

The old house creaked in the stormy night. Each gust rattled the windows and caused the kids to jump, and I held them tight.

"It's time," I whispered. Five minutes must have passed. I had no way of knowing for sure. "Maria, hold my hand. Nico, hold hers. I don't want you out of my sight."

Never in my adolescence did I consider what it must be like to have someone break into my home. I was the one who broke into others' houses. I snuck in, I snuck out. Everything as it was, just one fewer finger and a missing heartbeat. No time to think about fear, just doing the job at hand.

Now it couldn't stop happening. But last week's misadventure with Jacob Jordan meant I was more prepared. My discomfort in the dark was not our assailant's ally. I don't suffer anything twice.

We tiptoed down the stairs, avoiding the creaky spot on the step third from the bottom.

I froze on the bottom step. Sheets of rain were pulsing through the open space where our bay window had been. "Stay right here," I whispered. "On this stair. In my sight. Do not move."

I let go of the twins' hands and scurried over to the couch, continuing to keep my body low. With every step, shards of glass pinched and cut my bare feet like a thousand tiny crabs. When I reached the couch, I stood up straight to inspect the window. I hadn't seen what I was expecting—there was no brick, no rock lying on the living room carpet.

The entire glass window was gone. Every shard was now inside our house. No thrown object could do that. There would still be remnants, shards that stayed in the frame. This could only have been done with some sort of baton.

The glass embedded in the soles of both my feet told me all I needed to know. No one could have come inside after doing this. The entire living room was covered in shards. If there was anyone waiting in the darkness, they were outside.

What could have prompted this? My mind raced. This was too

violent to be just for association with Francisco. People on the internet have strong feelings, but not for this.

I tiptoed back to the kids, a futile attempt to avoid the shards of glass when I could already feel the blood on my soles. "What happened, mama?" Nico asked as a shiver racked his entire body.

"I don't know, little one." I pulled him close and grabbed Maria with my other arm. "Something broke our window. But what's most important is that we're safe, okay? There is no one here except us. And I know your father is out there somewhere and we're going to get him back too. Now, we're going to sit here together and let mommy think just for a couple minutes, okay?"

I pulled my phone out of the pocket of my pajama pants and raised it to my face to unlock it. Social media would tell me, I figured. One way or another.

I didn't even get that far. A text from Mikaela was on the lock screen. "I don't believe that is real. You okay?" it read. I touched to open the rest of the message. It contained a *Washington Post* link.

My jaw dropped. I swiveled away from the twins so they couldn't see what I was looking at.

A picture of me as a teenager, looking straight into the camera, grinning madly. That wasn't noteworthy. Teenagers smile. But most aren't pictured smiling while standing over a decapitated body, the blood still dripping off the carving knife held jauntily in my left hand.

I read the headline. "Veronica Walsh, Remorseless Murderer."

The public support. The bedrock of my continued existence in the country I'd grown to call home.

That would be gone. No way would they be on my side after this.

People like a redemption arc. People like messy, real lives. They want to root for an anti-hero.

But they only do so when they get to be several steps removed. The meat eaters who would never be able to kill an animal themselves. On the other extreme, the immigrant hater who has never actually met an immigrant. Most of us can only deal with the sanitized story, whether it is true or not. Not when a picture of their heroine shows up looking like a depraved lunatic. I would be willing to bet whoever destroyed our window was someone who supported me up until an hour ago.

Was that even a real picture? I certainly didn't remember any situation like it. But it didn't matter. It was out in the public eye, blazing its way through the internet before I'd even had a chance to try to stop it.

I'd learned that we all tend to block out—or reimagine—our worst memories, but surely, I would have remembered decapitating someone. But what could I do? Come out and say, "No, I swear I didn't do that, but yes, to answer the obvious follow-up, I did do plenty of similar and only slightly less gruesome things?"

The kids weren't safe here. I wasn't safe here.

Our address was clearly public now.

My husband was missing. My best friend was arrested for murder. And now my children's safety was compromised.

I shushed my sniffling kids. "It's going to be okay," I said, trying to keep my own voice from cracking. For the first time in my adult life, I truly didn't know if that was the case.

I hadn't felt like this since my kidnapping as a teenager. Since I heard my father tell them that I was expendable. The moment I realized I was on my own. I couldn't trust anyone but myself.

Now here we were again.

I had to get the kids to my parents. They then needed to go off the grid somewhere for a while. Keep them safe.

This was the only way. To keep those closest to me safe, I had to be on my own again.

CHAPTER 17
ELAINE

Morning, March 18

Elaine fidgeted in her desk chair. She stared at the open files on her computer without actually reading them. She couldn't figure out how to vocalize the feeling that had bubbled to the surface. She didn't know who to talk to, let alone what to say. Detective Brown was the obvious choice, but she didn't want to chance a negative reaction. She had only just begun to feel comfortable with her senior partner.

The evidence was there. Francisco Orellana—she'd finally learned his true last name from Detective Brown— was in the country illegally, had likely perpetrated many crimes, both here and in El Salvador, and his hair was found at the scene.

He was a bad guy, and the job was to stop bad guys from doing bad things. When it came down to it, there wasn't anything else.

But.

Was Francisco *the* bad guy here?

She worried she would sound ridiculous to Detective Brown. Would she ruin the credibility she had gained? It was a slam-dunk case. Right?

The nagging feeling wouldn't go away. But what would she even say? *I think all the evidence is wrong?* Based on what?

Knowing she didn't have another avenue to turn to inside the station, she made her way down to the crime scene lab. She shivered as she entered the sterile metal hallway leading to the lab. The interior needed to be kept clean, of course, but would it kill them to make it a bit nicer down here?

As soon as she entered, Zeke spotted her and waved her back, holding up his hand with his fingers outstretched. Five minutes. Elaine nodded back appreciatively and retreated to the cold hallway.

Unlike the people who say "five minutes" when they really mean ten at a minimum, Zeke emerged almost exactly five minutes later. "Hi, Detective, what's up?" he asked, pushing the door gently.

"I don't know how else to ask this but... do you think we could be wrong about Francisco Orellana?" She sighed deeply.

"How so?" Zeke's brow furrowed. What Detective Brown liked most about him, she had told Elaine, was that he always believed the most important thing was doing the work right. He didn't have an ego when asked if something could be wrong, and he took his craft deadly seriously.

"Look, it doesn't feel right." Elaine raised her hands in a defensive pose. "I know, I know. That's not good enough, but I just want to know if anyone else shares these thoughts."

"Have you talked to Detective Brown?"

Elaine shook her head. "I don't want her to think I'm stuck inside my own head. I wanted to see if there could be anything to it before I'd talk to her."

"Fair enough, but you can trust her with anything, okay? She won't judge."

Elaine pursed her lips. "I know that's how it's been for you, but that's not what she is around me. She watches me like a hawk, and I feel like I'm under the microscope every single time I make any move."

Zeke scratched his chin. "Okay, then. Let's get to it. The video that shows Francisco leaving with a gun, I'd give that alone a sixty percent rating. More likely than not it is him, but the quality is not high so you can't rule out it being someone else. Now that person would have to look very similar, though, and just how big a coincidence would that be?

"The other evidence," he continued. "That's trickier for your case. That is Francisco Orellana's hair. That's hard to fake, but not impossible to plant. I cannot fully rule out that it is an elaborate setup. But Occam's Razor would strongly dissuade that line of thinking."

Elaine took a second before responding. "What would you suggest?" she finally asked.

"If this is about Francisco and his relationship with Veronica Walsh," Zeke paused to look her in the eyes and confirm his thinking, "then I would say it doesn't actually matter, because he's either going to prison or getting deported. One way or the other, he's out of her life."

CHAPTER 18
VERONICA

Morning, March 18

"Look, mom, I really think you need to go somewhere. Get off the grid." I tried to keep the exasperation out of my voice.

My mother looked at me from across their mahogany kitchen table, calmly spearing a cherry tomato. "I've been keeping you safe for a long time, Veronica. Nico and Maria will be fine here," she said, placing the tomato on the top of her tongue and letting it sit there.

I didn't think I had any other choice. I couldn't have stayed at home any longer, definitely not for the night. If Francisco wasn't in jail, I could have asked him to come board up the window. He'd know how. I couldn't leave the house open like that. Old Town Alexandria was a reasonably safe place, but open windows will always attract trouble.

I had called my parents and told them the situation. They understood.

They always understood. They knew what they were getting into from the moment they adopted me. Or, as they like to put it, I adopted them the way a stray cat decides to adopt a family.

Last night I threw together a bag of kids' clothes along with their most important toys and stuffed animals, and we were on the road, driving down I-95, just a little before midnight. We arrived in Williamsburg at my parents' house at half past two in the morning, and we fell into their welcoming arms. I had told them they didn't need to be awake for us, but that just wasn't who they were.

We didn't speak much, they ushered us straight to our beds. Sleep blanketed me in the way it only can at your parents' house.

When I woke and came down the stairs, I found my mother sitting quietly at the table, sipping on her coffee, no newspaper or phone in sight. A second mug of coffee, dark green with the William & Mary cypher on it, sat in front of her, the steam still rising furiously out of the top.

Thirty minutes later, with my father and the kids still asleep, we remained stuck on the question of whether to stay or go.

"The crazies can easily find you here, mom."

Mom slowly chewed the tomato. "Honey, the crazies can find any of us, all the time," she finally said.

"This is different!" I slammed my hand on the table. Mothers always have this way. You could be unflinching in facing down a hungry lion, but no matter who you are, a disagreement with your mother will send sparks flying.

"Because of the image?" her mom asked, frustratingly calm.

I grimaced and rubbed my forehead. "You've seen it?"

She nodded, and reached her hand across the table, placing it gently on top of mine. "It doesn't look like anything you ever told us, but even if it is, this doesn't change anything for me or your father."

"It's not," I said quickly. "But how wouldn't it change anything?"

"Because you are not that girl. You left that girl behind a long time ago, so what does it matter what she did?"

How was I supposed to stay worked up when she says things like that? "Thanks, mom."

She nodded again. That practiced, maternal nod, that

conveyed more than a million words could. She always understood. "We're not going to subject Nico and Maria to any more upheaval than they've already had," she said, her tone final. "Their father is missing, and their mother is on the news for something no child should ever have to see. We will take care of them here. We will not run and hide. You do what you have to do."

What I had to do. Find my husband, maybe solve a murder in the process, and then come up with a way to get back into the good graces of the country lest someone on a whim decided to deport me.

No sweat.

The kids came down eventually, divulging that they'd been awake and just playing with their abuelo upstairs. My dad stood behind them, a palm on each shoulder. "Tell your mother what we were just talking about," he instructed.

"We love you mama, and that's all that matters," the twins recited together. Nico gave me a hug, while Maria waited patiently for her turn, before thinking better of it and joining in. My heart melted.

I felt the tears forming in my eyes, and the lump in my throat made it hard to speak. "You two are my world," I choked out. "And even though I have to go and find your dad, I know you'll be okay here with abuela and abuelo."

"But what about school?" Maria asked. "We have a math test tomorrow."

Mom gave me a smile accompanied by a shrug. *Kids.*

"I will call the school and tell them you have to be away for a little while, don't you worry." I reached out and pulled them both into an embrace, squeezing tightly until they complained.

I straightened and turned to my parents. "I better make moves." I took a deep breath but stood still. I couldn't physically make myself move away from my children.

My father walked over and gave me a gentle push. "Objects in motion stay in motion," he said, smiling. "Don't stop until everything is over."

I called the twins' teacher on the way out of Williamsburg, zipping west along I-64, appreciating, as I did every time, that Virginia had changed its interstate speed limit to 70 miles per hour. I needed speed, and what I absolutely didn't need was to be pulled over.

Miss Gordon and I had enjoyed a close relationship, but the first icy word through the phone made it clear to me that was no more. She politely informed me that if it were up to her, the kids would fail every single assignment they missed, and that murderers should get what's coming to them. I made a note to talk to the principal about Nico and Maria's continuation in that class, but that would have to wait until at least some portion of the country didn't hate me.

Social media is not real life, to repeat the ubiquitous mantra. But real-life people use social media and get their nicely packaged opinions from it. You have a slightly formed opinion, so you go online, type it in and *boom!* There's your set-in-stone view. This morning's consensus opinion was that I either killed my husband or didn't care that he was missing because someone like me couldn't have feelings anyway.

My husband. Somewhere out there.

I couldn't wrap my head around it. He went to Dan's house, something happened, and now he's gone. If he had been killed there, by whomever killed my friend, then where is his body? Who kills one person but takes their other victim elsewhere? Was it a planned kidnapping that turned into murder? If Ben was the target, how did they know he was at Dan Flint's house?

And what was he even doing there? What did he think Dan knew? Was he just going because of the Georgetown connection? He knew I was working on a case involving Georgetown and events that had happened years before and his mind went to my eldest colleague?

The thoughts swirled around in my head the entire drive back to DC—a food processor that kept getting stuck and couldn't blend all the ingredients into a cohesive idea.

I didn't stop at home. There was nothing for me there. I drove on up I-395 through DC, until I exited onto New York Avenue. A couple turns and I was in the NoMa neighborhood. I weaved my way around until I was heading north on a one-way street lined by thin but beautifully painted monochrome townhouses. I parked illegally in front of a house with a brilliant royal blue shade. Cyclists be damned, they could go around my car for a few minutes. And if any police showed up, well I had a few things to say to them anyway.

I approached the front door, slightly recessed next to the jutting living room. I watched the peephole darken after I knocked. I could've shot through the door and blown his head off if I wanted to. I told Ben about that in the past, that it's always best to put your hand up in front of the peephole just in case someone was ready to shoot. One of those life lessons passed down from my father that probably has no basis in reality. There are far better ways to break in. How do you know it's the person you're looking for? If there's anything I've learned in my decades of mathematical thinking, it's that controlling variables is what life is about. First, learn which variables are important. Then, control them.

Easy peasy.

The door opened slowly, a clear sign of his reluctance. Or so I thought.

"Hello, can I help you?" A woman's voice.

The door finally opened fully, and she stood in the frame, wearing jeans and a t-shirt with the American flag on it. Not Gary Tiller.

"Are you Mrs. Tiller?" I asked.

"Who are you?"

Smart. A reporter's wife would understand the value of information. "Veronica Walsh."

That reminiscent fear shot through the woman's eyes. It used to be reserved only for the name Alessandra Portillo. I sighed and held up my hands. "I just want to talk to your husband."

"I'm calling the police. How did you even find us?"

So much for valuing information.

"Your address is public record. It wasn't exactly hard."

"Get out." She pulled her phone out of her pocket and waved it in front of me. "I will call the police."

"For what?"

"This is private property, I don't want you here. That is trespassing."

"Okay, call the cops, then." Calling the bluff. Very few people actually want to call the police. They have to explain the situation without sounding like a crazy person, wait for the cops to come, make a statement, and then decide what to do next. It's a hassle.

She went to dial but hesitated. *Gotcha.*

"Look, what'll it take for you to leave us alone?"

Now time for the friendly, innocent-little-me, smile. "I am just looking for some information about a man named Jamie Simon, whom your husband might have worked with. He supplied a picture for a story, I believe," I added quickly. Her mouth had opened, and I could tell she was ready to trot out that stale old line about protecting his sources.

She exhaled slowly. "What do you want to know?"

"Anything you've got, I'd really appreciate it."

"Okay, hold on. I'll be right back." She disappeared back inside the house.

There was a nonzero chance she was calling the police. Easier to do it when not right in front of me.

She returned five minutes later, and with no sirens blaring in the distance, I took it as a positive sign. She held out her hand. "Here, just take this picture of him. My husband said to give it to you."

"Where did he get it?" I asked as I grasped the paper. It was regular plain matte copy paper, still hot from being fed through a printer.

"I have no idea. Just take it and leave," she said with finality, giving me one last look and slamming the door.

I make friends wherever I go.

I waited until I got back into my car to look at the picture. I had no interest in making a show for them peeking out from behind their pulled curtains.

Good thing I did. I gasped and put my hand over my mouth when I saw his face. Not dignified. Unbecoming of my persona.

But this man, Jamie Simon, could have been Francisco's doppelgänger.

CHAPTER 19
ARCHON

Midday, March 18

This wasn't going to fly. Veronica Walsh needed stopping. There is one true fear that anyone who has ever buried something lives with—that someone will come along who won't stop digging.

There was another lever to pull. He hadn't needed to do so yet, but he knew it was there for him.

Veronica Walsh still didn't understand what she was dealing with. The threads she was pulling had been intricately stitched together through years of painstaking work. Work that he was now repurposing.

The rest of the Princemakers understood the value of their organization. Money and power. As trite as he found it, Lin-Manuel Miranda was right. The only thing that mattered was being present at the table. There wasn't a decision-making table in the city where they didn't exert influence. Ulrich had almost exclusively focused on financial matters, keeping the prying eyes of the government away from his own affairs. He would throw a bone to other members, making sure a regulatory bill didn't get out of committee, or finagling a government contract to go one of their ways.

Archon had a different plan. But for now, he would let them think he was simply continuing the path that Ulrich set them down.

He twirled his lowball glass as he sat in his nook, watching the clear liquid slosh around. Stoli vodka was the only alcohol he would drink. He still wasn't used to the new abbreviated name, shortened from Stolichnaya after the Russian invasion of Ukraine—one of those things where the change brought more attention than if they had just left it alone. He could think of very few people in the States who knew that *stolichnaya* was a Russian word signifying capital city, ergo Moscow.

She would know of their reach, no doubt about it, if he pulled the lever. The groundwork had already been laid when he learned of her identity last year. You can never be too sure who won't become your enemy eventually.

Reverberations would be loud, but none would reach back to them. None ever did.

Another swallow of the Stoli. It wasn't a sure thing, but nothing in life ever was. The attempt would be risky, no doubt, and if it failed there would be hell to pay. But wasn't Hell about to come to their doorstep anyway?

By the time he finished his vodka, he was sure of it. Turning the public against her hadn't slowed her down at all. And she was too high profile to kill, what with her damned husband missing on top of her own infamy. Why did Ben Walsh have to involve himself in something he didn't understand? What was he even doing at Dan Flint's house?

For a moment, Archon had wondered if one of their own had killed Dan Flint. But no, it couldn't be. Not when they were in the midst of planning. Attacking each other wasn't unheard of—who didn't want more power? But not during a planning phase. Not when they all had agreed upon a common enemy, someone who needed to be slashed down.

In the meantime, Veronica needed a true cease and desist.

He picked up his phone. A friend's kid had taught him

Snapchat, and now that was the only way he communicated sensitive material. Forget Signal, just send a snap. He found the contact, a sleeper waiting in the wings for this moment, and typed out the short message.

Do it.

CHAPTER 20
ELAINE

Afternoon, March 18

"I have a question, but I need you not to judge it," Elaine said as she approached her partner's desk warily.

A smile spread across Detective Brown's face. "This is going to be good."

"How do you deal with the boring cases?" Elaine couldn't put her finger on it until after she talked to Zeke. She realized she just didn't believe this homicide should be so open and shut. Of course they were still investigating what happened to Ben Walsh, but that they already had the culprit? It just felt wrong.

"You don't think Francisco Orellana did it, do you?"

Well, guess she saw straight through that one. "I just realized that the only real case we've worked together so far was so high profile, I need to learn a bit how to handle the rest," Elaine said carefully.

"The slam-dunk cases. I do understand. What did you get in this for? Why police? Why homicide?"

"I grew up listening to all the politics and double-speak in my family. I never felt like anyone actually was speaking the truth. I told them that I wanted to go into a profession with absolutes."

Elaine felt her face burning as she spoke. Why did it sound so young and naive when she said it out loud?

"As good a reason as any." Brown shrugged. "But none of that has to do with looking a friend or relative in the eye and telling them that you caught the person who killed their loved one. No, it doesn't bring them back. It will never be enough. I saw how uncomfortable you were when we were talking to Veronica Walsh. But think of it this way: we are the clean-up crew after a natural disaster. We put the foundation back in place. And they are thankful for it because it allows them to move forward with their lives. That, more than anything else, is what this is about. It's not justice for the victim. They're gone. It's justice for those still living. It's closure and an assurance that it is okay to keep on living. That's what our job is. The evidence, the chase, the arrests, that's the nitty-gritty of it. What we really do is clear the path to allow those shattered lives to move forward."

"Detectives Brown and Iverson interviewing Francisco Orellana, 1500 hours." Detective Brown nodded to Elaine. "Go ahead."

"Francisco Orellana, you are here because you are under arrest for the murder of Dan Flint."

"David Rodriguez." Francisco's lawyer cut in. A man the shape and complexion of an unpeeled potato, he fittingly wore a dark brown suit over a starched white shirt and mustard yellow tie. "My client's name is David."

"His name is Francisco, but sure, if that makes you feel better." Elaine chuckled, before casting a quick nervous glance requesting approval from Detective Brown, whose eyes gave a silent assent.

"What's your evidence? You arrested David off the strength of a photo that could've been anyone, even me. I want to know what you have."

"We have some questions for Mr..... Rodriguez first," Detective Brown said. "We will get to that in due time."

"Nothing to say," the lawyer, whose name Elaine thought was Villa but couldn't be sure, stage whispered to Francisco.

Detective Brown's eyes found Elaine, prodding her to speak.

"We found blood from two different individuals at the crime scene. Want to tell us about the second victim?" Elaine asked.

"There is no way I would know that," Francisco responded, his tone verging on boredom.

"You don't seem to be taking this very seriously. At least one man is dead."

"People die all the time. Many deserve it, many don't. What do you want from me?"

"Why did you kill Ben Walsh?"

It was as if a vacuum had turned on. All the air was sucked out of the room. Francisco's eyes flashed menacingly.

Detective Brown sat back, letting a smug smile settle on her face. "You didn't think we knew that one, did you? Your old friend's husband. Did Yancey Portillo get you to off him after that whole moving-out situation?"

Francisco's voice was deliberate and filled with rage. "If you think, for one second, that I would harm any of Veronica's family, then you have no idea." He cocked his head. "Is Ben Walsh really dead?"

Elaine wasn't sure if they were supposed to answer that.

"You should know, we found his blood mixed in with Dan Flint's. Where did you put his body? Why did you hide it? Why didn't you hide Flint's?" Detective Brown asked.

"You have a lot of questions." Francisco held up his hands, showing the manacles. "Take these off me, and I can find out in a day what would take you a year."

His lawyer elbowed him in his side.

"Enlighten us, then," Brown said.

"Dan Flint. He's the victim. It's his house. Go to his funeral, log every person there. Note anyone who you'd expect to be there but isn't. Track down the connections. Figure out who gained by killing him. When you find that person, and I walk free, then you'll find your answer as to why Ben's blood is there, and if that's even real and not staged, itself."

"You're describing detective work. That's not clever, that's just our job," Brown said.

"Then why are you in here with me and not out doing that?"

"Because you were caught on camera near the crime scene with a gun."

"Do all Hispanic men look the same to you?"

Elaine was about to answer, when Detective Brown held her hand up, her fingers curled into a fist. Elaine glanced over and saw her partner reading something on her phone, her eyes so wide they were almost bulging out of her head. "What is it?"

"Interview ended," Detective Brown said quickly. "We have to see what happened." With a glance at Francisco, she added, "you'll want to know, too."

CHAPTER 21
VERONICA

Afternoon, March 18

The text came from the unlikeliest source possible. I couldn't believe I even had her number in my phone. I barely remembered any interaction we'd ever had.

I was sitting in a sandwich shop in Alexandria dedicated to rescue dogs. Having never had a dog, but having always liked the idea of a rescue—*how couldn't I?* —I had stuck my head inside when we first moved to the area. As long as the food was passable, I'd be happy, but I was pleasantly surprised by how much more than just passable it was. They had several dozen different sandwich options, and I hadn't yet found one I didn't enjoy. All hits and no misses.

I put down my sandwich when I saw the name on my phone. It was a short message.

Saw the news. You okay?

Okay, how? What news? My heart thumped against my chest as if it were a prisoner trying one last desperate attempt at escape.

I opened up Twitter/X, as good a local news app as you can get if you follow the right people, expecting to see the worst. My breath caught in my mouth as I scrolled, and I hurriedly pulled up the *Washington Post* app front page. This would be world news. I'd find the full story there.

Yancey Portillo Dead in Ambush.

Now my heart's thumps felt as if they were inside my head. I read on.

Salvadoran crime boss Yancey Portillo was killed today in a firefight in San Salvador. Based there, he ran a drug-smuggling and distribution empire and became the subject of intense international scrutiny when his long-lost daughter Alessandra, now Veronica Walsh, was discovered to be living in the Washington, DC, area. Witnesses claim that he was ambushed and that there are multiple other victims as well. This is an ongoing story..

This wasn't possible.

This couldn't be possible. My father was supposed to succumb to old age, safe in the knowledge he'd outlived every one of his enemies. Waiting until he heard they were all gone before he decided to go out on his own terms.

Not in an ambush. My mind raced. Where did it take place? Who would even be so brazen to attempt that in the first place?

I closed my eyes and leaned back into my wooden chair. I put the phone down on the table, next to the empty sandwich wrapper on a red plastic tray.

I spent my formative teenage years and then my entire adult life acting like he was dead. Why should it matter that he was now?

He was a horrendous father. In the cold light of day, that much was painfully obvious. But I now knew that he cared for me more than he ever could articulate. Our meeting last year, the chance at reconnecting that passed us by, had taught me that and flipped so many of my thoughts about him on their head.

I tried not to let my mind wander to who else might be dead. He wouldn't have been out of the compound without his inner circle of three men. Francisco's father, the Landaverde twins' father, and Orlando.

An entire world I left behind. But a world that never left me. A world I carried alongside me wherever I went, sometimes a parasite, sometimes a talisman.

The strength of the realization pulsed through my veins. I thought I had been alone. But with Yancey's backing, whether I wanted it or not, I would never truly have been alone.

That's the thing about staring into the abyss. It might look pitch black, but from up above you have no idea the different shades you're looking at. It's only when you've been plunged headfirst that you learn that the abyss can always get darker.

I was alone. No Ben. No Francisco. And now my own father was gone.

No one was coming to rescue me. It was only me. Just like all those years ago, when I was a handcuffed teenager with a newly severed pinky. I made a choice then. I chose to survive. My own survival wasn't at stake right now, but the choice was just as clear. It was time to fight.

The same number that had texted me flashed up on my screen. *Really, she's calling me?*

"Hi, Nat," I said, flatly. I couldn't muster any emotion, especially not for the ex-wife of the man I stopped from ascending to the presidency. Even if she was an international superstar.

Some singers' voices are unremarkable when they're talking. Not Natalia Rochev. Her voice sounded like a chorus of angels. "Veronica, I just don't believe all of this," she said.

"What's there not to believe?" I asked, mainly as a rhetorical question. I was done kidding myself. My past was my present. The little secret I hid for decades, now playing out in front of everyone I knew, and millions I didn't who still felt empowered to have their own say.

"I don't know what to say, or offer, in that text but I just wanted to let you know I'm here for you, whatever you need. Losing your father, I just can't imagine."

She sounded earnest enough. I wasn't sure of her angle, though. "You saw the photo, I assume?"

"It's clearly not you. Or it is you, but modified in some way," Nat said with a practiced confidence that suggested she knew what she was saying was true.

"That's not everyone's opinion," I said.

"Not everyone has been the victim of a million deep fakes and knows a thing or two about spotting them."

She had a point.

When Ben's best friend, Jeremy Wiles, had told us that he had gone on a date with pop star Natalia Rochev, we didn't believe him at first. Yes, okay, he'd become the type of celebrity who might cross paths with her, but dating? No way, that was just a funny 'imagine if' joke.

Then he brought her to dinner. Didn't tell us he was, just showed up at our front door. An understated "this is Nat" was all we got, which was of course exactly the vibe he always tried to present. *I'm dating an icon, but no big deal, why wouldn't I be?*

Despite how much Jeremy's fame grated on Ben, and by proxy, me, we couldn't help but love Nat. She was much funnier than we expected. She didn't take herself, or her fame, seriously at all. It was all a crazy game that she couldn't believe she was playing. She said she thought God had messed up and accidentally switched her out for whomever was supposed to be the singing sensation. She joked that there was likely some poor girl out there somewhere with the attitude of a diva combined with absolutely zero skills.

"Wait, Nat, where are you right now?" I had an idea.

"I'm on my plane, heading to Bratislava from Prague. Why?"

"You have a house in the area here, don't you?"

"I do."

"Is someone keeping up with it? Like, is it currently livable?"

"Yeah, my manager has someone who takes care of it."

"Okay, look, I need your house. I need somewhere to hide out and figure out how to fix whatever of this I can. Is that possible?"

CHAPTER 22
VERONICA

Night, March 18

Calling this just a house was quite the understatement. I stood in the foyer of the mid-1900s Colonial-style farmhouse in the Arcturus neighborhood along the West bank of the Potomac River south of Old Town Alexandria. The five-bedroom, nine-bathroom behemoth stood overlooking the river, the sole house on a cul-de-sac.

Nat had described it as "a nice getaway." It wasn't like I met her when she was poor, and I still couldn't come to grips with her riches. I knew who she was when she first appeared in Ben's, and subsequently my, life. But every once in a while, you get a glimpse of a life that is just so unnervingly different from your own. The house, named Tak Khoroshiy Den—Russian for *what a nice day*—had been hers for just over ten years. There for when she needed a private place as her fame exploded in her early twenties. The neighborhood was full of gorgeous houses with people who appreciated their privacy, so no one was going to come snooping around.

Nat had instructed me to find a key with a drop bag of other important items for me in an Amazon locker nearby. I didn't realize that people could access Amazon lockers for personal use, but then, she wasn't ordinary.

I was curious what items a millionaire—*billionaire?* —considered important. Turns out it was a plastic bag with a pack of tissues, a roll of toilet paper, and a razor and shaving cream. The rich, they're just like us.

I unpacked my single bag in the master bedroom. I didn't need much. It was time to go on the offensive. Time to rely only on myself once more.

My task was still the same. Track down Jamie Simon, this Francisco lookalike who must have been the one in the video.

I glanced down at my phone, thrown onto the heaping pile of throw pillows at the head of the California King bed. A notification appeared and I peered over to read it. An email, from a jumbled set of letters and numbers. The subject line simply read "Now You Know."

I swiped it open and read the rest.

Dear Veronica/Alessandra,
By now you will have seen what happened to your father. This was our doing and entirely your fault. Cease looking into what happened to Dan Flint. Give up on finding your husband. He will either come home or he won't. But now you know our reach. If we can get to Yancey Portillo, we can get to anyone you care about. You have our attention, and now we have yours.
–P

I read and reread it. It was signed "P" but was written in first person plural. This was a group.

They didn't want me to keep looking into Dan Flint. I wondered if that was an intentional comment, or a slip-up. Dan was my friend, but my interest in his death lay firmly in what I could find out about my husband.

These people killed my father. They went down to San Salvador and ambushed one of the most highly protected men in the world, just to show me they could. The sadness was gone, turned into a burning anger.

They clearly thought they knew who they were dealing with. But they left me alive, when I was much less protected than my father. Which told me there was a reason. Another underestimation.

They didn't want me digging into who they were.

Now I had two tasks.

CHAPTER 23
ELAINE

Night, March 18

Detective Brown pointed to the headline on the open *Washington Post* tab on Elaine's computer. "Yancey Portillo." She shook her head, disbelieving. "I was led to believe he was invincible."

"I wonder what happened," Elaine said, not truly meaning it. What did she care about what happened to a gangster in a foreign country? Was she supposed to feel bad because Veronica Walsh might be holding some lingering feelings?

"A rival. It has to be. The internet—famous for always being right—is abuzz with speculation. There's always someone trying to take down the top dog. It's crazy to think no one would ever succeed. Did you read how it happened?"

"No." Why would Elaine use her precious time learning more than she needed to?

"Yancey Portillo and three of his closest lieutenants, Orlando Garcia, Tomas Landaverde and Roger Orellana, were in a car driving somewhere through San Salvador. Two men jumped out in front of the car and opened fire. Nothing there yet that they couldn't handle." Detective Brown shrugged. "Both those men were shot and killed within seconds, with none of the Portillo crew hit. But now their bodies were in the road, blocking the way. The driver swerved to avoid them, pulling up onto the curb. But that's exactly what the plan was. A set of custom spikes, able to pierce even the strongest wheels, lined the sidewalk. The tires blew as they ran over the spikes, and six assailants approached with machine guns. Not even Yancey's men could get out of that jam. The shooters arranged themselves in a half circle around the car and fired hundreds of rounds."

"Jesus."

"I know. A coordinated attack. Eight present, plus whoever else might have planned it. That's not a crime of circumstance. So, who?"

"Who stands to gain?" Emilia asked the question her partner teed up for her.

"Someone within the organization wanting to rise, or someone outside the organization wanting to bring it down. Only two options that make sense." She glanced up and saw the immediately recognizable lumbering figure of Detective Martin Fahey come into view. "Fahey, you've surely got some thoughts on the Portillo assassination!" she called.

He grunted, shrugging his shoulders. "Someone got to him," he said dismissively as he headed out the door.

Elaine watched as Detective Brown's eyes raised in amazement as he left. "Didn't you tell me he was sort of fanatical about Yancey Portillo?"

"I did. That was weird. Why didn't he have more to say?"

Detective Brown stood at her favorite white board, laying out the latest details of the case to Elaine and the officers assigned to assist them. Elaine watched as she eased through the evidence against Francisco, acknowledging it was likely still a long way to a conviction, and how there was very little to go on in the search for Ben Walsh. Francisco hadn't spoken any more after learning of

Yancey's death. Elaine wondered if Brown had thought telling him would pry loose any extra information. If so, it backfired spectacularly.

"What we need is a lead. A clue, anything. Go out there and find me something about Ben Walsh that I don't know." Detective Brown turned to Elaine. "It's time for you and me to have another talk with Veronica. We'll track her down tomorrow."

CHAPTER 24
JAMIE

Night, March 18

There was still work to be done. The ongoing task at hand took up far more of Jamie's time than he liked, but it couldn't be helped.

He contemplated approaching Veronica Walsh. But to what end? His brother probably would have by now.

Jamie's brother had always been the go-getter. He was the one who had big plans. He didn't want a simple, quiet life.

"Look, don't you want your name to ring out beyond our own walls?" He had asked when Jamie was just ten years old.

Jamie could not understand the question. Why should he care at all what anyone but his family thought of him? He knew that it was nice if the other kids liked him, but beyond that, what did it matter?

And in chasing it, all his brother ended up with was a short life marred by a violent end. A death that had never been avenged. It wasn't like people didn't know who it was who killed him. There was just no way to get to them.

His brother would go straight to Veronica Walsh's doorstep. Knock on her door and face her himself.

Could Jamie do that?

CHAPTER 25
VERONICA

Morning, March 19

Relativity is a funny thing. Any characteristic of yours is only interesting, noteworthy, even relevant, based on who you are surrounded by.

To the public I was a murderer, sympathetic or otherwise, with a heavy emphasis on the otherwise after that photo. But when you are visiting a prison, the only characteristic about you that matters is that you are free. Who cares what you've done when you're breathing free air, while the prisoners languish away behind bars? Was there really no one in this prison who had done worse than me? Hard to believe.

I sat across from a face I had spent countless hours with. Your partner's best friend is a funny thing. They become a part of your life, and their approval means a great deal to your significant other. "Your new girl is hot" evolves into "of course your girlfriend can hang" and eventually becomes "you two were meant for each other." Jeremy Wiles liked me from the jump. Truth be told, I never cared about his approval. I wasn't a pick-me girl, I didn't need anyone to know I was different from all the other girls. Who cared? I was only ever unapologetically myself, an irony not lost on me considering just how much of myself was hidden away.

Jeremy always matched my energy. He was comfortable in his own skin, confident in his path. Little did we know just how intricately planned that path was.

Watching Ben's attempts to hide his jealousy had always pained me. Ben wanted to be the president one day—he made no attempt to hide that fact in private. And why shouldn't he? But watching his best friend, a, let's face it, anonymous Secret Service Agent, jump from obscurity to national hero status after he thwarted Jacob Jordan's assassination attempt was hard for Ben to manage. I still remember the day he came home and told me of Jeremy's desire to be president.

"What happened today, babe? You don't look okay," I had said, when he walked through the door at half past six in the evening.

"Work was fine," he muttered, sighing. We had an unspoken understanding of things not to discuss around the children, so I realized we needed to wait to continue the conversation.

Later that night, he sat down on the edge of our bed and looked at me, shaking his head like he couldn't understand what he was saying. "Jeremy is going to run for president."

I figured I must have misunderstood or heard him wrong. I put down my makeup removing pad and stepped out of our shared bathroom. "He... president of what?"

"The United States," Ben sighed. "POTUS."

"How?"

"Why not? He's got name recognition across the country and wants to 'leave a lasting legacy,' as he put it to me today." Ben's shoulders slumped, and he scooted back onto the bed and lay down.

"I know he's your friend, but he's not going to win. He can't," I said, hoping he couldn't hear the lie in my voice.

"I don't want him to win. But he's going to clear the field in the primary without even trying. The DNC is going to embrace him. How could they not? Who else would stand any chance against Leishear, a reasonably well-liked moderate Republican who now has the nation's sympathy after the assassination attempt? There's no one except a man he can't campaign against using the assassination. It blunts him."

"That doesn't mean he'll beat Leishear, though."

"So what if he doesn't win? He'll still be a power player on the national scale. Exactly what he knows I want to be."

I didn't have the words to console Ben that day.

I looked across at what had now become of this power player. Sitting behind plastic, several days' worth of scruff on his face, as pale as I'd ever seen him.

"Natalia must still have some sway with you, to get you to agree to meet me," I said.

Jeremy smiled wistfully. "She's a good egg. Pretty obvious to say about someone like her, but I picked wisely."

"She thinks you might be able to help. Did she tell you why I'm here?"

He steepled his fingers. "Just the bare bones. I wanted to build some excitement, something to look forward to. There's not much around here, I have to tell you."

"I want to know what you know about a cabal of movers and shakers in the city."

His cheeks filled with air as he tried unsuccessfully to stifle a laugh. "You're kidding, right? Take your pick. Everyone is either a mover or shaker or part of some group who believes they are movers and shakers. You're going to have to give me more than that."

"Was Dan Flint part of something, maybe a group that called itself 'P' or something similar?"

"Ooh. Okay, now we're talking. Dan Flint, as in the recently murdered ex-colleague of yours?"

I nodded.

"I normally wouldn't know, because by nature a shadowy cabal exists in the shadows," he said with a smirk. "But Dan liked to talk. I remember a department party that you hosted that I finagled an invite to. Dan had a quiet chat with me—this was while I was running for president—and he said he was part of an influential group and was curious if I wanted to get involved."

"But how would he be influential? He was a mathematics professor."

Jeremy grinned wide and chuckled. "Crazy, right? Can you believe a mathematics professor might have something else secret about their life? Unprecedented, I'd say."

Fair enough. "What did he tell you?"

"He wouldn't tell me any details, I think enjoying the secrecy. That's the thing about holding secrets. It's no fun unless someone else knows you have a secret. If you're just keeping a big secret and no one even bothers to ask, where's the enjoyment in that?"

He was clearly speaking from experience. "Okay, so?"

"He said his role was to watch over the Georgetown student body. Look out for anyone with special talent they could nurture. You mentioning the 'P' was the other part that puts this together. He called his group The Princemakers."

"The Princemakers? What does that even mean?"

"A play on kingmakers I assume. But catching people earlier in their career or seeing them through to positions of power? I'm not really sure, I never thought too much about it. What I do know is they have no hesitation to kill. These are some bad dudes."

"But this is true? His part at least?"

"Straight from his mouth to my ears."

"You wouldn't lie to me about this, would you?"

"Ben is missing, and it's somehow connected to this, isn't it?"

I sighed, realizing what happened. Ben and I had been talking about this cabal. He went out to look for answers, thinking that Dan Flint maybe had them. I wonder if he thought that since Dan had been at Georgetown for years, if anyone knew about a group that had ties to them, he would. But he didn't realize that he was walking into the house of one of the members. "His blood was found mixed with Dan Flint's," I said.

"Have you considered that maybe he wasn't injured at the same time Dan Flint was?"

"You're saying maybe Dan did something to him, and then whomever killed Dan came in after?"

Jeremy shrugged.

"But then where would Ben be right now?"

"Your mystery attacker might know," Jeremy said. "Although didn't Francisco get arrested for it?"

"He didn't do it," I said sharply.

"You seem very confident about that, considering the guy's backstory."

"Don't even go there," I warned.

He held his hands up in surrender. "Okay, fine. You came to me for answers. So, what I will tell you is this: there is one other Princemaker I know of."

"Who?" I felt my pulse quicken.

"Why, the president himself. President McAllister of your very own esteemed Georgetown University."

CHAPTER 26
ELAINE

Midday, March 19

Detective Brown called the number, and then put the phone on speaker and placed it on the center of the conference table. She and Elaine sat opposite each other, waiting as it rang.

"Did you find my husband?" Veronica answered without a greeting.

"No, Veronica, not yet," Brown said.

"Then why do I have multiple missed calls from you?"

"Where were you without your phone?"

"That's not an answer."

"We want to talk again about why your husband might have been at Dan Flint's house."

"Because he was a friend."

"Now you're the one not giving a real answer."

"Touché. All I know is that Ben thought Dan Flint could help him figure out who was behind this big cover up and conspiracy."

There was a tension in Veronica's voice that Elaine picked up on. Having a family full of politicians means no one ever gives a straight answer. You catch subtleties that others would miss. She waved her hand to catch Detective Brown's attention. Once her senior partner looked up, she quickly pressed mute on the phone and said, "there's something she's not telling us."

Detective Brown said a quick "thank you" and unmuted the phone. "Okay, we're running down that angle too. Anything else you got for us?"

The silence stretched as the detectives waited. Elaine realized she was holding her breath.

"I mean, I did find out who actually killed Dan," Veronica said, nonchalantly. "Is that something you guys might be interested in?"

"What do you mean?" Detective Brown's voice was icy cold.

"You and I both know Francisco didn't do it, and I found a man who has been trailing Ben who looks quite similar to Francisco. That sounds good enough for you?"

"Tell us."

"Is the baby detective not with us today?"

Elaine felt her face go red. She averted her gaze, knowing Detective Brown would glance over. "I'm here," she said, trying not to let her voice crack.

Why did she feel so ashamed? Everywhere she went people commented on how young she looked. Was it because she wanted Veronica to think of her as impressive?

"Oh, hey there, Iverson. Glad to hear from you."

"Who do you think was the true culprit?" Elaine asked. "I'm listening because I agree that it's unlikely it was your friend."

"Oh, look at you all grown up. I almost feel bad for the baby comment. This should help me out anyway, because I need to find him too and ask him where Ben is. His name is Jamie Simon."

"Do you have anything more for us?" Elaine ignored the backhanded compliment.

"More? You're the police, take his name and run with it."

"Run with it? On what basis?"

"I'll send you a picture. He's the spitting image. I'm telling you: Jamie Simon."

"If that's his real name," Brown offered.

"Here I was thinking I was speaking to professionals," Veronica said. "You called me. You wanted info. Jamie Simon. Find him, arrest him, find my husband. Don't make me do all your work for you."

CHAPTER 27
VERONICA

Night, March 19

I knew the detectives would assume I was hiding something from them. It didn't take all of my considerable wisdom to suss that one out. So I let them have Jamie Simon and think that was all. Left me free to do what I needed to.

I had a date tonight, although he didn't know it.

Sneaking into fortified buildings was a skill that didn't diminish with time or lack of use. Technology was better, but it was all the same. One guiding principle.

Don't be seen.

I knew that President McAllister was in his office late. That was well-known to anyone who spent time on campus. He was a smart man, a bachelor at the age of sixty-two. A Georgetown graduate himself, he took his business degree and a series of positions that helped him climb the corporate ladder until he was the CEO of one of those nameless Fortune 500 companies. The type you'd hear and think, 'oh, yeah, them,' but would never come up with their name on your own. When the previous president resigned almost a decade ago, he was the obvious candidate. He liked to stay in his office late, cracking the window and enjoying a

Cuban cigar. The no smoking rule didn't extend all the way to his office.

There were some campus security guards, of course, but no one with the skill or attention to notice me, clad in all-black, a skintight Nike top and leggings.

Healy Hall faced East overlooking Healy Lawn, itself extending to 37th Street NW and the edge of campus. The flagship building on Georgetown' campus, it was designed by the same people who did the Thomas Jefferson Building of the Library of Congress. With its Gothic spires, it would not look out of place in the center of an ancient European city, nor in the background of a horror movie, as it was in *The Exorcist*.

It was almost too easy. All I had to do was cross through an open area that had massive daily foot traffic and then sneak into a building that held not only the president's office, but a library, classrooms, full departments, and plenty of other administrative facilities.

I had an Uber drop me off down on M Street, several blocks away. No one remembers a rider going to the busiest street in Georgetown. I walked all the way west to where M Street turns into Canal Street and then headed north, up the famous *Exorcist* Steps. A tourist attraction, so again, no one would think twice about a woman dressed in athletic clothes climbing up those stairs. I even stopped to take a pretend selfie halfway up in case anyone was watching.

They weren't. No one cared.

Campus security is tricky. So much of it is predicated on cultural norms and niceties. You can't get into any residential building without swiping your ID card, so in theory those are safe. Other buildings are open during the day but then only accessible at night with that same ID card. But that completely fails when a well-meaning nineteen-year-old turns around and sees a pretty mid-thirties woman, her hood partially obscuring her face, stretching for the door and asking him to hold it for her. See, she can't pull her card out because of the stack of books in her hand.

He doesn't know they were bought in cash ten minutes ago at the newly opened Barnes & Noble on M Street. All he sees is someone holding books, presumably heading to the library, and he gets to feel good about himself for helping her.

Veronica Walsh one, campus security nil.

I dumped the books in a pile in a dark corner of a hallway. A bunch of disingenuous self-help trash anyway.

Sneaking into the president's office from there? Child's play.

Cameras would see someone dressed in black, possibly a woman but unclear, and then they'd go back as far as they could and lose the trail. There were too many people and not enough cameras to follow me all the way back to my Uber drop off.

McAllister wasn't nervous when I walked in. That was the first thing I noticed. He had the calm assurance of a man for whom nothing went wrong. Only when he recognized who I was did his eyes widen and I detected an initial fear.

"Dr. Walsh? What… what is this about?" He stuttered, trying to pretend his fear was mere confusion.

"Tell me where my husband is," I said calmly. I didn't show a weapon. I didn't need to.

"Why would you think I know?'

I looked him directly in the eye and I perched on the edge of his desk. "Hands where I can see them," I barked.

He slowly placed them on the desk, either side of his keyboard. "You haven't answered my question."

"One of your fellow Princemakers is dead and my husband is missing. I assumed this sort of organization would keep up with something like that."

"I don't know anything about that organization." Practiced liars think they are good at hiding it. But that ability is only for those for whom lying has become as natural as breathing. Even practiced liars have tells.

He was neither practiced nor a natural. His lips pursed inward every time he had to think about what he was saying next when it didn't just roll off his tongue.

"I just don't know why you even bother," I said. "You're the one who fired me last year. You know who I am. Hell, everyone does by now. Quit with the lying, I can see right through it."

He sat for a second, taking me in. A leer spread across his face. "You're right. And you just made a fatal mistake. We left you alive. But you just confirmed to me that you know about us. You signed your own death warrant."

I almost hoped that he wasn't high up in their organization. To do such juvenile one-step thinking was embarrassing. *You just confirmed to me that you know about us.* I got a letter from them taking credit for my father's death, and he thought I didn't know who they were? Either he wasn't part of the decision-making hierarchy, or this was the dumbest group I'd ever come across.

If you lose to a worthy adversary, you shrug your shoulders and say that's how life goes. A group that can get to my father, who was one of the most guarded and careful men in the world. But this? He thought that *I* was the one making the mistake here?

I let him keep blustering. "You know I once thought about recruiting you? That's how much we know about you. We know your entire life. We know everything there is to know about your father. Well, what there *was* to know," he added with a smile.

"Where is my husband?"

"You're still on about that, good Lord." He chuckled. "You really think you're going to learn something here? That we killed him and just happened to kill one of our own also? A man I've relied on for so long?"

"Tell me what you know."

"What do I know? I know nothing, you dumb bitch. Your husband found himself in the wrong place at the wrong time and now it's our mess to clean up because he stumbled into something with Dan. Hell, I'm not even convinced he didn't kill Dan." McAllister leaned back in his chair, beginning to feel more confident. "Whatever he did, it's now got you meddling around and showing up here having somehow convinced yourself you know something that you do not understand at all. You killed a few people as a kid, big deal. We've killed more people than you could possibly imagine, and rather than your juvenile antics and showing off, we stayed behind the scenes. We run this city, and not a damn soul knows. That's how it is, and that's how forever it will be. You are but a little bug to squash along the way. There's a storm coming your way. When you're gone, we'll get your adoptive parents too, and then, finally, just to make sure, your little twins, too, Nico and —"

I had my knife palmed in my hand, just in case. Black hilt, six-inch blade. My childhood weapon that my father had kept for me all those years. The last gift I ever received from my brother.

I didn't plan it that way. But what parent lets someone speak like that about their kids?

I swung my right arm in a backhand motion, hiding the blade until the moment it plunged into his heart. He fell back, his chair toppling behind him, the wheels spinning madly.

As he gasped his final, raspy breaths, I let my anger get the best of me a second time. I strode around his desk and sliced jaggedly across the two carotid arteries on the right side of his neck.

No one threatens my children.

CHAPTER 28
ELAINE

Morning, March 20

It's a beautiful day / Don't let it get away!

Bono pierced through Elaine's subconscious as she blindly reached for her phone to turn the alarm off. Every morning, she cursed her younger self who thought this would be an uplifting tune to wake up to each day. Every night she forgot to change the song, and the scenario repeated the next morning.

Maybe today would be the prophesied beautiful day.

She'd had plenty of them in the past; it had just been a while. College, probably? Plenty of good days there. But those who pine for long-lost college days are mistaken. It's a time and a place. You enjoy it while you're there, but you're doomed to failure if you try to replicate the feeling once it's over.

Freshman year of college, the first time she'd set foot on the wooded campus of William & Mary, was when she decided to eschew her last name. Attending the nation's second oldest college—a school only behind Harvard and Yale for number of presidents produced—while bearing the current president's uncommon last name was not a recipe for success. She enrolled as Elaine Iverson and kept quiet about her personal life as much as possible.

That lasted one week.

She shouldn't have signed up for that Intro to Political Theory class. Of course there was going to be some kid far too invested in politics who'd recognize her. She didn't get it. Who could possibly care that much?

"Hey, can I ask you a weird question?" the kid with the crisp button-down and gelled hair asked as they all filed out of the classroom.

"Go for it." Elaine shrugged.

"Are you the governor of Maryland's daughter?"

"No—" Elaine started. "Ah, what the hell?" She gave a rueful shake of her head. "Yes, I am."

His mouth dropped open. "Oh, my goodness! Wow. I'm Ricky, it is so nice to meet you. I have so many questions." He held out his hand.

"Hi, Ricky." Elaine shook his clammy hand. "I'd appreciate it if you didn't spread this around. I'm not trying to draw attention. Can you just let me come and go quietly?"

The twinkle in his eyes told her he was definitely not going to leave her alone.

He spent the entire semester making eye contact with her during class at any political mention that could at all relate to her. They 'accidentally' ran into each other at Swem Library over and over again. When her father came down at the end of the semester to help her move out, she let Ricky come over to her dorm room to meet him.

Ricky was now Richard, one of the youngest state delegates in Virginia, while she, with all her connections, was still just Elaine. Just someone else's daughter or niece.

As she lay in bed, Elaine's phone dinged. She looked down and quickly read the message on her lock screen. *Where are you right now?*

Elaine picked up the phone and called Brown, tamping down her fear of talking on the phone.

"Iverson." Brown's clipped answer as she answered told

Elaine exactly what kind of call this was. No pleasantries were going to be exchanged.

"What's up?" Elaine asked.

"Did you just wake up?"

Elaine glanced at the clock. 6:30 in the morning. "Yeah…"

"Not a dig, just asking."

"The president of Georgetown was killed last night," Brown said.

"Holy shit." Elaine jumped up out of bed. "Okay, where do I meet you?"

"It's not our case yet, but I've already talked to the chief. Fahey and Lockyear are on it, but we'll combine forces very soon if this goes the way I imagine."

Already? When? "What do you think happened?"

"I'm not forming any hypotheses yet. Remember always to be the enemy of certainty."

Elaine rolled her eyes. Detective Brown was just so over-serious at all times. If that were her personality, Elaine could accept it, but she had seen how Brown was playful and funny around Zeke and others in the department. Couldn't she let her guard down around Elaine, too? Was that too much to ask this early on in their relationship? The only hint of playfulness that Elaine ever got from Brown was when she called her Ivy. Even that, though, felt like it was delivered with a side of gentle ribbing.

"Okay, got it. What are we on, then?"

"What have you found on Jamie Simon?"

"Next to nothing so far." Elaine sighed. "Nothing useful, at least."

"Okay, keep digging. I want to know what Veronica knows about him. Tell me when you've got something."

CHAPTER 29
VERONICA

Morning, March 20

That wasn't supposed to happen.

Was that not exactly what I'd explained *ad nauseum* to Ben wouldn't and couldn't happen anymore? *You have to understand, the old me is gone. I won't revert back.*

I killed a man. Not self-defense, not an accident. Just straightforward murder. Did he unwittingly goad me into it? Sure. But as far as legal defenses go, that left a lot to be desired.

I snuck in like a cat burglar and murdered someone. I left his body there and washed my hands and face in the nearby bathroom and threw my coat on over my black clothing. No one looked too closely. No one ever does.

That's the death penalty. That's not an *'oh, you have to understand the circumstances'* sort of case.

What's even worse?

I didn't regret it at all. I regretted not keeping my calm, not getting more information out of him. But that split-second, violent strike? I spent the night tossing and turning, trying to will myself to be upset. But I couldn't do it.

He deserved it—not from me, through legal means, but when was that going to happen?

I sat up in bed and reached over to take a drink from my water bottle on the nightstand. What had I actually gained? Besides another visit from the police. I covered my tracks, I was no dummy, but it wasn't much of a logical leap to think I was involved. They'd find some circumstantial evidence if they looked close enough that I was in Georgetown. The Uber and the Barnes & Noble. But you don't get to arrest me for just that.

The less mature version of me would've cut off his pinky. Made it clear to everyone who was behind this. Strike fear into the heart of this dumb organization. The Princemakers? Come on, how utterly presumptuous.

But that wasn't me anymore. At least on that part, I remained truthful. The people who needed to know would understand. The rest didn't have to know.

The president of Georgetown University. A distinguished mathematics professor at the same institution. A Senator in the United States Congress. And the owner of a professional sports team. Was that almost all? Were there just a couple more, scattered around? Or was this the tip of the iceberg, an organization made up of hundreds or even more?

I considered that second possibility. Just about everyone has a favorite government conspiracy theory. They control our minds through the water supply, they could stop cancer but won't because there's too much profit, they did 9/11. Take your pick. But from what I'd learned from Ben, it just wasn't possible that so many people would be able to keep a coverup silent. A lot of these people are using ancient versions of Microsoft Excel and Outlook, trying desperately to keep up and sync their Microsoft Teams with the rest of their office. They're not hiding huge secrets in between trips to IT to ask why their software never works the way they want. Any secrets that the government might be hiding could only be held by a small number of people.

These Princemakers had to be the same. Power seekers and big egos often correlate. Wielding secret power wouldn't work for a big group. Someone would eventually go rogue. I'd be shocked if there were more than a dozen of them, and likely fewer.

But right then, what was most important to me was that they were a group who might not know what happened to my husband. McAllister was an idiot, but that felt truthful to me. They, themselves, were trying to find out what happened to Dan. Which meant they couldn't know what happened to Ben. Or at least not the full story.

What did Ben walk in on?

Something happened with Jamie Simon, Dan Flint, and Ben, and no one seemed to be any closer to understanding what.

Was Jamie Simon there when Ben arrived at Dan's house? What was the timeline? There was still too much I did not know.

Meanwhile, why hadn't the police tracked down Jamie Simon?

My phone started to ring, and I knocked it off the nightstand as I reached for it. I lunged over the side, bringing the duvet with me as I scrambled. The melody played in its entirety before I finally found it with my outstretched fingers. I gave the screen a quick glance.

"Hi, Natalia," I said.

"Hey, I just heard that you had a good conversation with Jeremy yesterday," she said without preamble.

"I did, yes." Don't confirm anything over the phone unless it can be easily confirmed elsewhere. You're never sure who might be listening. But a million cameras would have me at the prison, let alone all the admin evidence left behind.

"He said he tried to be as helpful as possible."

Where was she going with this? "I'm surprised you've already talked to him."

Natalia chuckled. "They let a lot of things slide when you're famous. Life moves faster."

"So, what's up? The house is great, and I can't thank you enough for a place to lie low. No news on who broke my window, and honestly, I don't think finding and charging one person really lowers the threat when an entire country's mad at me."

"No problem," she said in a clipped voice. "But, hey, so, Jeremy told me about the name he told you—"

"Nat," I cut in, my voice low and menacing. "Don't go any further unless you absolutely have to. Whatever you're thinking, don't."

I was playing with fire here. I really thought Jeremy would keep his mouth shut a little bit longer. Maybe asking for assistance from a murderer and the man who almost killed me wasn't the best idea. I needed this house, though. I could make do. I always had, but this was perfect.

"Listen, Veronica." Her tone was calm and measured. "I talked to Jeremy, and he told me about these people. I understand." She lingered on the final word.

"Thank you," I whispered, the words barely coming out. Why was I becoming so emotional about her external validation? Since when did I become so needy?

Maybe I was always needy. As a teenager, I devoured every succulent morsel of gossip about Yancey's assassin. And would I be lying to myself if I admitted some of my own checking for news of my disappearance was with a small hope that someone would put two and two together?

The only time I ever considered turning back, despite it all, was a couple years after I'd fled. No one had heard from me—*obviously*—and with no more victims with severed fingers, along with the whispers that had gotten me in trouble in the first place, it was starting to become a fact that Alessandra Portillo was the assassin.

Until some punk tried to steal my thunder. A copycat. I should've expected it, but reading a local news story from San Salvador about how a do-nothing lowlife—*correction: a high-ranking officer in an international syndicate*—had been found with his pinky severed made my blood boil. How dare someone try to pretend they were me this whole time?

My dad still believed I was out there somewhere. I could tell, because the very next day he told a friendly reporter that the severed finger had nothing to do with him or anyone inside his organization.

The story died, killed from up on high. It was all but an admission of who his own daughter was.

"I know something that could be useful to you, while you try to find your husband," Natalia said.

That brought me back to the present.

"Okay," I said. There was nothing else to say, she just needed an acknowledgement before continuing.

"Check the mailbox. You'll find a note in there. I think that should help you."

CHAPTER 30
ELAINE

Midday, March 20

A lot of detective work was just like any other job—too much time spent in front of a computer, typing your life away.

Elaine sat at her computer as she tried to track down any leads on Jamie Simon. That he had photographed Ben and it ended up in the news last week was interesting, but that lead was dry. She'd called Gary Tiller, and he didn't have any extra information for her. It had to be a fake name, so she needed to find his real name. A simple enough task to say out loud, far trickier in practice.

For starters, there was no Jamie Simon on any housing documents. No deeds, no leases, nothing. Where do you start with that?

Elaine jumped when her partner's phone rang. She whipped her head around as she heard the chief's phone ringing at the same time. Phones started ringing all over the floor. "What's going on?" she said out loud to no one in particular.

No one answered.

She looked on, bewildered, as fellow officers ran by. She heard snippets of conversation. *Hey, did you see? Yes, on it!*

Elaine grabbed Zeke as he went by, the only person who seemed to be walking at a normal speed in the building.

"Zeke, I can't get an answer. What's happened?"

"Xavier Henry just committed suicide."

"The Xavier Henry?" Elaine asked, her mouth hanging open. "That billionaire who's always in the news because he wants to buy the DC Metro?"

"Right? That one. Jumped out of that new building of his on the wharf. Caused a huge scene. That's why all your phones are ringing."

CHAPTER 31
VERONICA

Midday, March 20

It was going to be harder to explain away this one.

I really did just mean to go talk to him. I wasn't convinced the Princemakers didn't have a hand in whatever happened to my husband, but I was leaning away from them as the main culprits.

But since Nat's note left in the mailbox only gave his name and not a home address, and Francisco obviously wasn't available to help, I figured I'd follow the lead I did have.

Xavier Henry. Of course I knew who he was. Everyone in DC did. Probably everyone in the country, but I'd given up a long time ago pretending to be certain what the rest of the country was thinking about. Too many people in this city assumed that whatever was news here had to be nationwide news.

He had a gazillion dollars and made his money doing one of those nebulous hedge-fund type operations. Making money by moving money, the only goal in life to have the highest number in your account. He was probably happy enough, what with a disposable income that could've fed the hungry of the entire hemisphere. Well, until about an hour ago.

No one would have believed me that he actually did jump out

the window of his own volition. That I wasn't there just inside forcing him to do so. I wouldn't have believed me.

But I got lucky. He didn't throw himself out until after I was done talking to him. If he'd chucked himself out the window while I was standing there, in the middle of the day having had his secretary buzz me in, there would have been no explanation that could have gotten me off the hook.

But as it was, he jumped a couple minutes after I left. I hadn't left the building, so I didn't see it happen, but I heard the commotion. As soon as I saw the crowd I realized what must have happened, and that I was best suited far away from the scene.

Someone would come knocking soon—proverbially, at least, although I didn't put it past Detective Brown to have put two and two together and know where I was staying. I liked her. In a different life, she and I would have seen eye to eye a lot, I'd bet.

I would tell her the truth. I went there looking for my husband. A thoroughly decent man, a father to two lovely children. One of the men whose presence on this earth makes it a better place. The kind of man who noticed a potential problem before I even would. *Hey, I packed you a lunch that doesn't require heating since I know your schedule is too busy around lunchtime time to be sure you'll be near the microwave.*

A lot of men fell into the trap of only thinking those traditionally manly protective thoughts. How they'd face down an intruder, defend the home, that sort of thing. They'd miss the opportunities to take care of their spouse that flashed right in front of their eyes dozens of times a day. It became a joke in our family. I'd ask, "Ben, would you mind doing…?" and inevitably his answer would be, "already done!"

A good man.

As opposed to Xavier Henry. A snake in the grass. An immoral man who only cared about power.

But another snake who didn't actually have any info for me. Just like McAllister, he blustered and pretended he didn't know who I was, or what I could possibly be doing there.

Pretending not to know who I am was the biggest tell of all. If he truly hadn't been part of the Princemakers, he would have reacted differently. He would have legitimately had no idea why I was in his wrap-around office overlooking Washington Channel. True bafflement is easy to see. These weak men. Neither Henry nor McAllister had ever been hardened by having to do a job themselves.

I told him I'd be back, and he better sleep with one eye open until I returned. A bit cliché, sure, but a line that always did the trick. It never caused anyone to go commit suicide immediately afterward, though. That was new.

Death follows you wherever you go. Maybe that anonymous comment was right.

CHAPTER 32
JAMIE

Afternoon, March 20

He was going to have to stop her. Not a welcome proposition by any stretch, but this had to end.

He couldn't knock her results, though. Veronica Walsh was certainly effective. Two members of the Princemakers gone in as many days. Maybe the best bet would be to just sit back.

But he couldn't do that.

She was approaching a point of no return. He could feel the inflection point was approaching fast. He would have to make his move.

Time to come out of the shadows.

CHAPTER 33
ELAINE

Afternoon, March 20

A homicide detective is supposed to be able to tolerate dead bodies. Or at least not be horrified by them. Elaine shuddered as she stood over Xavier Henry's body on Maine Street SW. A sheet covered it, which almost made it worse in her mind. She'd never seen what a body dropped from the top floor of an office building looked like, so her imagination was running wild. Detective Brown had gone inside to talk to witnesses, so Elaine was left outside, steps away from what was a living, breathing human only an hour ago.

She remembered watching *The Departed* with her parents. She was definitely far too young for it, but they hadn't always been the tough-love, perennially disappointed parents they morphed into later. Back then, they were kind and empathetic, and the three of them shared quality time together every night.

Elaine had cuddled up between her parents, hogging too much of the communal fleece throw, and her dad shielded her eyes as the bad guys threw Martin Sheen's character from that Boston roof. She still remembered the *splat!* she heard, and how her entire body clenched in response to the sound. It hadn't occurred to her until later that her father must have already seen the movie to know to cover her eyes. At the time she thought they were all watching it for the first time together. But not seeing the aftermath, just hearing the sound the body made, made it worse inside her mind. She couldn't shake that scene from her brain for weeks after.

A large crowd milled just behind the ubiquitous yellow police tape. Elaine had often wondered if one company produced that. Is there some random CEO no one has ever heard of profiting from basically all police operations in the country?

The crowd was calm and hushed. No one pushes to the front to see a dead body. They were all there just to see it, but each individual had their own concocted story, telling themselves that they weren't *really* there to satisfy the gross urge to see death. They had to tell people what they knew, how they just happened to be nearby, inserting themselves into the story.

"That was a doozy," the officer near her said, shaking his head. She should have remembered his name, but she was terrible at putting names and faces together. Instead, she internally defined everyone by their outward-facing features. Cleft Chin officer sighed. "He was an inspiration, don't you think? It's always the genius minds that have something crazy going on inside. He would've saved WMATA and the metro if they'd just let him."

"A real pity," Elaine said, because she had nothing else to respond. She knew the name—who didn't? —but that was all she could muster. No other significant details about him sprang up from the recesses of her brain. "You were first here, right? What did they see?"

Cleft Chin nodded. "We were lucky. Someone was looking up and screamed and it gave the pedestrians enough time to move out of the way. One could easily have been killed if he'd landed on them."

"You think this was on purpose?"

His eyes widened. "You think it wasn't?"

Elaine shrugged. "I'm homicide. I always have to ask. Give me your impressions, Officer Hays," she said, finally getting enough of a glance at his badge to act like she'd always known his name.

He sighed. "Well, they did say he was screaming the whole way down."

"That doesn't sound like a man who meant to do that."

"I don't know, I've heard that there's often regret in those last moments."

"From whom?"

"Hm." He thought for a second. "Good point. I guess the internet?"

"The last bastion of truth. You'll never find something incorrect there." Elaine smirked. "Who was the last person to see him?"

"I've got his secretary right here." Hays called over and a young woman, dressed in a sleeveless blouse and far too short and tight a skirt, walked over. Elaine rolled her eyes. Of course he had a secretary who dressed like that. He probably forced her to do so. Too prejudicial? What did it matter? He was dead. It wasn't like she was going to stop investigating because he might've been a creep.

"There you are," the familiar voice behind Elaine said. She turned around to see her partner striding ahead. "Good, you've found Ann already," she said, glancing at the secretary, who was standing there trying to hide her shivering.

"Ann was about to tell me about who was last in his office," Elaine said.

Detective Brown shot her a mirthless smile. "I just asked that same question. You're going to enjoy this."

Ann took a deep breath. "I'll tell you, but like I told your partner, she had already left, so I don't know what she could have done."

"She," Elaine repeated, glancing at Brown. A knowing look passed between them. "Just what we needed."

"Veronica Walsh talked her way up to me, and then he buzzed me to tell me to let her in. She left about five minutes before he..." she gulped down a sob.

Elaine closed her eyes and sighed as it was confirmed. "Does everything that happens in this city end up connected to Veronica Walsh?"

"We need to talk to her again," Brown said. "She might be searching for her husband, and because of that we've treated her as a victim's family member, but that's over now. Veronica Walsh is now our main suspect in these two suspicious deaths."

CHAPTER 34
MIKAELA

Afternoon, March 20

Mikaela gaped as Veronica led her on a tour of Natalia Rochev's house. Everywhere she looked, there was something eye-opening. An ancient bust here, the recently found Vermeer from the Isabella Stewart Gardner Museum there (she was hastily informed that it was just there temporarily and would return back to its home shortly).

They arrived at the back patio, and Veronica offered her a chair. She sat down, marveling at the view overlooking the Potomac. The water glistened in the afternoon sun, and the flag atop Fort Washington across the water whipped back and forth in the wind.

"Not too dissimilar to the Belles' house, is it?" Veronica asked.

Mikaela gulped involuntarily. How had it only been a week since that harrowing ordeal?

She knew she had been venturing into the unknown when she knocked on the Walshes' door, asking to talk to Veronica about her missing husband. She had no way of knowing how they would react when they found out that she was Ben's half-sister, but she believed Veronica was the best chance at finding out the truth of what happened to her husband, Tony. She also selfishly needed reassurance that it wasn't her own actions that caused him to jump off the Woodrow Wilson Bridge to his death. That he felt guilt about his inaction at World's Edge years before had never been on her radar.

Nor had she thought she would discover she was pregnant.

It was still too early to feel kicks or to show, so the only proof she had to go on was the violent illness she felt randomly throughout each day. That morning sickness wasn't necessarily confined to the morning felt like a cruel blow. But every bout of nausea told her things were as they should be, and there was no greater gift.

Mikaela looked out over the Potomac, trying to banish the intrusive thoughts that invaded her mind. The river where Tony died.

"I think my newfound fear of heights is going to take a while to recover from." She offered a weak smile.

"We'll just stay here and drink our tea." Veronica picked up her mug and offered a toast.

"Look, Veronica, thanks for letting me come by…" Mikaela paused, working up the courage to talk to her newfound sister-in-law.

"What is it, Mikaela?"

"I saw that someone killed the president of Georgetown. I know there was this whole shadowy cabal, or whatever you call it, that Jacob Jordan talked about. You don't think he was involved in that too, do you?"

Veronica shrugged noncommittally.

"Wait, you do!" Mikaela pressed, not sure what gave her such confidence. "What do you know?"

Veronica shook her head. "I don't know anything. I'm just trying to find Ben."

"But maybe you went to talk to him because he might have info!"

"Spit it out, Mikaela," Veronica said with a ferocity that startled her.

"I…" Mikaela faltered. "What do you mean?"

"Don't try to pretend now. What is it that you're trying to ask?"

"Did you have anything to do with what happened to him?"

Veronica's face was stone. She took a deep breath and pushed the tip of her tongue against her top front teeth. "In all of human history there has been a common thread," she began.

Mikaela's mouth hung open. She hadn't actually believed Veronica had killed him. She was here to have Veronica tell her no, so that these intrusive thoughts in her mind about her sister-in-law could vanish.

"The ends justify the means. That's how it's been." Veronica held up her pointer finger as Mikaela was about to respond. "But only for men. Women have to account for their actions, their motives, their whatever. Men don't. You beat up your wife's lover? Good for you. A hearty pat on the back to you, sir. You killed the man threatening your daughter? Well that just makes you a good family man. You put your family above everything, and isn't that what the ideal male does? Where do we fit in?"

Mikaela stared before deciding Veronica was waiting for her to answer. "Well, we—"

"We don't." Veronica cut in. "There is no space for women's rage. For a woman's autonomy. Now, look. You'll probably tell me that this is 2024, we have some modicum of space for that now, but do we really?"

"Are you… are you trying to justify murder?" Mikaela now understood. She wasn't talking to Veronica Walsh, wife, mother of two. At this moment she was talking to Alessandra Portillo, serial killer. She knew the stories and rationally could reason that they had to be true, but she'd never seen Veronica show a glimpse of her previous self.

"Women are hysterical. Driven by emotion. Until as soon as you aren't, you're cold and calculating. There's nothing in between," Veronica said.

"Veronica, that can't be the way you see life."

"It's not about how I see it, it's about how life sees me. Sees us."

"I read all about you. I followed all the news. I told myself that you were a woman with steel, and backbone, and a determination that every one of us could aspire to. You clawed your way out, made a life out of scratch, and sure, you broke a few eggs along the way, but what else were you supposed to do? But if I'm reading between the lines correctly here, you're telling me you went and killed people. Two prominent members of this city. Murdered them just because you could. This is America, we have courts and laws against that sort of thing."

"You don't think El Salvador has laws?"

"No, I mean it's just that... you're established here. You have other options. You helped me find the truth about Tony, and you didn't have to go kill anyone to do it. Are you really still the type of person who would just kill in cold blood?"

"Cold blood? He threatened my children," Veronica said calmly, her face impassive. "He told me he would kill my children, so I made sure there was no chance of that happening."

Mikaela looked down and realized her hand had unwittingly gone to her stomach. What would she do if someone threatened her baby?

Veronica noticed it. "Exactly," she said. "Don't lecture me on what you would or wouldn't do in my shoes."

Mikaela stayed silent as Veronica's words hung in the still air. Could she actually have a point? Mikaela couldn't believe her mind was even letting her consider that possibility.

"Am I an accomplice now?" she finally asked. "After the fact, or whatever the legal wording is."

Veronica gave her a blank stare. "You wanted to know. You didn't have to ask questions."

"I wanted you to tell me you hadn't done it," Mikaela said, her voice soft.

Veronica looked up at the ceiling. When she brought her head back down, she said, "Look, I get it. I wish it wasn't this way either. But I live in a morally gray world that I never asked for. I was given tools and skills I didn't understand. If I'm being honest, I still don't understand what my role in life is supposed to be. Your husband is gone. My husband might well be too. All we both have for sure is our children. If your child ever is threatened and you know, deep in your heart, that they mean it, you'll do anything to stop them. You might not have a knife with you in that instant, but you'll protect your own. Because that's what we mothers have always done, and always will do."

CHAPTER 35
ARCHON

Afternoon, March 20

Archon looked around the oval table. It was rare to have the entire group together. They were three members lighter than last time they all gathered. The empty seats emphasized the somber tone.

"This has blown up spectacularly," he said, trying to project calm. No one needed to know how he internally felt. The fear that was bubbling up inside him that their entire world was on the precipice.

People who show their emotions on their sleeve never understand this. The people who look most calm, most in control, are often feeling the exact same things. It's just a coping mechanism. Some people express their feelings, some bottle them up, but everyone is trying to do the same thing: figure out how best to deal with them.

"How did Veronica Walsh get to McAllister and Henry?" the man at the far end of the table asked. If Archon had his way, they would have never met in person, leaving him the only one who knew all of their identities. But when you manage a group with egos this large, a little massaging has to take place. You had to let people think they were all equally important.

"Jeremy Wiles," another member responded. "Because Dan had to run his mouth to him, thinking getting him on our side would be useful when he won the presidency."

"Exactly the kind of naive thinking we don't do here," Archon said. "Wiles only knew about McAllister. Tell me about other vulnerabilities. Who else could know something?"

He watched as each member shook their heads in turn. None of them would say in front of the group that they felt unsafe.

"Is it time?" the one at the far end finally asked.

"Time for what?" Archon responded, knowing exactly what was going to be said.

"Time for Veronica Walsh to go."

"Absolutely not," came another voice before Archon could answer. "Too hot right now. She's being investigated hard. The connection is already there between her and Henry, what with her being at the scene. That, combined with the obvious ties with Dan Flint, is enough for the DC police to come down hard."

"I mean, couldn't we just push them in a different direction?"

"No," the man at the end of the table resolutely said. "We're not putting our hand on the scale when it comes to that investigation. We let that play out."

"She couldn't just have an accident?"

Archon scoffed. "If you want to be the one to try that, be my guest."

"We got her father. She can't be trickier than that."

"We got her father because we had an insider. We don't make moves without knowing how they will turn out. You all know that," Archon said, directing his voice to the entire group.

"So, what now?"

"Well, it's obvious there's another vulnerability," the man at the far end said. "Two, potentially, although they might be the same. Jeremy Wiles couldn't have known about Xavier Henry, and someone still killed Dan Flint. The one thing we know for sure is that it wasn't Veronica Walsh or Francisco Orellana. He was an easy patsy but that one won't stick at all."

"That's correct. And that's what brings us together today. Not because we need to rise up against Veronica Walsh, but because we are accidentally aligned. The last thing we want to do is kill her. Instead, we're going to follow her, because she's going to lead us right to the answers. Remember what's at stake here. D-Day is approaching. We need to be ready. Veronica Walsh may be a thorn in our side right now, but there's a much larger thorn that's finally ready to be plucked out and thrown away."

CHAPTER 36
VERONICA

Afternoon, March 20

There's no good way to tell your half-sister-in-law that you just murdered someone. But among all the ways, letting her work it out herself while you provide cryptic answers and talk about how it's the world's fault is probably high on the list of ways not to do it.

But what else was there? *Yes, Mikaela, I slit a man's throat when there was no active threat to my life.* I didn't even get to tell her that I didn't actually push Xavier Henry out the window.

It was snowballing exactly as Ben had feared. Every minute since he disappeared, my heart ached, but never before had I wished so hard he could be here by my side. I needed my calm, steady husband to explain everything to and have him tell me it was all going to be okay.

I thought back to my wedding day. That was the day I felt the worst about lying to Ben about my past. I felt great, personally, because it was the ultimate symbol of a new, fresh start. My past was over. Alessandra Portillo was gone, and now Veronica Aguilar would be too. Veronica Walsh. A white American-passing name that wouldn't catch anyone's eye if they were looking for the daughter of a Salvadoran crime boss.

That obviously was not why I married Ben, but it was a nice bonus. The ceremony at Holy Name Parish was beautiful. Not too small a wedding, but I didn't have too many to bring on my side. A handful of friends but nothing at all like the contingent of family members Ben insisted had to be invited. A big Boston Irish affair, complete with "Sweet Caroline" shouted out by loads of men and women drunk on too many Sam Adams.

I never thought of my wedding day as the best day of my life. I get why people say that, and there's of course a draw to the nostalgia of a day with all of your friends and family there solely to celebrate you and the love of your life. But it just seems to set up the rest of your marriage for failure to think that way. I don't want the first day of marriage to be the best. Where do you go from there? Only downhill. The best days of marriage are the hundreds of entirely mundane days where you each just exist together. A million little moments that make up true love, not an ostentatious one-day event that sparkles brightly before an inevitable fizzle.

The best day of your marriage should always be ahead of you. Even if everything else is failing, even if your own best days are behind you, I didn't ever want to think the best days of marriage were over. If you think that's the case, what is there left for you? You should look back at your wedding day, remember it fondly, chuckle a little bit about how young you were, wonder how you let that great hors d'oeuvre pass you by, and then think about how much better life is now. That's the dream. Sure, there's a lot outside our control, and loads of reasons why life might have lost some luster, but the goal should always be marriage, not the wedding.

That's not to say I didn't know how to throw down. There was a reason we put aspirin in the gift bags for all our guests.

There was the other reason it was an auspicious day, in hindsight. That fun little write-up in the local paper about Ben Walsh getting married, complete with a couple of the same wedding reception pictures you've seen a million times before. Revelry on the dance floor, a selection of the older guests forming an uneasy circle while a few of the younger crew vied to be the main character. Me giving a thumbs up to the cameraman as I get down.

Giving a thumbs up with my left hand. Where my missing pinky finger was easily visible. In a newspaper article posted online.

The internet is forever. Seeing that picture when Ben happily sent me the link caused my mind to refocus. There was a picture of me out there where anyone could see my missing finger.

I couldn't fix that problem, but I could assure there would be no more. From that moment on, I wore gloves every time I left the house. Ben knew it wasn't me being a germaphobe but couldn't ever figure out what my true reason was. I wasn't exactly convincing either. The happy-go-lucky, confident girl of his dreams all of a sudden never wanting to be out in public without gloves? And the only thing she'd say was that it *wasn't* because of germs? I knew I tested his patience with that one.

Well, now that was a thing of the past. Walking around without gloves had made me realize just how many people knew my story but didn't recognize my face. We'd be walking along the Potomac waterfront and a passerby wouldn't give my face a second look but as soon as they noticed my finger they stopped and gawked. Dining out turned into the trickiest experience. Everyone who recognized me wanted to say something. Positive or negative, they couldn't miss their chance to tell Veronica Walsh what they thought.

I really did understand how this had gotten so hard for Ben. He hadn't signed up for any of this. The spotlight, the whispers, the stares. That wasn't what he thought his life was meant to be. He was supposed to work his way up in congressional politics, a nobody on the grand stage but an asset to all who knew him, until one day he'd step into the public eye. From then, a straight shot to the top. Benjamin Walsh, president of the United States. That was the ending he deserved.

The phone rang. It would be the police, of course. Trying to find me to tie me to another murder. In fairness to them, they wouldn't be wrong. "Veronica Walsh," I said into the speaker.

"Hello, Mrs. Walsh," a nervous, shaky voice answered. "This is Officer Hughes from the Prince George's County Police Department, Division Seven."

Okay that was unexpected. *Where?*

"I'm trying to reach a relative of Benjamin Walsh, is that you?"

My breath was ripped from my throat as soon as I heard my husband's name. An ice-cold chill clawed its way down and took hold. No. It couldn't be.

"Mrs. Walsh?"

"Yes," I stammered.

"Are you a relative of Benjamin Walsh?" the officer repeated.

I took a deep breath and steeled myself. "I am."

A long pause followed by a quick exhale. "I'm sorry, Mrs. Walsh. We need you to come to Accokeek to formally identify a body."

CHAPTER 37
ELAINE

Afternoon, March 20

"She's not answering your calls, is she?" Elaine looked over to her partner, whose repeated huffing was drawing the attention of a few others.

"No." Detective Brown glowered. "And no one has been seen in her house in days. A neighbor said the bay window that was boarded up has now been fixed. My other question: where are her kids?"

"Where would they go?" Elaine asked. "Does she have family nearby?"

Brown pointed an approving finger at her. "Yep, good call. Parents in Williamsburg, Virginia. That's probably where the kids are. But what does that tell us?"

"She's on the run," Elaine answered without hesitation.

"Exactly. And people on the run are normally guilty."

"Except her, last time, I guess." Elaine allowed herself a small chuckle as she rose to join Brown at her desk. "On the run implies hiding, right?"

Brown arched an eyebrow.

"But she's not running this time," Elaine continued. "She can't be. She's searching for her husband. So, she has to be hunkered down somewhere, not away and on the run. Close by."

CHAPTER 38
VERONICA

Evening, March 20

There's a thing about me that very few people know. My heart rate doesn't slow down in times of crises like everyone pretends. I'm not super cool and calm at all moments. My heart rate does the opposite, in fact. It explodes. That I'm able to manage that, while doing everything I've done, I think speaks even more for me.

But it wasn't thumping today.

My pulse remained consistent. And honestly, that freaked me out. I drove as if on autopilot, my mind barely registering where I was until I arrived at the police station in Fort Washington. The officer had said Accokeek, but that was where the body was found, in Piscataway Park on the Maryland side of the Potomac, not where it was currently located. It would go up to Baltimore for an autopsy, unless Virginia or DC pulled rank and got it sent to their medical examiners instead. But for now, Fort Washington it was.

The little town named for the neighboring fort, built shortly after the Revolutionary War to defend Washington, DC, that I had stared at across the river for the last few days. Almost directly across from Natalia's scenic overlook, this was the place where my world was to come crashing down on me.

I pulled into the parking lot and drove all the way to the back end. I had scoped out the area and the dense trees behind the lot backed up to a row of houses. I could lose anyone in there. I always looked for exits, a trait that Ben used to rib me about. That ribbing stopped a few months ago.

I never once wondered if I wasn't loved. Isn't that what marriage should be about? The tagline, if it needed one. What is marriage? A relationship in which you never want for love. He'd poke and prod at me about all sorts of funny little things—like how I couldn't remember to close a closet or pantry door to save my life—but everything was joyful. He boosted me up, and every interaction, even the most charged, had the undercurrent of love.

Even in these last couple of weeks. He moved out, and I did consider what might happen if that was it because how could I not? But in hindsight, we were never close to a real fissure. We were a team. A partnership that could handle anything thrown at it and had the receipts to back that up.

A partnership that I was walking into a nondescript building to confirm was now over.

A kindly middle-aged man with round spectacles and a dark birthmark under his left eye met me at the door. "Are you Veronica Walsh?" he asked, his face showing me he already knew the answer and wished it weren't so.

I nodded and he ushered me in. I followed behind him as we turned and walked down a sterile hallway, lit by harsh ceiling lights.

"Have you ever seen a dead body?" he asked without looking back.

If I weren't about to see my dead husband, I might've laughed. Me? See a dead body? Well, yes, once or twice, if you're curious. Maybe not everyone kept up with the news in this town. "I have."

"I just need to warn you," he continued as if I hadn't said yes, "that it's not a pretty sight. No matter how much you read about it, or see it on TV, it can't prepare you for the real thing. And he was in the water for a while. There's bloating, discoloration, skin sloughing. We think the body was pinned down, possibly by a fallen log. It should have made it to the surface faster than it did. We're doing the best we can."

"I appreciate that." What else could I say?

We stopped in front of a set of metal double doors.

"Ma'am, are you ready?" He gave me a resolute nod and I returned one in kind. No point in prolonging this.

We entered a long, narrow room with closed coffin-sized drawers on each side. At the far end was a single table with the telltale covering draped over an unidentified body.

When we got to the table, he swept the covering back with an unnecessary dramatic flourish. Maybe his line of work didn't provide many wins for him, but what could possibly be helpful about adding a little pizzazz?

The face was bloated, as advertised. A horrific green discoloration had spread and small pieces of flesh on the cheek had been nibbled off.

The eyes were closed. I don't know why I assumed they'd be open. People who have never seen a dead body tend to think the eyes are open, because that's how movies show them. If they were closed, how would we know the person bleeding out wasn't just sleeping?

But I'd seen a fair few dead bodies. They don't all look like. Especially depending on what someone might have done to them first.

I really did think the eyes would be open, despite it all. Maybe because Ben's eyes were always my favorite part of him. With the light gone from his eyes, I'd truly understand that it was over. I'd see that what made Ben who he was had been extinguished.

But even closed, I knew.

My mind couldn't make sense of it, though. I shook my head, getting any cobwebs out, and looked again.

I knew these eyes. But these weren't my husband's eyes.

And the final face these eyes saw was my own.

CHAPTER 39
JAMIE

Evening, March 20

Jamie wiped the cotija cheese off his mouth with a cloth napkin. Despite not having anyone to cook for, he still enjoyed the craft of it. Why shouldn't he eat well and enjoy his meals? His tostadas weren't exactly a delicacy, but sometimes you just couldn't beat a mound of flavor on a flat taco shell.

And this time, he wasn't alone. He made a second plate, piling the shredded lettuce high and made his way out of the kitchen toward the front hallway and the locked door.

He pulled the small bronze key out of the zipped pocket of his jeans and slipped it into the lock, and with a click turned the doorknob and pulled the door open. The stairs down to the basement were treacherous in the dark, so he'd installed lights along the banister when he first moved in. He had survived too much to end up a scary story to tell about the neighborhood loner who disappeared and was found months or years later at the bottom of the stairs in his basement.

He gripped the railing—*better safe than sorry*—as he descended. The bare, cold room was empty apart from a pool table, futon, and TV. He crossed the floor and turned toward the door set in the brick wall at the end of a small hallway. The door here didn't need a lock on the outside—it was invisible to the naked eye unless you paid very specific attention. A classic push-the-correct-brick set-up that had been part of the house long before he bought it. The realtor said it was originally part of the Underground Railroad. He had no idea if that was true. One of these days he would look it up and find out for sure.

The door shifted backward, then slid sideways, revealing a small living space, complete with a toilet in one corner and a twin bed at the opposite end.

Jamie walked in, pausing to glance around the room, before heading over to the bed. When he got there, he reached an arm down and poked the man asleep on top of the covers. "Hey, Ben, wake up. We need to talk."

CHAPTER 40
ELAINE

Evening, March 20

Elaine's eyes bulged as she looked down at the name that popped up on her ringing phone. She quickly waved Detective Brown over to her desk. "Hi, Veronica. Where have you been hiding?"

"Veronica, it's Detective Brown on the line as well," her partner said, as Elaine shot her a glance. "We're on the verge of putting a warrant out, so get your ass down here and tell us about the bodies."

"The bodies." Veronica snorted. "That's a good one."

"What do you mean?" Elaine asked.

"How about you tell me about a body instead?"

Elaine looked to her partner for direction. Brown shook her head, a confused look on her face. "What body?" Elaine asked.

"The one that I was just called out by PG County to identify as my own husband."

"Oh my God, they found him—" Elaine stopped abruptly when she saw Brown raise her outstretched hand. "It wasn't your husband, then?"

"You'd think they'd have checked, I don't know, anything else, before calling me, wouldn't you?"

"What happened?" Brown asked.

"A cop from Fort Washington called, saying I needed to come identify my husband, who has been in the Potomac for days and so is bloated and looks bad, blah blah blah."

"Why did they think it was your husband and not Leonard Barry, a well-known missing person who fell into the Potomac?"

Elaine still wondered exactly what happened there. All they had to go on was Veronica's word that Barry had been the one up in the trees, acting as the sniper on Jacob Jordan's behalf. The tree branch gave way when Veronica tried to stop him, and he fell into the Potomac. A nice and tidy story. She wouldn't be surprised if he was found with a bullet hole or two, from some likely untrace-able gun.

"Wow, look at you asking the hard-hitting questions," Veronica said as the sound of a nearby car honking its horn blared through the speaker. "Sorry, trying not to die here. Asshole driv-ers. Anyway, they found Ben's wallet in the body's pocket, so they just assumed."

"Why would this body have Ben's wallet? Was it Len?" Brown asked.

"It was Len, and I have no clue," Veronica said. "Not my prob-lem, although you need to get with them for your own sake and reign them in down there while you're at it. That shit is sloppy. Also, since I seem to be the only one doing any real work around here, that cabal is called the Princemakers. Do with that what you will."

"Veronica—"

The line was dead. "Well, I was going to tell her we still need to talk to her about the other bodies," Elaine said.

"We'll get to that, but let's move." Detective Brown grabbed her coat. "We need a positive ID on Leonard Barry or else we've got another third homicide on our hands."

CHAPTER 41
VERONICA

Morning, March 21

I hadn't planned on continuing my circuit of visiting friends-turned-enemies in jail, but here we were. Of course I told the detectives that why Ben's wallet was on a dead man was not my problem, but how could it not be? What was I supposed to say, that obviously I'm going to investigate this whether they like it or not? They knew that anyway. We each played our role. I told them I wasn't going to follow up, and they pretended to believe me.

I sat down in my chair and watched Jacob Jordan shuffle in. His mannerisms were on the opposite end of the spectrum as Jeremy Wiles' had been. Jeremy had looked comfortable, like he understood what he had been getting himself into, and that he had adapted well to being inside.

Jacob's once floppy blonde hair was shorn, a buzz cut that showcased angry patches of red eczema across the top of his head. His bright, piercing eyes now appeared hollow and sunken. He had taken on exactly what I imagined prison should do to the average person.

What do you do when the monster turns back into a young man?

I couldn't help but look at him and see my pupil. I knew better than anyone that there are a million faces of evil, and staring at the pure, undistilled, form is rare, but it was still galling to me to see his face. He wasn't evil. He wasn't a 'bad guy' from the movies, with an armchair we only see from the back and a menacing studio where he plans his crimes. He was a kid, angry with the world for what happened to his sister.

Was that any solace for the families of his victims, though? Of course not. Bridget Lowe's loved ones weren't going to be grappling with her involvement in an incident in college, they'd just be heartbroken that their daughter, sister, friend, by all accounts a well-liked adult woman, was brutally murdered.

"Hi, Dr. Walsh." Jacob's distinct sing-song quality of his voice had dimmed, and he spoke barely over a whisper.

"Jacob, what happened?" I asked, unable to hide my concern. After everything, he was still just my pupil. The kid I had high hopes for.

"Oh, no, not what you're thinking." He put his hands up.

"No one hurt you in here?"

"No. I just... what's even the point? The rich and powerful win. That's what happens. I manage to permanently stop a couple of them who ruined Janet's life, but then what? Did the world stop? Did any institution, anything at all, skip a beat? No. Like, what are we even doing here? I *murdered* people, highly important people, and nothing happened. Why?"

"Because changing the way of the world isn't a job for just one person."

Jacob narrowed his eyes.

"That's not your role in life, save for a few specific examples," I continued. "But what you can do is light the first match. Inspire people until you have a critical mass. Break a stable equilibrium, introduce a perturbation." When in doubt, appeal in terms you know they'll understand.

"Change a parameter, force a new solution." Jacob nodded appreciatively.

I sighed. "But not your way. Not by killing people."

"Rich of you to say that."

"What change did I effect in any of my previous actions?" I asked. "Were any of them more important than what I inspired inside a classroom? People make the world a better place the tiniest increment at a time. That's all there is."

"Well, then it's just rigged."

"No one ever promised life would be fair. Never in human history has it been. We can decry the inequality, or we can take our station and make the most of it."

Jacob closed his eyes. I wasn't here for a lengthy discussion of right and wrong. I was here for one question only, but I knew Jacob. He wouldn't just give me an answer straight away and let me walk out. He agreed to talk because he wanted to, and I sensed this was why. Some sort of validation.

"Do you want me to tell you that you made a difference?" No point waiting around for him to eventually ask.

"I just.... I don't know."

"We're going after the people who Senator Billingsley was working with. How about that for a start?"

"You are?" I saw a flicker of emotion behind his eyes for the first time.

"We are. Jacob, I think you might know why I'm here. How much news have you kept up with?"

He frowned. "I don't actually keep up," he admitted after a brief pause. "I don't know anything about what's happened since I got in here."

I figured I might as well go for it. "Why did Leonard Barry have my husband's wallet?"

"Why did...? Oh."

I watched his face contort as he understood why I was asking. "Hold on. Did someone think Ben was dead just because they found Len?"

"That's exactly what happened. I got called to ID a body that wasn't my husband's."

"But why didn't you just tell them your husband was at home, or wherever?"

I didn't have time for the full story, so gave Jacob a brief recap of what he'd missed. He sat silent, his mouth gaping open.

"Holy shit," he finally stammered.

I gave a single shake of my head in return. "So, I want to know why, and how, did Leonard Barry have Ben's wallet?"

"I didn't realize he still was holding on to it," Jacob said, running his hand over his buzz cut, like I used to see him do so often in class. "I snagged it when I broke into your house."

"Wait a second," I said. "That timeline doesn't make sense. You broke in when Ben was at the hotel."

Jacob's eyes lit up. A spark of the old Jacob, just for a second. "No way, you never noticed I broke in again? Wow, that's like the highest compliment I could ever get from you."

"What are you talking about?"

"I came back. One night while you were all asleep. I didn't really have a plan, if I'm being honest, but it was after we spoke behind your house. I told you that something close to home was going to happen."

"You—" I started to rise out of my chair.

"Wait, wait, wait." He held his hands up. "I never meant it against your family. I was actually looking for some inspiration. I was stuck. I thought I'd find something on Francisco or somebody. Ben's wallet was on the table, and I snagged it before I left. Then I decided Mikaela was a better fit and didn't think about it anymore."

"Francisco would've ripped you limb from limb. You have no idea the bullet you dodged."

"Yeah, I met him when I got arrested. You're not wrong," Jacob conceded. "Anyway, I gave the wallet to Len, and just asked him to hold onto it. I assumed he probably just put it down somewhere, not that he was literally holding on to it. Wait," he paused. "Why wasn't his own wallet there?"

I shrugged and shook my head. "No clue."

"Damn." He cocked his head to the side. "Dr. Flint, really? I always wondered."

"What do you mean?"

"Do you know I never took a class with him?"

I thought back. "You know, he did mention that once. I always thought that was just some quirk of class scheduling."

Jacob exhaled a long sigh. "Nope. I knew that Dr. Flint had some weird thing about him and the Belles, so I did my best to stay away from him. I suspected he might have been part of the grander cover-up, but what was I supposed to say? 'I swear there's a shadowy organization and it's probably got a Senator and a math professor as part of it?' I would've been laughed away. I didn't even have any proof, just a weird feeling that he was included since I heard from my sister that she'd once seen him at the Belles' house when I talked to her about wanting to be a math major."

"You're right, no one would've taken you seriously."

"Wait, though. Where is your husband then? He was at Dr. Flint's house and must have been hurt in some way by Jamie Simon, posing as Francisco for some reason, but then what? I don't see why this guy would benefit from taking him as a hostage or something, and he hasn't contacted you anyway. Ben didn't crawl off somewhere because he would've been found and end up in a hospital. If he was dead, why would Simon move the body? I don't get it. Something else is going on here."

"That's basically where I am, yes," I said. I don't know what made me admit the next part. "I really thought he was dead this whole time."

"No way."

I chuckled and gave a quick shake of my head, as if I couldn't believe it either. "I know, right? He said he never gave up on me last year. He had no idea what I was capable of, all he knew was what I had shown him, and yet he didn't lose hope. He trusted I was out there, somewhere, and his faith was proven right. I think maybe it's the idealist in him versus the realist in me. I hoped, of course I did, but I wouldn't let myself fully believe."

I realized now that I had done a complete one-eighty. There wasn't any new evidence out there that Ben wasn't dead. If anything, the last day hadn't changed the status quo at all. But now I did believe. Ben was out there, somewhere, and there were only two options now. Either he would find his way back to me, or I would move heaven and earth to bring him home.

CHAPTER 42
BEN

Evening, March 21

Ben ate greedily, slopping up every morsel of the white chicken chili with his small metal spoon. Jamie, with all the grace of an award-winning host, had propped up a small tv table next to Ben's bed for him to eat on. Ben chewed the cannellini beans slowly, letting them melt in his mouth.

"Your wife knows you're not dead."

Ben snapped his head around. Jamie leaned nonchalantly on the open door. Ben had been so consumed by eating he hadn't noticed Jamie didn't leave after he dropped it off. "Is that what you really wanted to talk to me about yesterday?" Ben asked. "Not just more talk about how she needs to stop whatever she's doing that you won't even tell me?"

Jamie walked over to the bed. "I needed to be sure I wanted you to know. She's going to burn everything down searching for you. She got called out to see a body that was found with your wallet, but obviously wasn't actually you."

"How do you know all this? And what body?"

"I watch and I pay attention. Len Barry was found with your wallet, and the police thought it was you for a second."

"Jesus. Am I supposed to be upset that my wife is now looking for me alive rather than trying to avenge me?"

"Yes," Jamie said, matter-of-factly.

Ben sighed, exasperated. He pulled his legs back up onto the bed, a difficult act when his side was screaming at him. He pulled his shirt up and peeled back the bandage. Was it looking worse? Was that more angry red skin than yesterday?

It had been just over a week and Ben still had little idea of what happened at Dan Flint's house. He thought he had been doing a grand gesture of goodwill, going out to help Veronica find answers. An action to show he was back and fully on board. He loved everything about her, and even though all the new parts of her were hard to understand, he was going to be there for it all.

So he didn't even tell her where he was going, wanting it to be a surprise when he returned with useful intel. Not being able to find his wallet hadn't even slowed him down. It was just a quick hop from Old Town Alexandria over to Georgetown—highly unlikely that any cops would stop him, so what did it matter if he drove without a license just this once? Spending an hour fumbling around for his wallet would have ruined it. She would've come down, asked where he was headed while she helped him find it, and then the surprise would've gone away.

Dan had been surprised to see him but welcomed him in for a cup of tea. Ben had politely declined—*there was a reason they threw tea and not coffee into the harbor*—but followed him into his parlor and sat down beside him.

"What brings you over?"

"I was just wondering if you could help me out. You know about Senator Billingsley's death, I'm sure, and it looks like there might be some connection to Georgetown."

Dan's face scrunched up. "What do you mean?"

"Well, Jacob Jordan being the main suspect is the obvious part, but Veronica and I think there's something going on about a group of students who might have been at World's Edge a decade ago, and that's what this is all about."

"I—I don't know how to help you," Dan stammered as his face turned a ghostly white.

Of all the reactions Ben was prepared for, he had no answer for that.

"Well, I just thought, since you've been around the school for a long time, maybe you would know—"

"I don't," Dan cut him off. "I think that you should leave. There's nothing I can tell you." He stood up, taking a deep breath.

Ben watched, nonplussed, as Dan walked by him toward the front door. Dan paused and glanced at the fireplace, considering something. Ben frantically looked around the room, thinking of something to get Dan to keep talking. "Hey, wait," he said, turning and taking a couple steps into the kitchen at the far end of the living room. He didn't know what he'd find there but it was the opposite direction of the exit.

His mind still couldn't piece together what happened next. A jumble of split-second memories flitted around inside his head. The gunshot. A sickening thud. The searing pain. And then, finally, the light getting dimmer as everything faded to black.

Now here he was, sitting in a dark basement room. No idea how he got here or where here even was. The bed was surprisingly comfy, and this man who called himself Jamie had been polite enough, albeit unwilling to talk more than a few words while checking on his wound.

Ben had no experience with violence. He hid it well, but he was the guy who closed his eyes during violent scenes in movies and television. It was a world he wanted no part of. But now that world was on his doorstep. Finding his wife lying in a pool of her own blood last October had left an indelible stain on his brain. He would do whatever it took to make sure no violence was ever part of their lives again.

Those were a nice few months. They spent the first few weeks hunkering down. Veronica slowly recovered and Ben didn't like the idea of her out in public. She jokingly accused him of hiding her away, but she understood that it would be a while before she had her full strength back. So they implemented some new traditions. Homemade pizzas on Friday nights with the kids, long slow Sunday morning walks before the rest of the town was awake. Calm activities, as Veronica called them.

But as Veronica grew stronger—and happier—each day, Ben couldn't rid himself of his own growing fear that they were not out of the woods just yet.

And, well, look at him now.

"Look, Jamie, that's your name, right?" Ben said. "Now that you're here and want to actually talk, let's talk. Why have you been following me?"

"So, you did see me." A corner of his mouth lifted upward slightly. "The elevator, right?"

"Yes."

"I really thought that door had closed. That was poorly done on my part."

"You haven't answered me." Ben could feel his anger rising—anger that he hadn't had the strength to utilize since he ended up here. "What the fuck is going on?"

"What's going on is that you're dead, and I want to keep it that way." His voice was annoyingly calm. "Your wife, meanwhile, will stop at nothing to bring you back, and that's becoming a problem. I need to figure out what to do from here."

"Then why am I not actually dead? Why don't you just kill me and get it over with?"

"Begging for death this early? You're really not cut out for this are you?" Jamie turned for the door.

"Wait, where are you going?"

Jamie glanced back over his shoulder. "Not sure. But I'm going to go solve our Veronica Walsh problem. Sit tight."

CHAPTER 43
ELAINE

Night, March 21

"It's confirmed now."

Elaine looked up to see her partner approaching. "What?"

"The body those boys found in Piscataway Park was Leonard Barry."

"Okay. That's not exactly news, is it?"

Detective Brown shrugged. "Not our problem right now, unless we want to charge Veronica Walsh with homicide for making the tree branch break."

Elaine pondered that for a second. "Any chance she did it on purpose, do you think?"

"Probably." Brown waved her hand dismissively. "But there's nothing we can actually do there anyway. What we need is—oh, hi, chief."

Elaine whipped around to see Chief Branaman marching toward their desks. "Sir," she said, putting her bottle of Diet Pepsi down.

"Do you have anything that ties Dr. Flint together with McAllister?" He asked without a preamble.

"Not yet, sir."

"But you will," he said confidently.

"Well, if there's something that ties them together more than just the university."

"President McAllister was a close friend of the Belle family," the chief said, looking back and forth at the two of his detectives, an incredulous look on his face that he had to lead them all the way.

"Oh, shit," Elaine said. "The cabal, or whatever it is. Veronica Walsh said they're called The Princemakers."

"And why do we have her doing our investigating for us?" Branaman asked.

"You try stopping her," Brown said.

Elaine gasped. She wouldn't dare speak to their superior in that way.

But Branaman just sighed and shot a quick smile toward Detective Brown. "Fair enough."

"One other thing on that," Brown said. "I tracked down any reference I could to the Princemakers. As you'd expect, there's next to nothing, but I did find a weird little piece of information. It sounds like their leader goes by Archon."

"A pseudonym, surely," Branaman said.

"Yeah, Greek for ruler."

"Good work."

Detective Brown ignored the compliment. "Gregory McAllister, Xavier Henry, Dan Flint," she listed the names off as she wrote them down on a fresh pad of paper. "All connected to the Belles?"

Elaine glanced toward the chief.

"Check Henry and Senator Billingsley. You need to be sure," he said.

Elaine turned away so that he couldn't see her wince. She did not want the chief thinking he had to come over and bail her out, do her investigating for her. Especially not immediately after her partner had impressed him. He had given her this opportunity, and she didn't want him to have any doubts whatsoever.

She also knew there was a chance that she had been hired solely because of who her family was. She wasn't naive.

"So, Iverson," Chief Branaman had said the first time they met.

"Elaine Iverson, sir." She had shifted uncomfortably in the extra chair in his office.

He gave her a small, knowing nod. "Excited to have you on the team, Detective. I will be watching your progress with anticipation."

"You're not the only one," Elaine had sighed. Her mouth dropped open as she realized what she had said. "I mean, I just have a lot of pressure on me."

"I know who your family is." He offered a reassuring smile. "Just be the best detective you can be. But between you and me," he hushed his voice even though they were alone in his office, "I understand your family and your position, so if there's anything you need, just let me know."

The imposter syndrome never went away but it felt like a highwire act with a safety net. She knew that the chief had her back. He wasn't going to hand out favors, but he'd save her from failing.

Now here he was doing her job for her. Her face steamed as she listened to him. "This is all connected," she said. If a TV detective had said that line, the music would've swelled, and the camera moved in close while they gazed as some crucial piece of evidence. So why did it sound so juvenile coming out of her mouth?

"Everything you find. I want to hear it. Loop me in on every step," Branaman said. "This is big. Career-defining big. Whatever you need from me, you have it."

CHAPTER 44
ARCHON

Night, March 21

Archon sipped on his Stoli, sitting quietly in the near darkness of his study. The single tabletop lamp shone a soft light over his desk. Papers were stacked meticulously, pens tucked neatly in their holders, not a single item was a millimeter away from its designated location.

This was what it was to be him, he thought. This was the truest version. Solitude soothed him in a way nothing else on earth could. He put up with all the external noise because he had to, and he knew that even he couldn't do it all alone. But sitting in the dark, planning and scheming, allowing his brain to travel down a windy road, that was true bliss.

He allowed the Princemakers to meet together, and to pretend they all were equal partners. Pretend they made decisions together. They needed to feel important.

But their importance was only in what they could do for him. Once that was gone, there was nothing left. He wondered if this was the same power Ulrich Belle felt when he was Archon.

He knew Xavier Henry was a weak link. He hadn't recruited him. He had been happy with the relative size of their group, a close-knit team that wouldn't break no matter what they were up against. A team that placed important people into important positions and sat back and reaped the rewards. Sometimes those assets didn't even know they'd been targeted. They had no idea who had turned them into princes. But when push came to shove, they'd learn quickly. That was true power.

When Senator Billingsley said he had a great idea for a new member of their ranks, Archon was willing to hear him out. He understood internal diplomacy. Don't piss people off, especially when they might be of use.

Xavier Henry was an empty suit. A big talker who had been told his entire life that he was virtuous because he was rich.

But. He had loads of dispensable money. Archon never passed up the opportunity to use someone else's cash. All he would have to do was grease the wheels so that Henry's pet project of taking over the DC metro came to fruition.

Henry claimed that he hadn't told Veronica Walsh anything—that any of their plans that he knew were still safely concealed. But they were well past the 'trust but verify' stage. Archon calmly told him on the phone right after Veronica Walsh left that he needed to jump out the window.

"What?" Henry had blanched. "What are you talking about?"

"I'm talking about your daughter, Mimi, and your son, Walter. I'm talking about your wife, Lauren, and your two sisters, Jennifer and Terri. I'm talking about your dog, Muffler." Archon listed them off as if this knowledge meant nothing to him.

"What's going on?" his voice was quiet now.

"I'm simply offering you a choice," Archon said. "I'm providing you a detailed list of family members I will kill, one by one, if you do not jump out that window in the next ten minutes."

"I… you can't be serious."

"Veronica Walsh just came and talked to you. You're a liability, you could lose us everything. And for that, I need you to do the honorable thing."

"I will do no such thing! You pretend to be in charge, but

everyone in our group has as much power as you. You don't scare me."

Archon knew that assertion invariably meant the opposite.

"Lauren first, I think. That would be best. I'll send a car over. She's probably just finishing teaching that hot yoga class she enjoys so much over on 14th Street, so she'll be looking for an Uber back to your house in Chevy Chase. We'll tell her you sent for her, and she'll think it's a sweet gesture that you don't do often enough. Then…" He paused, drawing out the tension. "…About 30 minutes or so from now, she'll realize something is wrong. The car will turn east on U Street. She'll try the door and realize it's locked. She'll yell and scream and the driver won't even look around."

Archon listened to the frantic breathing on the other end of the phone. This was true power. "Shall I continue, or have I made myself clear?"

Henry was hyperventilating now.

"Do it now." Archon pressed forward. "Work up the nerve, and don't hesitate. Your wife and children will be compensated, and no harm will come to them. You have five minutes. If I do not hear on the police scanner then we will move forward with our plan for Lauren. Rest assured there will be unspeakable pain before the end."

He hung up the phone before there was a response. The sirens he heard from outside his window a few minutes later told him all he needed to know. He hadn't even bothered to turn his scanner on.

Now that Xavier Henry was gone, the group was getting small. Back to our roots, he thought. No matter, he liked it better that way anyway. His mission mattered far more than the individuals.

And it was almost time for the next step.

CHAPTER 45
VERONICA

Night, March 21

Among the many perks of using Natalia's house was the proximity to the Mount Vernon Trail. Running from Mount Vernon northward along the Virginia bank of the Potomac River, it passed through Old Town Alexandria and continued all the way to Theodore Roosevelt Island. Only sparingly lit, some sections were treacherously dark at night, most notably so in the wooded section just north of Arcturus.

I didn't mind. I enjoyed the solitude. And the lack of light helped me continue to work on eradicating my only weakness: fear of the dark. Although fear of reckless bicyclists was a new one while out here.

I walked along the trail, a single headphone in, listening to Blackmore's Night and thinking about my husband. He was at Dan Flint's house. He wasn't dead on the banks of the Potomac. So, what happened?

He was hurt and was moved. But to where and to what end?

"Stop right there. Don't move."

I didn't stop. Not my modus operandi. I whirled around, trying to see through the dense vegetation that covered the steep incline just off the path. I couldn't ascertain where the voice came from.

"Hands above your head, palms open."

I still couldn't see well enough to tell who was there. I sighed. Sometimes you just have to accept the situation for what it is. I slowly put my hands up in the air and spread my palms wide.

"I know you probably have some weapon still within reach," the voice said, and this time I was able to pinpoint what I hadn't been able to before. It was coming from below. Someone hidden down the bank. "I have a gun trained on you. But more important is what I know. So, you'd be wise not to try whatever you're planning."

Someone who had been able to sneak up on me and yet understood the unique threat I could still possess? If I didn't know better, I would've guessed it was Francisco. "Whatever you know better be worth your life because that's what you're risking right now."

A hammer cock was the only response.

"Is that meant to scare me?"

My eyes were adjusted to the darkness, but he must have been out here lying in wait for me. Which meant he knew I'd come out on a late-night walk. He had watched me in Natalia's house.

Who would know—or care—enough to do that?

Only one answer.

"Is this whole charade even worth it when I already know who you are, Jamie?" I asked, doing my best to sound as bored as possible. Assailants abhor a bored tone. They mean to strike fear and letting them know you're just not too bothered is the easiest way to rile them up into a mistake.

I heard rustling, soft but loud enough in the still, crisp air. "You can go ahead and turn around now. Slowly," he added.

I did as instructed and found myself facing down the barrel of a gun from only a few feet away. He was smart. If he had put the gun any closer, I could have knocked it out of his hand before he had a chance to react. As it was, I might still be able to kick it, but he'd see me coming.

He did look a lot like Francisco. The tall, slender, distance runner's build. The defined jaw, even the soft eyes.

"Finally, we meet," I said, holding out my hand as if to shake his. "I'd appreciate it if the gun were lowered."

"You need to stop."

"Why did you kill Dan Flint?"

"You're asking too many questions."

I shook my head and pulled my hand away. "If I don't get answers I keep asking questions. That's how it goes."

"You want an answer? Here's one. I know your husband is alive. If you want him to stay that way, you need to come with me. Right now."

CHAPTER 46
ELAINE

Night, March 21

"This is lovely, isn't it dear?"

Elaine acknowledged her mother with a simple grunt. It was the same Ethiopian restaurant they'd been to a dozen times.

"You seem down. What's the matter?" her father asked, swallowing a mouthful of injera and doro wat.

"You guys always think I seem down." Elaine rolled her eyes. Anything to insinuate that her job was beneath her. Elaine knew that was the real reason her father had gone around crowing to everyone about how she'd been the one who stopped Jacob Jordan. Not because he was immensely proud, but because it was finally a moment of consequence in his daughter's life.

Well, maybe they were right. Maybe this job wasn't a good fit. But not because it was beneath her—because she might be the one who couldn't cut it.

The chief liked to take an active role in cases, despite his overwhelmingly full plate. She knew she didn't have to take it personally that he had jumped in to offer his thoughts, to give them a nudge as needed. But why did it feel like a vote of no confidence?

Every day she was learning more about this job that she

always wanted, but never truly understood. She imagined herself as Hercule Poirot, Sherlock Holmes, Nancy Drew. The dashing and debonair crime fighting detective. The intellectual, who broke down clues and motives and spotted that one piece of evidence that no one else could, wrapping the entire mystery up in a nice bow. The satisfaction that would bring. The dopamine.

But maybe that wasn't her.

Maybe she wasn't cut out for it after all. Wasn't she the one who almost heaved when she was next to Xavier Henry's body? And that was after it was already underneath a sheet.

She fiddled with her injera, trying to decide what to grab a bite of next on the family-style spread in front of them. "The only food you eat with your hands that remains dignified," her dad would say. She never understood what exactly he meant by that.

"Dad, when you helped me get this detective job, how hard did you have to push Chief Branaman?" she finally asked.

He smiled at her with rare warmth. "Not very hard at all. You know that we don't love your career choice, I think your mother and I have made that clear, but your talent and intellect are all your own. You could be whoever you want to be. The chief saw that very clearly, and all it took was a small push in the right direction. I cracked the door for you, that was all."

The words would have been more meaningful if she couldn't easily read the disappointment behind his eyes.

"I don't think he trusts me," Elaine said.

"Of course he does," her mom scoffed. "Don't be ridiculous."

"Mom, the toxic positivity thing isn't going to work. 'It'll all be fine' doesn't do me any good right now."

"Well, excuse me for believing in you."

"But how is your investigation going?" her dad asked, patting her mom on the hand, as if he also could not believe her insubordination. "It's Veronica Walsh terrorizing the city, isn't it? In cahoots with that slimy character from her past."

Cahoots?

"Well, I do think that she's involved," Elaine said carefully, measuring out each word. "The 'how' is where I'm not sure yet."

"If you ask me, it's pretty simple. She sent out her lackey to do her dirty work, and then when he messed up, she decided it was time to take it on herself. I know why your uncle felt compelled to pardon her. Well, not pardon, but push prosecutors not to press any charges, and it makes sense politically, but the country would be better off with her gone. Once you catch her, then you can make it right, and my brother still gets to keep his high approval rating."

That was the thing with political families. Everything was politics. No conversation could stay contained within itself. Even the smallest discussion or argument turned into an event that could have long-lasting consequences. *Do your job well, and the president gets to hold onto his mandate.* What kind of police detective could work well under that sort of pressure?

"I've been meaning to ask you, dad. I think what the chief was trying to get at was that these people are all connected, and possibly are that cabal that Jacob Jordan was talking about. You don't think Senator Thresh could possibly be involved in that, do you?"

Her mom's eyes grew wide, and she threw her hand up in front of her mouth. "I dare say!"

Her father wasn't one to overreact, and certainly not in public. He gave her a once-over before saying, "Shadowy, behind-the-scenes groups don't actually exist here. That's a myth that people from outside the city make up to fit their own agendas." He rolled his eyes at her mother before continuing. "What makes you think there is such a group? And why would Thresh be a part of it?"

"We've got Flint and McAllister from Georgetown, and Branaman said that McAllister was close with the Belle family. I pulled some records and found out that Xavier Henry donated to Senator Billingsley's re-election campaigns and we know he ran in the same uber-rich circle as Ulrich Belle. Every one of them is dead now. That's enough smoke that it's our job to look for fire. To your point, when I mentioned this to Thresh, he was really weird about it."

Her father closed his eyes and gave her a patronizing shake of his head. When he reopened his eyes, he spoke. "Just because you're a detective doesn't mean every story has some secret to be detected. Thresh is a half-wit, but he's our half-wit, and family sticks together."

"He's technically not family," Elaine pointed out.

"We get to choose family, too," her mom said.

"Well, clearly Veronica Walsh thinks there's something up, or else why would she be doing what she is? And if I can think that Thresh is a possible suspect for this group, then how do we know she won't and that he might be in danger?"

Her father reached his hand over the food and set it on top of hers. "I'll handle it," he said, looking her square in the eye. "I'll go talk to him. He can make a public statement—or a tweet or TikTok or whatever. We'll make sure it's clear he knows nothing about anything, and ain't that the damn truth." His country twang that Elaine knew he worked hard to tamp down as a teenager and into adulthood still came out every now and then.

"What if there is this underground group, dad? Isn't that the sort of thing that by definition you wouldn't know about?"

He sighed, and an easy smile settled over his face. "My dear, there is nothing in this city that my brother and I do not know about. Power rests exactly where you think it rests."

CHAPTER 47
BEN

Night, March 21

Ben could feel his strength returning to him. He could stand up and move around within his confinement without struggle. The pain remained, but he could just about handle it.

What would Veronica do?

His captor had been borderline kind to him so far. He dressed and treated the wound, and Ben even got the sense that the food he brought down was the same food he was eating upstairs.

But.

He was still in captivity. Veronica had been on the hunt for Jacob Jordan when he made his ill-fated drop-in at Dan Flint's house. Where was she now? Had she—or the police—caught him? What about his half-sister? The twins?

He had to get out. He was a father. A husband. He had to get back to his life.

With a groan he lifted himself from the bed, clutching his side as he wobbled before steadying himself.

He wore a thin black tech shirt that felt like something out of a Costco 5-pack, and a pair of sweatpants with no branding. They weren't the clothes he went out in. He didn't ask but assumed

Jamie had put them on him. Luckily, they wore similar enough sizes. After several days in the basement, they were quite ripe, and he was anxious to get back to his own wardrobe.

The thought unnerved him ever so slightly. Why did he care so much about his own clothes? Shouldn't he be spending every waking moment thinking about Veronica and Nico and Maria?

The room was pitch black. The sort of impenetrable darkness only an underground room can achieve. He hadn't heard any footsteps from upstairs for hours, so he had to assume Jamie was asleep.

What would Veronica do?

There's always an exit.

In the immediate aftermath of Jeremy's betrayal and attempted murder of Veronica—*twice!* —Ben had peppered her with an almost unending series of questions. He couldn't stomach all the violence, and after hearing her tell her story fully he regretted ever asking. But he needed to know the other details. How do you get out of handcuffs? When stranded in the woods, what should, or shouldn't, you do? If you're all alone in a city, where is the safe haven that others don't know about?

How do you get out of a locked room?

She hadn't had all the answers, but they enjoyed a succession of nights as she was convalescing. He would ask a question, and they'd work through the permutations for hours, cracking each other up with outlandish scenarios.

"There's always a second exit," Veronica had said. "Every room has our villain's exit but will also have yours too."

"What about a jail cell?" Ben had replied, a smirk on his face.

"All right, smartass." Veronica playfully swatted his temple. "Remember, I'm talking about my own life, and I don't need to remind you I've never seen the inside of a jail cell and I'd be very happy to keep it that way. Barring some obvious exceptions—" she cast him a side-eye— "rooms aren't built to only have one egress. There's another door, a window, a weak spot in a wall.

Something. Your job is to find it. After that, it's just a matter of using your wits to figure out how to escape."

Ben looked around the room, his eyes having adjusted to the darkness but still providing scarce help. Why hadn't he asked her more follow-up questions? What kind of wits do you use?

He was underground. No secret door to lead out into the backyard. The ceiling, then. But how? A vent. Did that work in real life? Could people actually fit inside vents? The grated opening in the far corner of the ceiling was barely wide enough for him to get his arm through.

No way.

Ben felt despair creeping in. He was already feeling woozy. Maybe it would be best just to lie back down. Live to fight another day. What was the alternative, that Jamie came back to find him passed out on the floor?

He felt himself slipping and leaned an arm against the wall to keep upright. The wall abruptly shifted, sliding away, and he fell hard on his shoulder into the empty space.

The hell?

His fuzzy brain struggled to wrap itself around what had just happened. The sliding door that Jamie used to get in and out. It was just... unlocked? This whole time? The implications flooded his mind, and he scrambled to his feet. He tip-toed through the basement, fear and darkness slowing his stride.

He felt his way along the wall until he reached the stairs. Sitting down to conserve energy, he scooted up each step on his backside.

No noise from upstairs.

Could it be this easy?

The door creaked as he pushed it open at the top of the stairs. Ben froze.

Still nothing.

As confidence flowed through his veins, he took a deep breath and hurried down the hall toward the front door. He was almost out.

He had to get back to Veronica. To Nico and Maria.

The rain teemed down outside, but he didn't care. Freedom was worth anything.

He took a deep breath and turned the doorknob.

A small click told him it had been locked, but it unlocked as his wrist rotated, and he pushed it open, stepping out into the deluge.

He walked out to the edge of the driveway.

No possessions. No money. Drenched and getting wetter by the minute.

But he was free. He didn't know at all where he was. It looked like an American suburb, but that was pretty much the point of suburbs. They all looked the same. He could be anywhere, and in this nighttime rain, there wasn't much more he could make out. He walked down the street, solely because that way was downhill.

A car drove by, the headlights momentarily blinding him. He looked down and realized just how disheveled he looked. It was the middle of the night, and he was walking alone through a storm. No one in their right mind would open their door for him if he knocked. They'd call the police, which might be preferable, but Veronica's recent insistence against ever going to the police had taken hold inside his brain.

He needed a phone. He needed Veronica. Once they were together, they could take on anything.

CHAPTER 48
VERONICA

Night, March 21

Everyone knows the line. The warning. *Don't get taken to a second location.* Being Kidnapped 101. Stand your ground where you are. If you're taken elsewhere, your chances are slim to none (*and Slim's leaving town,* as Ben would quip).

The reason that has to be pounded into us by parents and the random law enforcement officials who visit schools and scare small kids with their stories is that it is inherently contradictory to our instincts. The instinctual reaction is to stay alive, to prolong. Why fight now if you can give yourself more time, another chance to fight later? Live to fight another day.

But living to fight another day in most cases means choosing an eventual death over the immediate chance to escape.

Would you take a one in four chance at freedom over a one in one thousand chance? Of course you would. Even the least mathematically minded of us could understand that. But would you choose that same twenty-five perfect chance over the one-hundred percent certainty that you were not about to be killed this instant?

That was where math and philosophy ran into each other.

My mind continued to make up these specifically enumerated

scenarios as Jamie Simon waved me into the passenger seat of his Toyota SUV, parked on the side of Northdown Road. What if the odds were five percent chance of freedom and ninety-five percent chance of being immediately killed? Would you still make your move?

I made my mind up as soon as I turned around and saw him. He wasn't bluffing about Ben. And that's why superheroes hide their identity. You can be the strongest, toughest, baddest out there, but as soon as your family is threatened, everything changes. You're not going it alone.

He knew that Ben was alive. Likely because he knew where Ben was. I was no idiot. Could I have taken him there on the path? Probably. But that's the added incentive not included in the warning. Don't go to a second location. But what if not going means that the would-be kidnapper kills your husband, or your child? What if they say the only way your family member lives is if you get in the car?

You get in.

Every time. With zero regrets. Would going along with Jamie Simon possibly end in my death? I didn't know for sure. But I knew getting in the car meant my husband was safe, at least for a second longer. And that was worth everything to me.

"Do you have a lair?" I asked.

He gave me a side-eye as he climbed into the driver's seat. A 'knock it off' eye roll that my twins saw often. Smart of him not to put me in the back seat. Short of sticking me in the trunk, this was his safest bet. He could keep an eye on my hands.

"What? Just asking how far you're going with this whole villain thing."

"I'm not a villain." His voice was already exasperated.

"Tell that to Dan Flint."

"That mother—" He clenched his fists around the steering wheel as he stopped himself from saying more. "You're not making this easy."

"Who placed the moral imperative on me to do so?"

He didn't respond. We drove the rest of the way in silence, his eyes glued to the road ahead. We headed north up the George Washington Memorial Parkway, then merged onto the Beltway, heading west. I did my best to look uninterested while I kept a keen eye out, watching exactly where we were going. We exited at Springfield, and we took several small roads, making what appeared to be a series of indecipherable turns. If he knew me like it seemed, it couldn't have been on my behalf. He was making sure we weren't being followed. Droplets of rain quickly turned into a downpour. I'd pity anyone trying to follow him in this.

Maybe he did me a favor. I wouldn't have gotten back home before this rain started. When your husband is missing and you've just committed a murder, you tend not to stop and think about what the weather might be. I never was bothered by the rain anyway. Complaints about the weather were the sign of an angry mind. Climate change notwithstanding, weather happens, and you move on. As my favorite poet, W.H. Auden, put it, "weather is what nasty people are nasty about and the nice share a common joy in observing."

Funny the phrases that can pop into your head when you least expect them.

Finally, we pulled in front of a large house in the Crosspointe neighborhood of Fairfax Station. Jamie shut the car off and pointed at the passenger side door. "Go."

"You're not going to at least offer me an umbrella?" I asked with a sly grin. Keep him off guard. Make him understand that I did not fear him.

"You're not touching anything that can turn into a weapon. What's the matter? Are you scared of some rain?"

"I don't run from storms." I threw the door open and jumped out. I waited with my arms folded as Jamie came around the car, complete with his own umbrella, swaying against his hands in the wind.

He walked up the driveway and turned to follow the small footpath through the yard up to the front stoop.

"I have to admit, this is nice, as far as lairs go" I said, looking around, making a note of everything I could see through the rain. "Was that a small lake we passed? I bet it's a lovely place to go for morning walks."

Jamie stopped and faced me. "Look," he said, his arms out in front of him. "I get it, you're not scared. You're the famous Alessandra Portillo, you've done things I could never dream of. I know all this. Will you please just shut up for a second?"

A light turned on across the street. He hadn't been shouting. Could someone really have heard him? The front light was on in his house, so we were decently well illuminated.

"Shit," he said, reaching for my hand. He grasped it and pulled me to the front door. "Get inside."

A dim light was on in the entryway. A Persian rug covered much of the floor, and I could see a hallway leading toward the back of the house. To my right was a small, seemingly unused, living room, with what appeared to be an office behind double doors beyond it. To my left was a dining room with a full-sized dining table and a stocked China cabinet on the far end. Stairs straight ahead led to a second floor, where I could see several bedroom doors.

This was not the house of a villain. This looked like someone's grandmother's house. Knickknacks covered every flat surface, and I could see matching Turkish-style rugs and table runners. Was I going to walk into the kitchen and be accosted by the smell of a freshly baked loaf of banana bread? Did grandpa stock the extra fridge with all the family's favorite beers just in case?

"Where are we? Whose house is this?" I asked.

A confused look spread across his face. "Mine, of course."

"You kidnapped me at gunpoint, and brought me to… your house?" The feeling I couldn't shake continued to grow. Why wasn't he acting at all like a criminal? Like he was the one under extreme duress, not me?

And why was he giving me a look like I was the weird one? Like I was behaving in some way he didn't expect?

"Take your shoes off." He pointed down at my feet and then to the doormat by the front door. "They're soaking wet."

"Oh, I'm sorry, Mr. Kidnapper. Did I offend you?" *What is going on?*

"Common decency." He shrugged.

I understood criminals. I understood crime. I knew that he brought me here for something to do with Ben. Was Ben here? Was Ben alive? I didn't know, and his frankly confusing demeanor was throwing me off. Why did he seem more nervous than I was?

Without another word, he walked further into the house, stopping at a door at the end of the hall. He pulled on the knob and the door swung open with a creak. I could see only darkness and a faint hint of stairs leading down.

"What's down there?"

"Answers," he said, and descended into the dark.

I clearly wasn't being kidnapped. I could have just turned around and walked out the door. His keys were hanging on a key right at the entryway.

He got the drop on me, which has only happened a handful of times in my entire life, knew enough about me to understand the threat I could still pose, and then just decided to leave me to my own devices?

He held the trump card, though. And he knew it. He knew about my husband, and that knowledge was more potent than any physical threat he could make towards me.

There was nothing else to do. I leaned down to my right foot and pulled my trusty knife out of my sopping-wet sock. Palming it, I followed him down the twisting staircase.

CHAPTER 49
VERONICA

Night, March 21

I followed the bend in the carpeted staircase and watched as Jamie flicked on a light, the basement now fully in view. A wide finished room, with bright white brick walls and a low ceiling. A pool table stood directly in the center, with mountains of papers lying on top of it. A small futon, complete with a hideous orange slipcover, faced a flat-screen television that must have exceeded seventy inches.

"What am I looking at?"

Jamie looked over at me and raised his hand in a calming gesture.

"Don't raise your hand to me like that, as if I'm somehow being impatient with you," I said.

"There's nothing to see here. Hold on," he said, exasperation clear in his tone. "Follow me."

As he walked further into the room, I could see that it was bigger than I'd originally thought. The far end had a hallway off the side that continued toward the back of the house. I walked behind him, and we passed a small bathroom before stopping in front of what looked like a plain brick wall.

"What's here?" I asked, gripping my knife tight.

Jamie ignored me. Instead, he pushed a single brick and called through the door that appeared, "Ben, I'm coming in!"

I knew this must be who he was taking me to, but my heart began to race as I heard my husband's name. He really was okay, and just beyond this door. Days of heartache, missing, longing, and the acute pain of thinking that he was truly dead were all about to be behind me. My husband was on the other side of this door. It was about to be over.

The door slid open. I stepped forward onto a hard concrete floor and felt a chill as we entered.

"Ben, are you awake?" Jamie asked, as he reached a hand up to a dangling light fixture. He glanced back at me, and there was just enough light from the hallway that I could see him give a small shrug. He pulled the string, and my eyes darted around the space.

It was small and bare. The concrete floor indicated this was meant as some sort of utility room. Instead, it had been converted into a makeshift bedroom.

A cell.

There was a twin bed in one corner and a beanbag chair lumped in the center of the room. Some paperback books lay strewn around.

But no Ben.

I pulled my knife and crossed the distance between myself and Jamie before he realized what I was doing. I whipped the knife up to his throat and spun him in one motion, pinning one of his arms behind his back. His gun toppled down the floor beside him and I kicked it away. "Tell me why I shouldn't just kill you right now," I growled. "Give me one reason I shouldn't slice you open for whatever psychological bullshit you are pulling."

I let him tilt his head toward me. His eyes were wide and frantic. But as I looked into them, searching for deception, I realized it wasn't my knife that was the source of his panic. His eyes were flitting back and forth, looking into the corners of the now-lit room. I let him go and stepped back.

"He got out," he finally muttered, and I could tell he wasn't lying. No one can fake true surprise. Actors might get it right for shots in movies, but in real life it's impossible to hide if someone is looking for it. His pinky finger twitched. He took several short breaths that he thought I couldn't see. Fear replaced panic in his eyes. He gave up all pretenses and put his hands to his head. "Why would he leave?"

I pulled the knife away. He barely even noticed. I grabbed his shoulder and forced him to face me and look me in my eyes. "Tell me everything. Now."

CHAPTER 50
ARCHON

Night, March 21

"Everything is still in place." Archon used his most reassuring voice.

"You're sure? I don't mean to be callous, but we're dropping like flies here."

Archon studied the man seated across the table from him. They shared a bottle of Stoli on the back veranda, taking advantage of the unseasonably warm night. When at all possible, Archon loved to sit outside. A small light allowed for them to sit comfortably, but not to disturb the rest of the yard and the woods that lay beyond the back fence. He liked to immerse himself in nature. That was how the earth was supposed to be enjoyed. Without the flora and fauna being aware of your presence —or at least, concerned about it. That had been the only real renovation project Archon had overseen after buying this house. The backyard was too curated, with its perfectly manicured lawn and infinity pool. He wanted real nature. He wanted the backyard to seamlessly flow into the woods beyond. An animal should think of it as only a clearing, nothing more, he had told the landscapers.

The man fidgeted with his lowball glass. Whether he was

waiting for more reassurance or validation, Archon was not entirely sure. "Are you still able to do your role?" Archon asked.

"Of course. It will go down exactly as planned on my end."

"Then what are you worried about?"

"Well," he put his hand out, palm facing up, as if he were stating something painfully obvious, "three of our members are dead..."

"And what roles did they play?"

"I don't know."

"Which is exactly the point, isn't it? You don't know, because you don't need to, and because information is a virus. But I will throw you a bone here. Flint and McAllister? Solely for recruitment, for putting the right people into the right places when we need them. Accomplices placed into positions where their actions help our causes. And even of those people they've recruited, the people who don't even realize their importance? Not involved in the immediate plan anyway. Xavier Henry? Just for finances, and we've already had some positive talks with a replacement. Short-term, nothing to worry about. Long-term, we'll have to be more creative with our reach, but I'm not concerned."

Archon didn't like saying more than he had to, but he was talking to the most vital cog. If the man facing him didn't do his part, the entire plan would fail.

The man wasn't, strictly speaking, a member of the organization. But over the years, he became a go-to, to the point where he was eventually read in. That's what happens when you use the same killer over and over. At some point, he learns enough information that it's less dangerous to give him the rest than to let him run free with only tidbits.

"How did it work with our last problem?"

"The neighbor?" the hitman asked. When he saw Archon's eyebrows raise slightly in confirmation, he continued, "I've got to tell you, one of the easiest tasks of my life. The man was absolutely desperate to be important. All I had to do was tell him that the new Archon was calling on him and he didn't even look back, he just jumped straight into my car."

"He always was worming his way around, finagling invitations to World's Edge. Ulrich was a little too lenient there."

The hitman nodded tentatively. Archon appreciated that he knew his place. He didn't try to rise above his station. This particular hitman used the moniker Bedrock, a name Archon felt fell flat in the two necessities of a hitman's nickname: sounding both cool and scary. He told him the first time they met that he would not be calling him that. But he couldn't argue with the man's results over the years.

What he was asking of the hitman—*Bedrock, ugh*—this time was much more. He needed precision, he needed perfection. They had one chance to pull this off and the chips would fall exactly as required. Even the slightest deviation, though, and who knows how much of their already wobbling tower would crumble?

CHAPTER 51
VERONICA

Night, March 21

Jamie sat down on the twin bed, and for the first time I wondered why there ever would be a bed in a room like this. I looked closer at the sheets, wrinkled and piled in a heap, like someone had woken up too hot and kicked them off in the night. I was about to snap at Jamie to quit stalling and start talking when my eyes focused in on one spot.

"Is that… blood?"

"Yes, but wait!" Jamie held his hands up quickly. "It's not what it looks like."

"Is that my husband's blood?"

"Well, you have to hear me out—"

"You better have a really good story. I will kill you. Don't doubt that for a second."

"Look, come, sit down, and I'll tell you everything." He motioned to the empty spot next to him on the side of the bed.

"When my husband, who is hurt, is out somewhere having just escaped from your basement dungeon?" I shook my head. "No. You talk while we find him."

I marched back into the main room toward the stairs, not

looking back. I made it up to the main floor and was squelching my feet into my running shoes before he caught up.

"Okay, look, I was following your husband."

I stared at him, my eyes giving nothing away. "Go on."

"I know you and your story, and I was upset at him for having left you. I followed him, and that's why I took pictures and sent them to that reporter. I was mad at him for what he was doing."

Enough with the lies. "You said you'd tell me everything. You just happen to know my story and care so deeply that you *followed* my husband? If you do know me, you know I can spot bullshit pretty easily."

"Do you want to hear about how your husband was shot or not?"

I didn't have the high ground. He had information I needed, so I reluctantly backed down. The rain had slowed to a drizzle as we stepped outside onto the front stoop.

"I followed him to Dan Flint's house. He ran out quickly from your house—"

"You were at my house?"

A nonchalant shrug was all I got in response.

How was he at my house? How couldn't I have noticed?

"Wait, where is our car?"

He smiled, his eyes glistening slightly. "I wondered when you'd get around to asking that question. Right in here." He pointed to the closed garage.

"You drove him back here in his own car?"

"I did. Once I was sure he was secure here, and the car was hidden in the garage, I took the metro back up and got to my car and brought it back."

"I'm taking that car back."

"Go for it, but if you want to drive together, you're parked in behind my car. Anyway," he continued as I grudgingly accepted, and we got into his car. "He knocked on the door, and Flint opened up, and they shared what appeared to be a friendly discussion. I stayed outside, figuring there was nothing interesting for me. I walked around the block. I smoked a cigarette or two."

"Can you drive around the neighborhood slowly?" I cut in. "He can't have gotten very far."

He had the gall to roll his eyes at me. "Yes, wow, great advice. I'd never once think that an injured man on foot in the middle of the night wouldn't get very far."

"Get on with your story."

"Dan Flint has one of those big bay windows. The curtains were open, so when I walked by again and glanced, I could see right in. And I saw an angry confrontation. Your husband was just standing there, looking a little confused if I'm honest, and the professor was upset and pointing for him to leave. It still wasn't my business. I was about to keep going when I saw your husband turn around and head out of the living room, further into the house. I don't know where he was going, but I saw Flint pick up a fireplace poker."

I gasped.

"The door was unlocked, so I raced inside and got there just as Flint was about to swing the poker. He was in the living room and Ben was just out of my eyesight, in what I now know was the kitchen. I fired two shots into his back. He went down and dropped the poker. I just wanted to get Ben out of there. I didn't have a plan, I just knew I had to act."

He paused as we turned around at the end of a cul-de-sac. I was trying hard to listen to him while scanning the dark streets. It was futile, and I knew it. The only way we would have found him out here was if he ran in front of our headlights. When Jamie didn't pick the story back up, I asked, "And so when did you shoot him?"

"I—"

"You just described a situation where Dr. Flint clearly did not have a gun, and you did. My husband was shot—that's what you told me. So, when are you going to get around to the truth that you shot him and then locked him inside your basement dungeon?"

Jamie sighed and squeezed his eyes shut. "I didn't mean to," he said as he reopened his eyes, his voice soft and brittle.

"What, you just got so excited about it you decided to shoot some more after you'd killed Dan?"

"One of the bullets went straight through him—in and out—then sliced through your husband's hip. He passed out. I knew Dan Flint was dead, but I had no idea how badly hurt Ben was. I frantically checked his body and was relieved to see that it was just a slice, it didn't even fully hit him. I dragged him out to my car and was going to take him to a hospital, I swear. But I needed to know what happened, so I took him home and patched him up first. I took care of him well. I swear I did."

He shot my husband. He shot him and then kidnapped him. The man who shot and kidnapped my husband had convinced himself he was the hero in the story. "What changed? You obviously didn't take him to the hospital."

"What changed?" Jamie sighed deeply. "What changed was that Ben told me about their conversation when he woke up. And I realized this was all much bigger than I'd anticipated."

"The Princemakers," I said.

He gave me a knowing look. "It was you, then."

"Was me what?"

"Who killed the Georgetown president and caused that CEO to jump out the window. They were both involved, weren't they?"

"I have nothing to say on that." He wasn't in a position to be questioning me. "Tell me why you kept my husband locked up. Tell me why you framed my best friend. And you better have a good reason why we're out here searching for my missing husband when you could have let him come home days ago. Do you even know what it's like to have a family member snatched away from you? Do you have any idea how I felt? How my kids felt?"

We circled around a cul-de-sac, lingering for an extra second on a house with a light on in the top floor. Nothing to see, though. If Ben had gotten someone to open up their house for him, there would be more lights on. Plus, if he did, then he'd be calling me any minute anyway.

"I know a thing or two about family members dying," Jamie said, breaking the silence. "But for Ben it was better that he was dead. I was trying to keep him *dead* to make sure he stayed alive. What do you think was going to happen? One of their members is shot, there's likely clear DNA evidence that Veronica Walsh's husband was there—you don't think they'd retaliate immediately? You don't think his life would be in great danger the moment they found Dan Flint's body?"

"More in danger than when you shot him?"

He ignored my jab. "He told me what he had learned, and I realized that Dan Flint's death needed to be black and white. I went back there that same night—before the police found him—and left some of your friend's hair at the scene. I have nothing against him, but your husband needed them to stop wondering who killed their partner. He needed to be a victim, an interesting coincidence but nothing more."

I could see how it made sense in his mind. He'd created a situation where he told himself he was the hero. He was the guy who had saved the day, acting on the side of the angels. But we were getting nowhere. Ben was nowhere to be seen, and I needed to go it alone again. But one line he just said was ringing in my head. I turned to face him in the driver's seat, taking in all his features, noticing just how similar they were to Francisco. "Did you... just happen to have my friend's DNA on you, just in case?"

"I..." he faltered momentarily. "It's good to be prepared."

I stared at him, momentarily giving up on scanning the street. "Who are you?"

CHAPTER 52
ELAINE

Morning, March 22

Elaine pulled her leggings on and grabbed her refillable water bottle. She didn't enjoy her apartment building but loved the little gym on the fourth floor. She knew one day, if everything went well, she'd be living in a single-family home, complete with the picket fence and kids and a dog, but she knew she would always miss the proximity to a gym.

Plenty of runners loved to hate on treadmills. Like it somehow made you less of a runner if you didn't find a perfect trail near your house to run on every day. The treadmill was boring, and the easy way out. Elaine never understood them. The point was exercise, wasn't it? Lengthy, repetitive motion. A heightened heartbeat. To her, runners who could only run outside were the weak ones. You need your specific playlist and your nice little scenery to set the mood, allowing you to drift off into endorphin-land. Give her a treadmill, TV screen turned off. Headphones optional. The purest form of running.

She groaned as she pulled the gym door open. Of course, today all the treadmills were taken. Seven in the morning and all of a sudden everyone is into fitness? She glanced out the floor-to-ceiling windows at the far end of the gym.

Ahh. It was raining outside.

Another gripe of hers about outdoor runners. Guess there was only one recourse here. She scooted back up to her apartment, threw on her rain jacket, and headed off to run in the rain.

Without stopping to consider it at all, she knew where she would run. A few nice downhills to get her going. A route she'd curse on the return leg when she was fighting gravity as well as tiring legs. Down Western Avenue, the northwest border of Washington, DC, and Maryland, and then 49th Street NW straight south through Spring Valley. Right on down to Kent, one of the only true competitors with Spring Valley for the most prestigious and upscale neighborhood in the city.

Also, where her parents lived.

She had only recently begun therapy, right after becoming a detective, and her therapist quickly confirmed what she'd assumed all along. She had severe daddy issues, although her therapist groaned when she used that term. It wasn't like they were novel or exciting, either. She craved approval from a man who rarely gave it out. A dime a dozen.

So, despite all his misgivings, all his patronizing talking down to her, she needed to know what he thought. She craved the validation.

She wanted to know how to find Veronica Walsh and she wanted to hear from him again about Senator Thresh.

His whole "power belongs to exactly who you think it does" speech from the night before had made her realize that she wasn't utilizing the power she often wished she could escape from. Why should she hide from her family's power and influence?

She wasn't interested in doing a one-eighty and embracing the Leishear name professionally, but what was the point of having a powerful dad and uncle if she couldn't ask for some advice every once in a while?

Yes, technology makes being outside in the rain harder—*got to keep your phone safe*—but why didn't everyone love this feeling? The rain pouring down, like going for a run while in the shower.

She had once mentioned to a friend in college how much she liked to run in the rain and got a stare as if she'd said she enjoyed walking through cities alone at 3 am. After that, she kept those thoughts safely inside her brain.

Only a few miles, and at a decent pace, spurred on by the joy of feeling the elements. Just under twenty-five minutes later, she stopped her running app as she came to a halt at the end of her parents' driveway. A quick run in the rain, some answers from her father, and then trying to match her pace on the return journey with elevation gain. Hard to beat that for a morning workout.

She rang the doorbell, wiping competing droplets of sweat and rain out of her eyes.

CHAPTER 53
BEN

Morning, March 22

Ben must have been walking for hours. Day was beginning to break, not that there was a huge difference with the layer of cumulonimbus clouds blocking out the sun. But how did he not get to any store, anything that could have a cell phone? He was stuck in suburbia and felt like he was exactly where he started when he escaped. Each turn down a street had eventually taken him to yet another cul-de-sac. He thought of the story of the woman who got lost in the woods and died, her body found years later within meters of the path she'd been looking for. Exhaustion does funny things to the mind.

He shivered violently and attempted to peel his shirt away from his body. No use. But now that dawn was approaching, he felt more hopeful. He'd made it through the night, which made the ordeal sound more epic than it probably was. What was your greatest triumph? Well, one time I walked around suburbia in the freezing cold all night long.

But it was all about to be over. People would emerge from their homes soon. Someone would see him and take pity, stopping to find out what was wrong. That was the best way. Someone had to come to him. Not vice versa. There was no telling how a person might react to seeing a wild-looking wet man at their doorstep.

His best bet was likely just to sit down on the sidewalk. Wait for someone's dog to sniff him out. But he was so, so, cold. He had to keep moving, just to keep the blood flowing.

Time was of the essence, too. If Jamie Simon hadn't found him yet, there could only be one reason. He had gone after Veronica. He had to find out what happened. So, he carried on his march, past million-dollar houses, waiting for one of them to transform into salvation.

When he saw her, he first thought it was a hallucination. Probably just a runner out too early, one of those intrepid types who didn't care about the cold, the dark, maybe even their own families. Only the endorphins.

It couldn't actually be Veronica, running down the sidewalk towards him. That wouldn't make any sense. How could she even be here, in some Fairfax-type suburb?

But she came closer, and didn't slow down. The hallucination didn't go away. The hair, the running stride, the nine fingers, all perfectly her own. All perfect.

"Oh my God," she said, as she got within earshot. "I've got you."

She ran the rest of the way, and he collapsed into his wife's arms as her embrace engulfed him. He could feel her heart thumping against his chest, and knew she could feel the same.

"I'm... I'm sorry," Ben managed to fumble the words out. "I should have left the sleuthing to you."

Veronica looked up into his eyes, her own brimming with tears as a wide smile spread on her face. "That doesn't matter at all, my love, nothing else matters. We're back together."

Ben lay on the king bed, propped up by two memory foam pillows, and marveled at how he'd experienced both extremes of comfort levels in the few hours. Veronica sat on a velvet bench by the foot of the bed, watching him closely.

"Nat really let you use this place, just like that?" Ben asked, even though she'd answered that question multiple times already on the way over.

Veronica grinned, nodding. "It's not bad, is it?"

"Does anyone else know that you're here?"

"Mikaela does, and I imagine a few of the staff because Natalia said she had to tell them to stay away for a bit. So they at least know something's up, which could get problematic. To answer your next question, yes, I already called my parents while you were sleeping and told them and Nico and Maria that you were safe and that you were with me."

Ben felt a wave of relief surge through his body. But as soon as it subsided, fear settled in again. "But why can't they come back here then? What else is going on?"

Veronica grimaced, and moved onto the bed next to him, patting his thigh. "How much do you know?"

"I don't know how to answer that without knowing how much the maximum is."

Veronica broke into a smile. "Look at you, half-dead and yet comparing relative quantities." She explained everything that had happened since the day he left, up to leaving Jamie back at his home when he gave up the search. Ben sat in silence, listening and experiencing the déjà vu of once again hearing his wife talk about killing people.

This time was different, though. Because he was no longer the naive sap he had been in the past. They'd been through too much now. They were a team.

She noticed his resolve too, he could tell. Everything about her was sharper, like she didn't need to hide anything about herself anymore.

"How did you find me?" He asked.

"I know you better than anyone. Of course I'd find you!" She gave him a playful swat on his foot.

"But I didn't even know where I was."

"I left that house and at each intersection asked myself where you would go. Knowing that you were desperate to be found, I just followed along. Took a few turns I wouldn't have taken myself, and then there you were."

"That's incredible."

"Well," Veronica shrugged self-deprecatingly, "it didn't hurt that I found you on Argent Circle, a road that—as the name would suggest—curls back around on itself."

"I got really lost, didn't I?"

"That subdivision is not that big, so yeah, you must've been walking in circles for a while."

"I'm no good at any of this." Ben tried to stifle a yawn and failed badly.

"You're not supposed to be." Veronica patted his ankle. "Look, now that you're back, full transparency: I think the police know it was me with McAllister. Brown and her sidekick, Iverson, at least do. Innocence is out of the question, we need to show I was stopping them. Make it clear there is no reason I should be prosecuted even if they do get enough evidence, which I doubt they'd find anyway. But lack of evidence won't stop them arresting me, and nothing good can come of that."

"Okay. What do we do now?"

CHAPTER 54
ARCHON

Morning, March 22

"What do you think? Time to do it?"

Archon looked around the war room, hesitating only slightly over the empty chairs. There would be time to do a proper remembrance later. Not now.

"Didn't you say it would bring too much heat?"

He looked over at the man who had been his friend for decades. "It would. And it will, although less now that she doesn't have the public on her side. We've created a situation whereby it could be any number of people who were upset with her."

"But what has changed in your thinking?" Another man asked.

Archon considered the question. The state of play wasn't measurably different. They were still on track. A piece would be taken off the board, and none would be the wiser as to their involvement. It would once again be as it always was. What had changed? It wasn't his resolve, that was as strong as ever. His belief in their mission would never waver.

The true answer, he realized, was something he could never

speak aloud. What changed was that Veronica Walsh stabbed Gregory McAllister in the heart and slashed his throat for good measure. What changed was that he got a first-row seat to the kind of decisive action that she could take.

Killing her father hadn't stopped her, and seemingly hadn't made her pause at all to take stock of their own prowess.

What changed? He was scared.

For a man whose persona relegated fear to the sidelines, he had a responsibility to maintain the devil-may-care confidence he brought to every Princemakers interaction. Most of being infallible and unstoppable is believing that you are.

"What changed is that we're coming up on D-Day, and I think that she is the only person who can stop us, for obvious reasons. Does anyone disagree?"

Quiet murmurings of assent shuffled around the long oval boardroom-style table.

"If she is alive, we have a chance of failure, and gentlemen, we will not tolerate failure."

"How do you propose we do it?"

He looked his friend in the eye. "The only way we can. Without her ever seeing it coming. And don't we know exactly the man to do it?"

A loud jingle came from upstairs, as his Ring camera announced someone was at the door. "Honey, you got that?"

No answer.

"Honey?"

Nothing. "Alright, guys, you know the drill. No movements, no noise. No one knows you're down here."

Archon rose and walked to the corner of the room and pressed his hand against a palm reader he had installed when their meetings moved from World's Edge, the Belles' cliffside mansion, here to his multimillion-dollar DC home.

He climbed the spiral staircase and pushed his way out into the utility room. He paused, checking the cameras showing the hallway outside. No movement, no one who shouldn't see him leaving the room.

He opened the door and marched over to the front entrance. He smiled when he saw in the security camera who awaited him just outside. He swung the front door open and said with a genuine smile, "Hello, my daughter! Come on in!"

CHAPTER 55
ELAINE

Morning, March 22

"Hi, Dad. Good to see you," Elaine said as she stepped over the threshold. "Is Mom here?"

"She's out at some workout class, I think," he said dismissively. "Coffee is in the pot."

She followed him into the kitchen and perched at a barstool by the kitchen island. Everything in the kitchen gleamed. Her parents were born to live a life of luxury. No appliance besides the coffee maker had been touched, probably since they were bought. The kitchen was for showing off, not for cooking.

She remembered a time when that wasn't the case. Growing up, she used to love getting flour everywhere as she made sugar cookies with her father. He was the one who would let her go wild, making messes and leaving handprints all over. He'd always promise her mother that any mess she made while he was with her, he would clean up fully and on his own. She loved Christmas cookies so much that she wanted to use the cookie cutters year-round. As a compromise, they bought—sometimes custom-made—cutters for every holiday so it was never too long between cookie baking sessions.

Elaine liked to imagine what it would be like having a sister to decorate cookies with. To steal a spoonful of icing from while she looked the other way. To drop her favorite star-shaped sprinkles all over the perfect cookie her sister was decorating.

She only asked her mother once, when she was eleven years old, why they never had more children.

"You..." her mom faltered, her eyes flitting around looking for anything to distract her. "Your father and I decided that it would be best to devote all our attention to you," she finally said.

"Does that mean that my friends with brothers and sisters don't get as much attention from their parents?"

"Well, honey, it's just math, isn't it? There's only so much time to go around in one day, so why would we want to spend any of that time on anyone else but you?"

The words might have rung true if her mother actually seemed to enjoy being around her daughter. But her mom never wanted to be around. Most nights she would retire to the parlor after dinner, taking a book and a glass of wine.

Her dad had been the one who engaged with her. She didn't understand what he did, except that people called him a "media mogul." They had a beach house in Maryland right on the Chesapeake Bay where she would spend weekends as a teenager laying out or searching for blue crabs. This was the house that allowed her father to claim full-time Maryland residence for his first governor's race, she learned as an adult, despite them spending the majority of their time in Washington, DC.

Rules didn't apply to the rich.

Her favorite place, though, was the *other* beach house, their condo on Hilton Head. That was luxury. It made the Chesapeake Bay seem downright podunk. The two weeks they spent there every summer felt like heaven. Every day she would take their speedboat over into Braddock Cove to eat at Salty Dog and watch everyone stop and stare as she sashayed out in the hottest new look of the summer.

She knew she was lucky. She knew her father provided opportunities that most children only dreamed of, even if all she wanted was his love.

Then her uncle was elected president, and it all changed again. After that, when she took the speedboat out, she always had an unsmiling sentry tag along.

Elaine watched as her father poured her a cup of coffee, snagging the half-and-half and adding in a small dollop of vanilla syrup. "DIY vanilla latte, or close enough," her dad said. "Never really understood the draw of those home espresso makers. What happened to just having a cup of coffee?"

Elaine didn't respond. It was a tired refrain at this point. Her dad had his views, and he was less interested in a conversation than a pontification. "Dad," she said after taking a sip. "I wanted to talk to you more about Senator Thresh."

Her father puffed out his cheeks and sighed. "You think he's part of some secret group running the world still?"

Elaine knew she would have to be resolute. That's what dad always responded to. He appreciated power, so of course he should understand her trying to stop those who seek to gain power illicitly.

"You're working hard to make things better in this country, aren't you, dad?"

"Yes, of course, that's what public service is."

"So, if there's some group of people acting against the will of the public, in it for their own benefit, then that's something you'd be against?"

"Sweetie," he laughed, "that group is called Congress. No one in government is actually out there doing what they claim to do."

"Not even you?"

"What can I say? There's an exception that proves every rule."

"Why are you so sure that Thresh is not involved in anything?"

"Do you want my honest answer?"

"Yes." Why else would she be asking?

"Because he's not smart enough. He lucked into his position

because he tricked voters as dumb as him to believe he was on their side. He has no tact, he couldn't keep anything secret. They vote for him because they believe in me, and he's allied to me. If I cut him off, he'd be driven out with his tail between his legs."

"Well, isn't that lack of tact exactly what happened when he called me? He explicitly told me to stop investigating. That seems to me like the perfect example."

"No. That's a perfect example of him thinking about re-election only. He only stands when I back him. If his constituents learn about my daughter investigating impropriety, they'll probably take it out on him rather than me."

"Wouldn't they take it out on the offenders?" Elaine wasn't following her father's logic at all. Better to just switch tracks. "Where do I find Veronica Walsh?" she blurted out.

"What do you mean?"

"I need to find her, and I can't. Do you have any, I don't know, insider knowledge?"

"Check her network of friends. You'll find her." He shrugged, as if that was the simplest task in the world.

"Yes, obviously, dad," Elaine groaned. "Do you think I was born yesterday?"

"Well, have you found her?"

"No."

"Then you missed someone. Go back and try again. I wouldn't fret too much, though."

"And why is that?"

"I have a feeling she'll pop her head above water soon enough anyway."

CHAPTER 56
ARCHON

Morning, March 22

Archon watched as his daughter stretched her muscles for a few minutes in the driveway. She waved after she finished, turning away and beginning her jog home. He kept his eyes on her until she was out of sight.

Finally satisfied that she wasn't going to double back, he walked back to the utility room. To any visitors, it was just one of those ubiquitous rooms with a key lock in place of a doorknob. A closet-sized space that held a water-heater and nothing else. Nothing that required a second glance.

Archon pressed a switch inside the shade of the small tabletop lamp and the door swung open. He walked in, passing the washing machine and dryer, before getting to a hidden button, this one inside the wall and painted over to be invisible. Set up as a push door, but only opening if the correct spot was pressed, it blended right into the wall.

When the Belle family died in the car accident caused by Jacob Jordan, the Princemakers had to scramble for a new location. Not only was there a change in leadership, with Archon taking over the position Ulrich Belle had held, but the perfect isolated location along the Potomac was gone with them. No more sweeping views while they planned—now they had to make do with a basement lair. Archon did his best to make it feel powerful, with torches in each corner lending a medieval touch (fake flames, of course; he wasn't about to burn his house down over some extra gravitas).

Archon had taken more than just Ulrich's position at the head of the table. He'd taken the title as well. It had been Ulrich's idea to call himself that, and when he died, it felt natural to continue with the epithet.

Archon thought back to that fateful, and utterly stupid, day at World's Edge that changed the trajectory of the Princemakers, and ultimately led to the current upheaval.

Senator Billingsley had caused all this trouble, all these deaths, up to and including his own, because he couldn't hold his liquor —or his bladder. They had been seated in Ulrich and Yvonne's stately dining room, far enough away from prying eyes that they didn't need a secret door. The room had floor-to-ceiling glass windows along one side, with a view overlooking the backyard and the Potomac beyond it. For privacy, Ulrich had gotten those one-sided mirrors installed, so that no one could look up and see in, but they could still enjoy the view.

Ulrich's compromise with his daughters to make sure that they were left alone whenever he had a "business dinner"—to use his euphemism—was to let them bring a small set of friends over and have free reign of the backyard and the first floor. His compromise with his own people was that there would be no ogling, no inappropriate behavior of any sort when his daughters were by the pool.

A reasonable rule, and one easily followed by all involved. They had bigger fish to fry.

Except Andy Billingsley. He couldn't help himself. A sign of weakness if Archon had ever seen one. Andy's wandering eyes were on the receiving end of many a glare from Ulrich over the years. He seemed harmless enough, a philandering serial cheater who had enough affairs not to need to attempt to dip his toe into the forbidden pool.

And yet.

The night Ulrich plied them all with far too many margaritas, Andy abruptly stood, claiming he needed to go to the bathroom. They all rolled their eyes as Andy shuffled out, one or two stage whispered comments about what a lush he was.

The rest of the group went back to drinking and toasting to previous successes. Not every gathering had to be all business.

"Hey, is that…?" McAllister had started to ask before swallowing the question. They all rushed over to the windows and peered out, watching the scene unfold before their eyes.

Andy was on a golf cart, laughing away as he tried to pull a bikini-clad college girl onto it with him. She wasn't one of Ulrich's daughters, but a friend they'd seen there a few times before.

From Archon's vantage point, it looked like two of the other kids were helping Andy drag this poor girl onto the golf cart. God knows what his plan was. But Archon watched, as Andy swung the golf cart around and around, doing large donuts on the lawn as the co-conspirators sat in the back and held the girl in the front seat.

All of them were mesmerized, watching in a line against the windows. All except Ulrich and Yvonne, who had sprinted downstairs and were running across the yard. Archon never considered Andy would take it too far. He was more worried for Andy's sake than anyone else. The punishment he'd face for this transgression would surely be getting kicked out of the Princemakers, at best. Ulrich might just call their hitman right then and there. There was no room for such puerile, impudent behavior.

But then the golf cart lurched closer to the drop, and he watched on helplessly as Andy lost control. The cart teetered and slid, and the back right wheel dipped over the cliff's edge. It hovered, frozen in motion for a second, before gravity and the weight of the students in the back took control, and the entire cart pitched backward out of sight.

But not Andy. A gardener or outdoor worker of some sort had sprinted in from around the side of the house and lunged for them as they fell. That he succeeded only in grabbing Andy's arm and pulling him to safety was a cruel and ironic blow.

They all took off downstairs and ran out onto the lawn. Privacy be damned, this was an emergency.

But this was also part of what the group always prepared for. You must be ready to mitigate any circumstances that come your way. As soon as they realized the golf cart and the co-eds hadn't been saved, and had tumbled down into the Potomac, they sprang into action. One member immediately started calling the friendly police officers they had on speed dial. He explained the situation and said their search and rescue mission was tantamount to the president of the United States being stuck in the Potomac. They needed to pull those bodies out *now*.

A shout from the edge alerted them to the fact that not all three students had made it to the water. Archon hustled to the edge to peer down. Far below, in the midst of a tangle of branches, lay the girl Andy had originally forced into the golf cart.

"Fucking hell, Andy. What the fuck did you think you were doing?" Ulrich exploded, leaning over the Senator, who was lying on his back gasping for air.

"I... I just," Andy's head lolled backward. "Are they okay?" He managed to croak out.

"No, you imbecile! You killed them!"

Ulrich raised his fist and moved to strike Andy, but Yvonne stepped in the way. "No, no. Don't," she said. "We have to fix this."

Archon watched as the wheels turned in Ulrich's brain. He looked around at the group, one by one. The college students were huddled off to the side of the yard near the tree line, tears streaming down their faces.

"Opposite direction, move, they can't see your faces. Yvonne, their phones. Now." Ulrich pointed at the students with a sudden urgency. "Grab them."

Yvonne rushed over and tore their phones away from them. They didn't put up a fight. They were too stunned. Ulrich glared at Andy as they made their way to the opposite tree line and addressed the group. "Not a word of this leaves these premises. All of us are in danger now. We cannot have anyone poking around World's Edge for any reason. Our group, our mission, is too critical."

"Are you saying we just cover all this up? How?" One of them behind Archon asked.

Archon didn't hang around to find out all the details. He didn't care, that wasn't his role. He just knew he wanted nothing more to do with Andy Billingsley. How absolutely juvenile could one man be? One of the most important men in the country put them all in danger because God only granted him a brain the size of a pea.

Archon only learned the extent of the bribing and hush money when the Belles died and he took over control of the group. Ulrich had been meticulous with his bookkeeping, so every dollar spent was catalogued and itemized. *So that's where most of our money has been going,* Archon had thought.

Archon thudded down the stairs, letting his footsteps echo down below. His very own entrance music. When he reached the table, he didn't bother sitting. "Gentlemen," he said. "It is time to call a hitman, but not our usual one. Not for Veronica Walsh. We move now. Once Veronica is gone, Chamique Moore is next."

CHAPTER 57
VERONICA

Midday March 22

"Here's where I'm at," I said as Ben walked into the dining room, snapping my fingers to wrest his attention away from the sparkling chandelier hanging over the center of the table. He looked at the large poster board I had laid out.

"You weren't kidding about this. You really are trying to map it out."

I was, as ever, a woman true to myself. How do you figure out who else is part of an underground conspiracy? Math, of course.

A little graph theory. Not my main area of expertise, but I wasn't over here trying to solve Conway's 99-graph problem. I just needed to study the connections between the members we knew of, and I hoped creating a network of all connections and relationships would yield some interesting patterns.

"You look like a madwoman, you realize that?" The tone told me Ben meant it lovingly. He peered at my map, pausing on certain individuals. "I don't know what I'm looking at here. How do you even have all this information?"

He had a point. There was too much going on to see any connections with the naked eye. "I scraped a lot of data. I pulled loads of social media info, who is friends with or follows whom, work connections from the Hill, who might be neighbors, all that sort of stuff. We're in 'throwing all the darts at the same time hoping for a bullseye' territory here. Then we'll narrow it down as needed."

"On this giant paper here?"

"No, silly." I swatted his butt. "On my computer. Why do it by hand when an algorithm can do it for you? This map is for you, to show exactly what we're looking at."

"I wonder if we should talk to Jamie again," Ben mused.

I glanced up sharply, taken aback. We hadn't spoken of Jamie since I found Ben. Jamie hadn't told me anything more after I asked him who he was. He just dropped me off to continue my search alone. Ben hadn't been interested in bringing him up, and I wasn't going to push it. My husband was a smart man. If he thought Jamie could help us in any way, I knew he'd say so.

"Why do you say that?"

"I just," he paused, trying to come up with the words, "I think he was following me for a while, and there's a chance he can help with a connection or something."

"Oh, he was definitely following you. He said he was outside our house the day you went to find Dan Flint."

Ben smirked, noticing a lilt in my voice. "Is that annoyance I hear? He was outside and you didn't ever see him. Isn't that supposed to be your thing?"

By the time I responded his grin had spread widely. "You're enjoying this too much," I grumbled, but I couldn't keep the smile off my face. We were back together, and now, for the first time in our lives, we were both open books. Nothing left to hide. Working together. As soon as we stopped this group and cleared my name, we could go scoop the kids and be together once again. Fixed, whole. Everything visible.

Everything visible.

"Ben, look at this," I pointed down at the poster.

"What are you pointing at?"

In his defense, I wasn't actually pointing at anything specific. "A connection that isn't there," I said.

"What do you mean?"

"A connection that should be there but isn't." *Not everything was visible.*

"I don't understand."

"There is no connection in any way here from a cabal member to any member of the police."

"Okay…" Ben trailed off.

"You don't see it?"

"I don't, sorry." He offered a chagrined smile. "Help me out here."

"There has to be a connection. They covered up the deaths of students. There has to be a relationship somewhere here."

"Okay, but we don't see any."

"Exactly. Sometimes it's the relationships we don't see. The ones that have been hidden. Because they don't want us to see it."

"So what are you saying? That there's likely a cop who is part of this organization?"

"That's exactly what I'm saying."

Ben's mouth quivered. "I'm headed to the police station tomorrow to be interviewed."

CHAPTER 58
ELAINE

Afternoon, March 22

Detective Fahey loomed over Elaine's desk, a startling eclipse over an otherwise sunny day.

"Hello, Fahey, how's it going?" Elaine asked, keeping her eyes on her computer.

"Where's Brown?"

Elaine shrugged, pretending it wasn't a big deal that someone she'd never seen take a sick day hadn't shown up for work. "Texted that she had a family emergency, had to dip for a while. I didn't ask for details."

"Family emergency, huh? Never once heard her talk about her family," Fahey said, pulling Brown's chair around from her desk and plopping himself down next to Elaine.

"She's told me a little about them," Elaine said noncommittally. No need to get in a pissing contest with Fahey. "I think almost all of them still live in Farmville."

"Farmville?" Fahey barked a laugh. "That's not a real place."

Elaine didn't know how to respond.

"Branaman asked if I could look over what you've got, keep an eye on you if you will, while Brown is away," Fahey said.

"What?" Elaine finally pulled her eyes away from her computer. She turned to face him. "I don't need looking after."

"Of course you do. You're a junior detective working on the murder of the president of Georgetown. I hear you're also trying your best to add more doubt into the arrest for Dr. Flint's murder. That's too much for one person."

"I can handle it."

"Have you arrested Veronica Walsh yet?"

Elaine felt her face flush. "No."

"Why haven't you yet? She obviously killed McAllister," Fahey scoffed. "She was a danger last year, she was a danger last week, and she's still a danger now. First order of business, we go scoop her up. A holding cell for forty-eight hours might help clear her mind."

"We don't know where she is right now."

"See, there you go. What were you going to do about that?"

"Police work." Elaine shrugged. Why did the chief have to saddle her with Fahey? There were plenty of others who could jump in after Detective Brown's unexpected absence.

"Okay, what other leads do you have? Who else do you think is breaking into his office like a cat burglar and slicing his throat? Just a normal Georgetown thing, could be anyone?"

"DNA analysis isn't back yet, and all campus security has is someone dressed in all black with their face obscured."

"Wow, wonder who that could've been." The sarcasm dripped from his voice.

"Look, what do you want from me?"

"I want you not to look a gift horse in the mouth. We can work out the details, find the evidence that pins her to this, but don't slow walk this just because you're one of her adoring fans."

"I'm not."

"I get it. I used to be obsessed with Yancey Portillo. People love bad guy—*or girl, could be girl*—antiheroes. But this is murder, and that means something. Let's cut the crap and go handle this."

"You knew Detective Brown wasn't here," Elaine said, studying Fahey's face. "You pretended like you didn't. Why?"

Fahey's mouth widened into a boyish grin. "Just trying to get some background on her. She's a tough nut to crack, isn't she?"

Elaine didn't respond, just grabbed her coat and followed Fahey as he bounced away sprightly, as if the idea of arresting Veronica Walsh had put a spring in his step.

CHAPTER 59
BEN

Afternoon, March 22

What do you do when you think the police aren't the answer?

Ben knew the answer from prior experience. Go it alone.

When Veronica had disappeared in the fall, only to be named the prime suspect in a multiple murder, he realized that he could only rely on the authorities for so much. It also caused him to take a step back and realize the inherent privilege of his life up to that point, where he had never had a reason to be concerned.

But first he had a separate agenda. He understood the reasons why they shouldn't, how there was a chance it could be risky, but he had to see Nico and Maria.

Veronica had told him that she did her best shielding them from the news when he was first shot and didn't come home. She explained that dad was unexpectedly away for a little while. But when that picture of her came out and someone shattered their window, there was only so much they could do. Even kids of that age weren't sheltered enough from the internet. "If there's a way to be sure we aren't being followed, can we drive down just for the day? See them, tell them I'm fine and that we love them, and that their vacation with their abuelos will be just a little longer?"

Veronica sighed. "We won't be able to guarantee their safety, but then I guess that's just part of life, isn't it?" She looked Ben in the eyes and gave a resolute nod. "Let's do it, but we're not calling them first. No paper trail, we use cash, no one knows we went down there."

"We can use one of Nat's cars, I assume?"

"Yeah, she left the keys and said the Mercedes AMG had a full tank of gas. It's probably the least conspicuous of the three she keeps here anyway."

"Imagine this being your least conspicuous car," Ben said, as he climbed into the driver's seat a few minutes later.

They were still on East Boulevard Drive, not yet out of the neighborhood, when Veronica did a sharp intake of breath.

"What is it?" Ben asked, looking over at her in the passenger seat. She was completely still except her eyes, which were scanning this way and that.

"I need you to forget all your safe driver training," she said, her voice low and tense. "None of this driving slowly shit."

Ben started to turn his head. "Face forward!" Veronica hissed. "Don't let them know you see them."

"Who are they?" Ben asked, bewildered.

Veronica shook her head. "I don't know. But this isn't Jamie getting me to come see you. This is something sinister. Turn north on the parkway when we get off this street."

"Like we would anyway?"

"Yes, but keep going into Old Town. We need public. We need people around. They were in this neighborhood. That means they know where we're staying. They're about to act."

"What do you think is happening?"

"Ben," Veronica looked him dead in the eyes, "someone is here to kill us."

CHAPTER 60
VERONICA

Afternoon, March 22

I wasn't surprised. Of course it was going to come to this eventually. The police might need pesky things like motive and evidence, but this cabal of powerful characters? Absolutely not. They knew it was me. McAllister even said as much. They left me alone until they decided they couldn't anymore.

They planted a fake story to get the public to turn against me. They killed my father. They drove me from my home. Now it was time to end it. They'd kill Ben too, for whatever they thought he knew about them.

No one was going to leave my children orphans.

"Drive to Market Square," I said. The large square fountain in front of Alexandria's Town Hall was the centerpiece of the oldest continuously running farmer's market in the country. It was also the location where Jeremy Wiles coerced Jacob Jordan into his ill-fated assassination attempt on President Leishear. But most important for me, it was rarely empty. I needed witnesses. I needed something to make whoever was following us pause, even if just momentarily.

Because the truth of life is that if someone decides it's time for you to die, and has enough resources, there is little you can do to stop it. I was a master in exactly that back in my teenage years. There's an arms race, and an individual will never win that. What could I do if someone planted a bomb along a road I had to travel? There was always a way if you were creative enough.

But now I had been alerted. Chances of assassination success plummet once the target knows something is coming.

I didn't like it, but we would have to split up. Ben would go past the square then circle back and drive south on Fairfax Street, pausing just enough to give me a chance to dive out of the car at the entrance to the parking garage below. He would keep driving, and head straight to the DC Police. Detective Brown only. Whoever was back there would have to make a choice, and of course they'd choose me. But they wouldn't be able to see if I went into the garage or not. Did they know there were two egresses? Would they consider who I am, and what they know about me?

My mind raced, gaming and evaluating the possibilities as we drove alongside the Potomac River. It was a dark Dodge Durango following us. No one was in the passenger seat, but that didn't mean the driver was alone.

My phone rang, and Ben jolted, the car veering onto the gravel for a second before he corrected. I raised an eyebrow. "Let's not do the job for them."

I normally wouldn't pick up a call from an unknown number. Let them leave a message and I'll decide whether to get back.

But this could be them.

"Hello, who is this?"

"Alex, it's me."

There's a thing about hope.

It can break through every barrier that fear and anxiety put up. Even the tiniest hint of it, and those walls can come crashing down. *The Shawshank Redemption* had it *partially* right. Hope can set you free, but only in the right circumstances. Relatives of those who are missing, presumed dead, will tell you that hope is itself an anchor, and they'd be perfectly right to say so. But sometimes the dark sky does pale, and a flicker of light begins to shine through, telling you that everything will be okay.

My best friend was on the other end of the line.

"Francisco? How did you…?"

"I'm sorry it took so long, I had to spend a few days planning this out as soon as I heard that our fathers were both killed. I sprung myself from jail, and I'm headed to San Salvador as soon as humanly possible. I need to fix whatever has happened down there."

"Francisco, I'm so sorry about your father," I said.

"I appreciate it, Alessandra."

I let the mention of my old name go. He needed my empathy right now.

"I'm going to kill anyone who knew even the tiniest thing about this." Francisco's voice came out as a low snarl.

"I don't doubt that. I would do the same," I said. "You'll meet up with the Landaverdes down there, won't you? Tell them I'm sorry too."

"I will. We'll burn the city down."

"Hi, Francisco," Ben called, and I put the phone on speaker. "Sorry about all this, but I'm glad to hear you weren't the one who killed me!"

Look at my husband. A tense, life-or-death situation, and he's cracking jokes. He'd come a long way.

"Guys, that's just it. That's what I'm calling about."

"What is it?" I asked.

"I found this out days ago, but I had to confirm it. Then I got arrested before I could tell you."

"What is it?" I repeated.

"Jamie Simon is not his real name. That name is an anagram."

My mind raced. I was supposed to be the puzzle master, the queen of solving the unsolvable. How could I not have seen this? "He's someone we know. That's why you had to confirm, and you went back home to check."

"Yes. He flipped the first and last name, I think that's what made it not so obvious," Francisco added.

There was a long silence as Ben sped into Old Town proper. I knew Francisco was letting me figure it out on my own.

Jamie Simon. Simon Jamie.

Simon.

Minos.

Osmin.

It hit me with the force of a freight train. "Holy shit," I said. I felt a swell of heat and pressure rush through my head.

"Exactly," Francisco replied.

"Who is he?" Ben asked.

A flood of memories poured into my brain. I never had heard what happened to him. Where he went. He just disappeared all those years ago. After a while, none of us even bothered to care where he was. Why spend any time worrying about someone who was clearly no longer a threat? Everyone knew that his brother had been the ruthless one. That organization was a two-headed snake, but all it took to kill it was cutting off one head.

Which I did. Of my own volition, at age thirteen. The act that started everything and changed my life forever.

I took a deep breath and turned toward my husband. I could see in his eyes that I must have had a shell-shocked look on my face.

"Ben, he's Osmin Mejia."

CHAPTER 61
VERONICA

Afternoon, March 22

I remembered it like it was yesterday, not over two decades ago.

I was standing at the tree line behind the Mejia compound, blood dripping down my leg from Maynor's finger in my pants pocket. The adrenaline coursing through me was causing me to shake uncontrollably. My head was spinning. I had just killed Maynor Mejia.

The Maynor Mejia, our greatest rival, was gone.

And it was entirely my doing. Nothing would be the same now. I took several calming breaths, eventually stopped the shaking, and checked all my appendages to make sure I was physically fine. I turned for one final look at the house, my very first homicide.

That was the last time I saw Osmin Mejia. It had to be him. He looked just like his brother. He was supposed to be away. But there he was. Standing on the third-floor balcony, staring right at me. Motionless and expressionless.

I froze. How much could he see? How well hidden was I in the woods? His face didn't give anything away. Was he watching me go or just looking out into the void?

I stayed completely still for as long as I could bear it. They must have found Maynor's body by now, so any second, his people would come streaming out the door looking for me.

I was struck by just how young he looked. I knew he and Maynor weren't many years older than me, probably in their early twenties at oldest, but Maynor had a hard edge that aged him. That was a man I had killed. But the figure I was looking at was more like a lost boy.

If I moved, Osmin would see. Even if he couldn't make out who I was, he would see movement in the woods.

I couldn't chance it.

I had to chance it. *Run!*

With one final glance and a deep breath, I turned around and plunged through the trees. Stealth didn't matter anymore, only distance. *Don't look down. Don't look back. Only straight ahead, towards safety*. All the way until I made it out the other side of the trees.

My anonymity was my safety once I was around other people. No one looked too closely, why would they?

I didn't tell my father about Osmin. Not that day, or ever after.

Initially, it was self-preservation. I needed him to think I had done something so incredible that there was no turning back. I needed to appear infallible. If I just said, "Oh, by the way, the victim's brother might've seen me," I would never have been accepted into the inner circle.

But eventually there was no reason to talk about him. No one ever heard from Osmin Mejia again. We weren't exactly on speaking terms with the Mejia henchmen, so we never got the full story, but in the ensuing days after I killed his brother he just disappeared.

We fretted, but only a little. We weren't the type to fret, if I'm being honest.

Years passed, and all memories of him flitted away.

Until now.

Jamie Simon. Osmin Mejia.

One and the same. The name that I feared for the years I spent making everyone else fear me.

"What did he tell you?" I asked Ben. "Anything at all you can remember. I need to know."

Ben's face was strained. "I don't think he told me anything… Umm… Wait, he did tell me one thing. He said he was following me and took those pictures from the hotel room and leaked them because he was mad at me for leaving."

"Mad at you? What does that even mean?"

"I don't know what is going on," Francisco said. "But you need to watch your back. I have no idea what his game is, and him killing Dan Flint shows he is willing to be just as violent as his brother was."

"I can't believe I didn't put this together earlier." I glanced back at the SUV still behind us, making no attempt to hide itself. "Okay, look, Francisco, thanks for telling us, and I'm so glad you're free, but we might have a situation here." I filled him in on where we were headed.

"Understood, Alex," Francisco said. "I'd help you, you know I would, but I need to lay low. I'm keeping this number, even back home. Please keep me updated. *Buena suerte.*"

"I don't understand," Ben said as Francisco hung up. "He saved me from Dan."

"Did he, though? What do you actually remember?"

Ben's eyes dilated as he came to the realization. His memory of the incident was entirely based on Jamie's—*Osmin's*—account of how it went down.

"Who is this guy?"

"Remember me telling you all the details of my violent teenage career?" Of course he did. Those conversations were probably seared onto his brain forever. "Maynor Mejia, the first one," I said.

"I remember."

"Osmin is his twin brother. No one knew what happened to him, he just disappeared after I killed his brother."

Ben thought for a second. "Did everyone know you did that? Why would he be coming after you now? Why not last November when your story came out and you were in a coma in the hospital?"

I took a breath. "That's the thing," I said. "I saw him as I was escaping from their house. I still don't know if he saw me or not, but he stared right out into the woods where I was. He could have easily seen me. He might have known all along it was me. That still doesn't answer your second question, though, I know."

Ben stared straight ahead. I could see him gripping the steering wheel with enough force to rip it off if he shifted his hands. "I thought everything about your past life was behind us," he spat out through gritted teeth. "But instead, there's another psycho murderer who shot me and has pretended to help me for days. Why didn't he just kill me?"

"I really don't know," I said truthfully. Ben's tone was rimmed with anger, but I knew him well enough to know that it was just masking fear. I didn't begrudge him that fear. How could I, when I felt the same?

"Do you think that's Osmin in the car behind us?" Ben asked.

"I really don't know," I repeated. "But if he is, he was one of the most dangerous men in all of El Salvador, and he's possibly been holding a grudge against me for decades."

"Fuck," Ben mouthed.

"Look, whoever it is back there, we'll handle it. And if it's not Osmin, then we'll handle him after." We drove through the stop-start blocks of Old Town, and I waited for an intersection to force Ben to look at me. Once he did, I said, "You will be fine, and I will be fine. I promise you that. If you believe nothing else right now, believe that."

As we drove past the little bookstore that the both of us loved on the corner of Royal and Prince streets, I grabbed my husband's hand. "Okay, Ben, you know the drill. You drop me off on the next block, right as we reach the square, and you keep driving. You call this number," I showed him my phone, pre-dialed to reach Detective Emilia Brown, "and you don't talk to anyone else. She's the only cop we can for sure trust right now. You get the hell away from here and you go straight to her. I'll be fine. I'll do my thing. You get out."

CHAPTER 62
BEN

Afternoon, March 22

Ben did as he was told. He dropped Veronica off, watching her roll out as she hit the pavement, bursting back up in an instant and rushing off to his right, hidden by the exterior wall of the elevator down to the parking garage. Whoever was following, Osmin or someone else, would see what happened and assume she went down into the garage.

But that was the extent to which Ben planned on listening to Veronica. He wasn't going to run away, seeking out help elsewhere. He couldn't leave his wife in harm's way on her own. He called Detective Brown's number and when a recognizable gruff voice answered instead, he hung up immediately. Veronica had said to talk to no one but Brown. Not Fahey, the detective who had made his feelings on his wife very clear during her disappearance.

That was that. No way was Ben going to get back on the parkway, head north, cross the river into DC, find Detective Brown's building, and go get her in person. There would be no cavalry coming. The Ben of even a few weeks ago would have chafed at Veronica's surety that only Detective Brown could help. He would have nodded along, but then raced to the nearest police officer to help, promises be damned. He was past that now. Complete trust. She'd earned that from him.

Ben could feel his heart pounding as he searched for a nearby parking spot. It felt churlish to have to think about parking, but he didn't want to illegally park and bring any more attention to the car. After doubling back, he finally found a spot on the corner of Duke and Royal Streets, on the block that held the town's main Catholic church. Thanking the Lord that it wasn't Sunday and the spot was open, he parallel parked and jumped out of the car, running north on the cobbled sidewalk as fast as his legs would carry him.

He arrived at Market Square and scanned the area.

Oh, God.

A pale man was standing inside the fountain—empty of water for the winter—holding a young boy around his neck, a gun pointed at the side of his head. "Veronica Walsh!" he called. "Step forward or else I will kill everyone in this square, starting with this kid."

Not Jamie/Osmin.

Ben couldn't see Veronica but knew she must still be close.

"Don't tempt me!" the shooter yelled. He swung his gun arm quickly around and fired off a shot at a fleeing young woman. The shot missed but the crack of the bullet flying by sent her tumbling down the stairs at the southeast corner of the square. "I've changed my mind! If anyone moves, I shoot them and then shoot him."

Ben watched as Veronica emerged from behind the elevator building. Her arms were raised, palms extended. *No, don't,* Ben whispered under his breath.

"You're only here for me. You were sent to kill me," Veronica said, a calm, self-assured smile plastered across her face. "Don't make this any bigger than it has to be."

"There she is. The woman of the moment! Everyone take a good look. This despicable woman is your only hope now. If she isn't willing to give up her life for you random people, then you will all die today. And you'll all know it was because Veronica Walsh is exactly who you think she is. Your dying thoughts will be cursing that you ever were hoodwinked into thinking she was redeemable.

"Or," he continued, "Veronica Walsh will save you all. You can regale your children and grandchildren that you'll get to see grow up with the tale of how she did finally redeem herself in the eyes of the world. She'll be gone, but she'll have gone out a hero. Finally, fully loved by everyone."

"*Dios mio,* shut up, dude," Veronica said, slowly stepping closer. She moved her arms away from her, parallel to the ground, presenting as big a target as possible. "I'm here. Make your move. Earn that money."

He held her gaze but didn't move his gun away from the boy.

"I will keep moving toward you. If you don't shoot, eventually I'm going to just take that gun right out of your hand." She cocked her head. "What's the matter? Not used to confrontation? Are you the type who just shoots your victims in the back of the head and runs off? Barely even counts as getting your hands dirty where I come from."

Ben watched, frozen in place. She glanced over and made eye contact, giving him a quick reassuring nod.

"Who is that you just acknowledged? He's now first!"

As soon as the gun began to swing toward Ben, Veronica took a long stride toward the hitman. The stride turned into a sprint and before he had a chance to fire at Ben, he whipped his gun back around and let off several shots in her direction.

Ben's heart jumped to his mouth as he watched her flinch but keep going, making up the distance before plowing into the gunman with the force of a middle linebacker. She grabbed his gun as he lay there, winded, and smashed him across the forehead with the butt. Blood gurgled out and his eyes closed.

"V!" Ben cried as he rushed to her side as the boy ran past him in the opposite direction.

"It's okay, I'm okay." The words tumbled out of her mouth.

She leaned into his hug, keeping her gaze and gun pointed at the assailant.

"Holy Mary, Mother of God."

Ben whipped his head around to see an old woman with her hands clasped together, being hugged by a younger woman—probably a daughter. Her eyes were brimming with tears and her body was shaking. A quivering, bony finger stretched out toward Veronica. "She saved us," the woman said. "She saved everyone."

CHAPTER 63
ARCHON

Evening, March 22

Archon pinched the bridge of his nose, trying to stave off the migraine coming his way. He used to get them often as a child. Dehydration induced them when he didn't drink enough water while playing whichever youth sport he was dominating at the time. His parents used to get annoyed at him since he knew how to prevent them, yet still forgot often because he was, well, a kid.

Now as an adult he only ever got migraines in times of high stress. His primary care physician had suggested he try to limit the external stresses in his life—*doesn't everyone try to do that?*

This was supposed to be a 1-2 knockout punch. Take care of Veronica Walsh and then make their move. Things were already in motion, there was no stopping now.

But Veronica Walsh was still in play. And on top of that, the leading story this evening was that the picture of her holding the decapitated head was proven fake. That nasty actors were at work trying to sully her name.

Sully her name. As if she were a squeaky-clean Disney Channel child actress.

One fell swoop, and she was on the way back into everyday Americans' hearts.

"What happened?" He spat into the phone.

"She spotted him."

"The fuck did you say? She spotted him? I was led to believe—*by you*—that that was impossible. He was going to sneak up on her and take her out. A quiet kill, that's what we said. Instead, we get this shit? What is our entire raison d'etre? We stay in the fucking shadows! I ought to—" He stopped himself before he finished the thought.

"I never led you, or the Archon before you, to believe that he was infallible." The voice on the other end of the phone was so calm, he could've been ordering takeout.

"You said he came with a guarantee of success. I don't take guarantees lightly."

"I have never once said he guaranteed success. I just said he had always been successful, which was the case up until now. She got away, we'll get her next time. Don't worry about it. He will complete the task at hand, as requested."

Technicalities and double speak. The mark of a man who would never be in the running for Archon.

"He's been arrested, you dimwit." Archon squeezed his eyes shut. The migraine was definitely on its way. "What went wrong?"

"It was too public. That's all. No big deal, she'll be on her guard now, but that's no issue."

"No big deal? We are moving tomorrow!" Archon shouted through the phone.

Archon slammed his phone down onto the couch. What was the point of having hitmen at your beck and call if they couldn't finish the job? Archon had found Ulrich's encrypted notes detailing exactly who to call in such situations, and all the hows and whys of it. He stayed up late one night not long after Ulrich's death reading the copious pages on every confirmed kill that had happened under The Princemakers' watch.

Bedrock—*shudder*—probably would've been successful. But there were obvious reasons why he had to go with a different shooter, and they'd never before had a problem when switching it up.

Tomorrow there would be one more name added to the list. It was time for an old-fashioned approach. Brains, not brawn. This time tomorrow night, Archon would be enjoying a nice highball of Stoli, watching the news recap the tragic events of the day. He'd probably even go on one of the circuit shows, make some asinine comment that the press would lap up. Wouldn't that be a laugh? He couldn't help himself, he started wordsmithing in his head. *You really never think it would go that far. We're just lucky that there are enough good people out there to outweigh the bad.*

More good than bad. That would be a nice touch.

CHAPTER 64
ELAINE

Evening, March 22

"What happened down there?" Fahey thundered, weaving his way through traffic as they headed back to the station.

"I don't know. Not our business," Elaine quipped.

"Except it literally is our business, because our prime suspect was at the heart of it!"

Elaine couldn't argue with that, so she remained silent.

"We should be down there, arresting Veronica Walsh," Fahey said, banging his hand on the steering wheel. "Rather than this bullshit."

"I mean… the chief called us back to talk to him. That feels important. And it's not like Veronica is going to get away this time anyway. Whoever is down there will handle it."

Fahey snorted and glanced at Elaine to check if she was serious. "You have so much still to learn, it's unbelievable," he said, when he realized she was.

"What do you mean?"

"No one is going to 'handle' it unless we do it ourselves. That's what this job is. A bunch of blundering oafs and every once in a while, a diamond who can do some real, no fooling, detective work."

"Are you a diamond?" The corners of Elaine's mouth crept up into a sly smile.

"I have my moments. This is the thing, though, and I don't know if Brown is going to teach you this: there is no room for sentimentality or emotion here. You find a clue, you log a clue, you catch a killer. That's it. There's nothing else, no narrative, no story to be told. All that is around the outside, stuff to distract you."

"Alright then, Lester Freamon."

Fahey's eyes shot over to meet hers. "You know *The Wire*?"

She felt his respect for her rise in real time. He wasn't hard to figure out. Play to his vanity, speak his language. "*Real po-lice*. My parents watched it over and over. I heard you compared Yancey Portillo to Marlo Stanfield. Or was it Omar?"

"It doesn't matter what I thought about Yancey Portillo." Fahey frowned.

"Sure, it doesn't. I thought that comparison was a little nonsensical anyway. A bit melodramatic for my taste."

Fahey took his eyes back to the road and said nothing.

"So, you're saying not to have an ego."

"Exactly." His eyes didn't waver.

"Well, weren't you friends with the Belle family?"

Fahey's grip on the wheel tightened.

"And didn't you get really upset when you were pulled off the Billingsley murder and everything that followed there?" Okay, maybe don't always play to his vanity.

"Aren't we feisty?" Fahey said, each word laced with venom.

"I'm just saying, I'm not sure you practice what you preach."

"Fahey, you track down wherever Veronica Walsh is now; Iverson, let's talk," Chief Branaman said as the pair of detectives walked into his office. No pleasantries. Straight to business.

"I— very well, sir. That's a good idea," Fahey said, wheeling away and stomping through the station.

"He seems upset."

"He ranted the whole drive about how we need to be out arresting Veronica Walsh. It's probably not going down well that you brought him all the way back here just to tell him to find her."

"On what evidence?"

"Circumstantial only, sir."

"I figured. Lord knows if we had evidence on her, I'd be right there leading the charge. Murder is murder, but we can't be hasty here. Especially after what happened this afternoon."

"How so?"

"There's a groundswell of support for her now. All that public outcry after the doctored picture of her, it's all gone. Switches have flipped, just like that, and she's America's hero once again."

"How do we know it was doctored?"

Branaman shrugged. "I don't know, but apparently enough experts are saying it is, and that the original picture is benign. I try not to keep up with all that crap on the news. But it's hard not to look away from what happened down in Alexandria."

"That she had a chance to get away and then turned back to stop that shooter? That's not the action of a villain."

"True enough, but I think you and I both know that everyone lives somewhere in the gray, especially in this city."

"Did you call me in to talk about her?"

"No, actually." He rested his chin on his fist. "I want to know more about Detective Brown's absence. I was hoping you could tell me more."

"More? All I know is that she had to leave quickly for a family emergency."

Branaman sighed and put his hands behind his head. "That's all she told me too. She deserves her leave—God knows she doesn't take enough. Do you think we should send her something?"

"Like to her parents' house in Farmville?"

"Is that where they live?"

"Yeah, I think so."

"Maybe. It just feels a little strange not knowing where my star detective is. No shade meant," he hastily added.

"None taken." Elaine chuckled. "As if you'd think it was me."

"Hey, there's a reason you're rising quickly, and it has nothing to do with your family. Don't talk yourself down. You're here because everyone knows you're a good detective and everyone trusts you."

Elaine tried and failed to tamp down the smile on her face. External validation from a superior. As far as dopamine hits go, it was hard to beat.

"Chief, since you trust me, I did want to say something to you." Elaine glanced behind her.

Branaman got the message and walked over and pulled his door firmly shut. "Go on."

"You know how Detective Brown and I are supposed to be looking into this 'cabal' or whatever it is?"

Branaman sat, stone-faced, waiting for her to continue.

Elaine took a deep breath. "I'm worried that Detective Fahey might have something to do with it."

Branaman chewed on his bottom lip. "That's... a strong accusation," he finally said.

"I know."

"You must have more to say."

"There has to be a cop involved. I mean there's no way what happened at World's Edge could have been covered up otherwise."

"It's highly likely you're right, but that doesn't mean it's any of us."

"Sure, but this is a man who had an unhealthy obsession with Yancey Portillo, ranted to any and every one about how the Belles and Senator Billingsley were good people, and has now been itching to lock up Veronica Walsh for killing people who I think were likely members of this cabal. Doesn't that all seem a bit suspicious to you?"

"Look, when you line up a bunch of decisions or thoughts any of us have in a certain way, we all can look suspicious. Take the cleanest person in here and I bet I could find a pattern of behavior that would make you question them. But," he raised his hand to stop Elaine from jumping in, "I am willing to admit that this is concerning, if not alarming."

"We should watch him. I can do it."

"No, hold on. We're not doing anything like that yet. I will have a talk with him."

"You can't let him know that we're on to him!"

"Detective, this isn't some perp, this is one of our colleagues. I will speak to him, and I will decide how to take that further."

"How am I supposed to work with him in the meantime?"

"How long have you considered him to be part of this cabal?"

Elaine hesitated. "A day, I guess?"

"And how were you with him today?"

"Umm, it felt awkward but fine."

"There's your answer then. I appreciate you bringing this to me, you know you can always come to me whenever you have a concern. You can keep an eye out, of course, but take no further action until you hear from me, is that clear?"

Elaine nodded, trying to determine if this was the first time she was ever willfully lying to her boss.

CHAPTER 65
ARCHON

Night, March 22

"Everything is in place, do I understand correctly?" Archon sometimes wondered why he even bothered having a home office. All he recently used this space for was phone calls away from prying ears. There was plenty of space in this house for that. Maybe he should have left it as his daughter's playroom. Maybe a grandchild would eventually come along, not that she'd ever made that seem likely.

"Yes, sir. It will be done tomorrow at five-thirty in the evening. The schedule works perfectly, and it'll go down exactly as we have planned."

Archon rested his head back, satisfied. "Your man will be there?" he asked, even if he already knew the answer.

"He will, and he too will do exactly as planned." His old friend sighed, weary of the questioning.

"I know, I get it. We're almost there, and then we can breathe."

"I just want a day to relax, is that too much to ask?"

"We'll all have a celebratory drink together very soon. Those of us that are left, we'll meet, and we'll decide how we move forward. Veronica Walsh will need to be next, but that's now a problem for another day." Archon slid his tongue back and forth across the bottom of his incisors. "When the moment comes, it has to be precise. There cannot be any cracks at all. We've set the stage, the pieces move as planned. The public will jump on the story. This is the social media age. Truth is what we make it. Our truth will hit first and hardest and anyone trying to argue differently will look like a crackpot."

"The maddeningly vague but ultimately damning police statement that follows will seal the deal. I'll make sure of that."

"We won't speak again until after. You know the drill, destroy your phone as soon as we hang up. Call me on your new phone as soon as it's done."

CHAPTER 66
BEN

Morning, March 23

Back at it. On foot with his boss. His favorite part of his job.

Ben breathed in deeply, letting the brisk air fill his lungs. He needed this. A tiny slice of normalcy. He'd begged his boss to let him come into work, despite it all. The first time he called, she'd hung up as soon as he asked the question. The second time she waited long enough to tell him he was a fool. By the fourth time, she relented and told him she wasn't going to wait if he fell behind. They had a full schedule, mostly just inside the halls of Congress, but she had one mid-afternoon meeting at the White House that would likely last until close of business, not that anything stopped at five in the evening in this city.

Veronica had been on board with him going back to work. She'd laughed when he suggested he should stay home to help keep her safe. "That shooter is in jail now," she had said. "They'll send another eventually, I'm sure, but they're going to lick their wounds a bit before trying something so doomed to fail again."

Ben tried his best to mirror her confidence.

"Ladies and gentlemen, our hero returns!"

Ben rolled his eyes as he stepped back into Moore's office for the first time. She had balloons up around the room and a Hallmark-style card on the entryway that read, "Congrats on escaping a kidnapping!"

He pinched the bridge of his nose and chuckled appreciatively as fellow staffers gathered around. "Tell me you didn't just happen to find a card that said this?" he pointed at the happy little cartoon figure with a cheesy thumbs-up gesture next to the word "kidnapping."

"The internet never disappoints," his boss said with a smile. "Well, you know, except continuously every single day."

Ben took some time to regale the team with stories and show off his hip, which was healing well but still looked ugly.

"Okay, wrap it up, everyone," Moore eventually said, clapping her hands together twice. "Work to be done. Ben, you stay here," she mouthed as he started toward the door.

After everyone else filed out, Ben sat down on Moore's couch. She liked to joke about being everyone's therapist as well as boss. For Ben, he just was happy to take the weight off. His hip was throbbing already.

"Alright, Ben, not much to catch you up on," Moore said as she poured herself a cup of coffee. "There's only one thing I care about today and that's avoiding Senator Thresh."

"Wherefore?"

"Ben you can just say, 'Why?' You don't have to impress me with your erudition."

"I can't turn it off. I am who I am."

"Good to see being kidnapped and shot hasn't changed your personality at all. Anyway, look, Thresh and I are in the middle of a relatively public spat."

"About that spending bill still?"

"That's where it started, but I made a dumb comment in public, basically insinuating that all is not above board when it comes to him. Plus, he's mad about my comments about this so-called cabal."

"Well, it's clearly not all above board. He's bought and paid for."

"Yes, but you know the game. We have to dance around that, not say it explicitly. So, now we've had a bit of a back and forth, and, I'll be straight with you, the public seems to be veering toward siding with him."

Ben leaned forward and put his elbows on his knees. "What's the play, then?"

"The play?" Moore snickered. "The play is that there is no play. It's to avoid any mess and concentrate on things that actually matter today. To that end, I'm telling you this just so you can play bouncer in case anyone tries anything, from the media or otherwise, today."

CHAPTER 67
ELAINE

Afternoon, March 23

Elaine couldn't figure out where her sense of urgency was coming from, but she felt it coursing through her veins. She had to do something now.

Dan Flint was dead, and the killer had escaped. McAllister was dead—*what was his first name again? She really should remember*—and his apparent killer was running around scot-free, aside from a highly public assassination attempt. Ben Walsh was back, found by Veronica herself. Elaine felt a bit of chagrin over that.

It was now just over twenty-four hours since she had heard from Detective Brown. She hoped that whatever had caused her to leave so suddenly was okay. She had never known her to miss work. The single text explaining a family emergency was tripping warning sirens in Elaine's brain. She couldn't tell for sure, because she'd never been in this situation, but it didn't seem like the way that Detective Brown would leave. She was diligent, organized, a workaholic even. Why didn't she take a second to do some handover? If it was that important that she had to leave immediately, why didn't she leave a voicemail or something?

Not checking in was weird, too. Maybe it was insensitive of her to think that. Before she could stop herself, she searched for any news in Detective Brown's hometown just to see if she could find a reason.

Nothing. No tweets, no Instagram pictures, nothing on TikTok. Okay, so there wasn't a fiery car crash or something. Was a relative sick?

She pulled herself out of it before she could go too far. It didn't matter where Brown was right now, it only mattered what Elaine was going to do next. Where to go, who to follow?

Detective Fahey was the lead. She was sure of it. But what was she to do? Could she really follow a fellow detective—one who far outranked her?

She glanced around the room from her workstation. Generic police station buzz. A couple officers sharing some coffee in the kitchenette in the corner, holding matching cracked Washington, DC, novelty mugs. Chief Branaman's door was closed, blinds ever so slightly askew, offering just a glimpse of him leaning over his desk, inspecting something.

Fahey's desk was empty, as was Brown's.

The thought popped into Elaine's head as if it were the most natural thing in the world. After all, why shouldn't she? As long as she played it the right way, no one would be suspicious.

Act like you belong.

She rose from her chair, grabbing her notebook, and walked nonchalantly over to Fahey's desk. If she were right about him, this would be easy enough.

Everything about the big detective screamed that he didn't like inefficient things in his way. That would definitely include his computer password.

The department had recently changed their security protocols and now everyone had to type in a sixteen-digit-plus password manually each time they logged in. There was the option for two factor authentication, but Fahey wouldn't have taken that.

If she sat down, it would attract attention, so Elaine leaned over the computer instead. A quick glance to make sure no one was eyeing her actions. This was natural, wasn't it? A detective checking her partner's computer for a piece of information. That was all.

There it was. Exactly as she expected. A Post-it note, stuck to the bottom of his monitor. A string of random-looking numbers and letters. Her fingers flew across the keyboard as she punched the password in.

What now? She looked at the unlocked monitor. What was she looking for?

Anything that looked strange. But what did that mean? It wasn't like Fahey was going to have a folder labeled "My Personal Crimes." She checked his desktop folders. He wasn't a man who would hide something big deep within his computer. He'd want it nearby, discrete but easy enough to get to.

Emails, maybe. She had heard of people subverting prying eyes by writing emails and saving them in their drafts. Then all it took was someone else logging on to the same account elsewhere, reading the draft, and then deleting it. No email ever sent, no breadcrumbs to follow.

No drafts in his inbox, though.

Recent emails likely wouldn't have anything, but what keywords to search through his entire inbox? And surely, he'd delete any incriminating emails anyway.

Feeling a wave of defeat, she let her eyes wander through his emails. Nothing crazy.

Except.

Why was Detective Fahey emailing asking about Representative Moore's schedule?

CHAPTER 68
BEN

Afternoon, March 23

"You're sure you're good after that?" Ben asked.

His boss looked him directly in the eyes. "Ben, of course I'm fine after the White House meeting. Barring Senator Thresh ambushing me, I think we're pretty well set for the rest of the day. You have your interview at the police station and then you need to go home. You were shot and kidnapped. Someone tried to kill your wife. Pardon the language, but you need to get the fuck out of here." She smiled at him and shook her head ruefully. "I still can't believe I let you come back in today."

"I'll have my work phone with me if you need anything," Ben said, wondering what made him so desperate to appear useful. It wasn't as if Representative Moore had ever suggested she thought otherwise. Even when she'd benched him, she had taken the time to sit him down and explain her reasoning. It wasn't anything about him, she just needed his wife's newly uncovered past not to derail her own work.

"I'll walk home tonight, and check in with you about this weekend," she said. "Just get me info on whatever I need to know for the next couple days and that's all."

"You're walking home alone?"

"Like I always do, Ben. I don't need the chivalry here. And anyway," she winked slyly, "I've got a companion waiting in my locker who keeps me safe."

Ben chuckled. "Good point. Pity anyone who'd try to mess with you."

Ben looked around the room as the memories flooded in. "Did you really have to put me in the same room that I was in when Veronica was missing?"

"Sorry about that." The young female detective shot him an incredulous look, making it clear that she wasn't sorry. "We don't have loads of rooms."

"I know you weren't part of that, but still. I don't like being in here." The pit in his stomach had only gotten deeper since Veronica voiced her theory. Was he in the lion's den? Could any wrong word to the wrong person spell doom?

The fresh-faced detective seated with her pencil and notepad had a familiarity about her that he couldn't place. She cleared her throat several times, priming her voice like a lawnmower before the blades began to spin.

"Ben Walsh," she finally said. "My name is Detective Elaine Iverson. You were there at the scene of Daniel Flint's death. You are not a suspect. You are here as a witness."

Ben took a deep breath before recapping everything he could remember for the detective. From leaving the house to ask Dan Flint if he knew anything that could help Veronica stop Jacob Jordan, to being shot and held in captivity, albeit in relative comfort as his wound was tended to.

"How is it, your hip?" Iverson jumped in.

"Loads of pain if I shift the wrong way, but with round-the-clock painkillers, I'm doing okay."

"You should go get it checked out."

"I know, I know." Ben allowed himself a quick smile. "As soon as this is all over, I will."

"Jamie Simon. Your wife mentioned his name previously, what else can you tell me?"

Ben sucked in air. What else? That Veronica wasn't the only missing and presumed dead Salvadoran residing in the area? That everything he thought he understood about the last few days had been flipped on its head? "How about you tell me what you're doing to stop my wife from getting killed?"

"We'd be doing a lot more if she'd come turn herself in."

"Turn herself in?"

Iverson lifted an eyebrow. "Has she told you any specifics about what she's been up to?"

"I—no." Ben almost let the old, trusting version of him come out. "Except finding me when you guys couldn't."

Iverson sighed. "Look," she said. "Let me be real with you. I would like to talk to her for exactly that reason. I have a problem."

"I don't—"

"I promise, I just want to talk to her."

Ben looked the detective over. He couldn't help himself. He trusted her. Part of what made him so effective for his boss was his ability to read people and understand their motivations. All that had changed when he found out he had never truly known his best friend and his wife.

It was the eyes, though. She was trying to hide it, but he could tell. She was pleading. She didn't just want to talk to Veronica, this wasn't just her doing her job. She *needed* this.

"Okay." A compromise. "I won't tell you where she is while we're inside this building, but follow me outside once we're done, and I'll let you know where we're staying."

CHAPTER 69
ELAINE

Evening, March 23

Elaine drove slowly and deliberately down the long driveway, passively admiring the view. A previous version of herself would have been astounded by the grandiosity, but after everything she learned about World's Edge, she had soured on mansions.

After looking on Fahey's computer, she realized she needed her own backup. With no word still from Detective Brown, she knew who she needed to talk to. All she had to do was find her. Enter Ben.

She rang the oversize doorbell, noting the lack of a camera on it. The rich, she thought, probably don't just rely on Ring cameras. There was likely some other hidden one showing the occupant exactly who was on their front stoop.

Veronica Walsh opened the door after a few seconds and gave an immediate huff. "Are you finally here to arrest me, or are you just fucking around again?" she asked.

Elaine pursed her lips. "I want your help," she said plainly.

Veronica's face softened. "Where's Detective Brown?"

"Some emergency. She's away."

"Huh, didn't get a sense she had a life outside her job."

Elaine shrugged.

"So, what's causing this whiplash of a relationship here? Why are we back to working together? And how did you find me here?"

"Ben." Elaine shrugged again.

Veronica threw her head back and looked toward the sky. "Incredible. He goes to the police station thinking that you could have a mole or some sort of intelligence leak, and what does he do? He gives up where we're staying. What a guy, right?" She chuckled and shook her head.

"I think my father knows you're here, too. He made some comment the other day about you poking your head up or something."

"How would he know?"

"No idea. The grapevine of people who have that amount of influence? Anyway, that's not why I'm here. You know Detective Fahey, don't you?"

Veronica rolled her eyes. "I still don't know if he wants me in jail or wishes he were me. Probably both."

"He is who I'm here about."

Veronica raised an intrigued eyebrow.

"I think he might be involved in all of this somehow."

Elaine didn't know what response she was expecting but it wasn't a smirk.

"Of course he would be."

"I don't know what to do next," Elaine admitted.

"So you came here."

"I couldn't figure out who else to talk to. If I'm not certain here, I'm ruining my career by bringing these thoughts to him. I've already talked to the chief once. He said he'd check in on Fahey, but I don't think that's enough. I can't have the chief thinking I don't trust him. He's the reason I have this job in the first place."

"It sounds like you do know what to do next," Veronica said. "You're just looking for validation."

"Sort of. There's another aspect here. Detective Fahey was trying to track down Representative Moore's schedule today. Is there any innocent reason you think he'd be doing that?"

Veronica's eyes flashed. "Chamique Moore?"

"Yes."

Veronica sucked in a breath. "Ben was with her today. He said he needed to take a step toward normalcy. I'll call him." She checked the time on her phone. "It's just about five. He'll be wrapping up."

"Wait, he came in to be interviewed today, I saw him this afternoon."

"Shit, you're right. Sorry." Veronica pulled out her phone. "He probably went back to the office after, even though I'd bet all my savings that Moore told him to go straight home. He can't help himself." She smiled and shook her head ruefully.

"He didn't say anything about where he was going."

"All good, I'm calling him now."

Elaine stood on the front stoop, cognizant she hadn't actually been invited in yet. She listened as Veronica relayed to Ben their concern about Moore. She left Detective Fahey's name out for now. Elaine was thankful for that. The fewer people who know her suspicions, the better. She wished Detective Brown would check back in. She would know exactly how to act.

"Be safe." Veronica emphasized the final word as she hung up. She turned back to face Elaine. "He had returned but then left again. He was still near the National Mall. He said he'll try to go back and check on her, but she's probably walking home by now."

Elaine hesitated, weighing up their options.

"What are you doing?" Veronica's eyes bore into Elaine's.

"Thinking."

"The time for thinking is long gone." Veronica pushed past Elaine down the front stairs. "We have to move. Now."

"Without telling anyone?"

"Look," Veronica said. "You're young, but aren't you tired of cleaning up messes? Arriving after the deed has been done and just trying to catch whoever did it? It's time to be proactive. We go find Moore right now."

"But your husband is checking on her."

"He won't be able to stop something on his own, and, anyway, wouldn't you go after a loved one if you knew they might be in harm's way? Get in the car."

CHAPTER 70
BEN

Evening, March 23

Ben ran east on Independence Avenue SE, dodging between bewildered pedestrians.

"Hey, watch it!" a young woman in a sharp suit scolded, clutching her briefcase as papers spilled out.

"Sorry!" He called back, keeping his eyes ahead, scanning the street. Independence Ave was his best bet for now, but he hadn't gotten to the intersection with Pennsylvania Ave. Independence became a small one-way residential street after that, while Pennsylvania was the busy throughway. Would she turn onto Pennsylvania?

He figured if he got to Eastern Market, he could then wander around until he spotted her. She had only left a few minutes before he got the call from Veronica, so she couldn't have made it home yet.

His boss loved her routines. Her phone would be safely tucked away, deep inside her work bag slung over her shoulder. Even though her official workday had ended, she was never truly off. So, she told Ben she never kept her phone close enough for it to be a distraction while she walked home. If there was news she needed to hear, well, it could wait the extra fifteen minutes, couldn't it?

Not right now, it can't.

He made his mind up as he bounced on the balls of his feet impatiently, waiting for the light to turn. She'd go down Pennsylvania. Unless you live on one of these next few blocks of Independence, it makes no sense to stay on that street.

As he went farther down Pennsylvania, the initial adrenaline rush post-phone call with Veronica began wearing off, being replaced by fear. Did Moore really know how to use that gun she kept in her bag? Surely, she had never used it in anger before. Not since he had known her. Could've been before. No doubt less extreme than Veronica, but his boss did have a life before he met her. But still. Would she be aware enough to defend herself with it?

Would she even know to defend herself if the assailant was a cop?

Adrenaline masked pain. Fear did not. A fire was steadily burning in Ben's side. He pulled his jacket away and glanced down and saw a streak of blood. Fuck. He'd pulled out the stitches. He wasn't supposed to do anything strenuous for weeks, but what was he meant to do?

He stopped in Seward Square. Nothing out of place. The bustle of the evening commute. Cars, bicycles, buses, pedestrians. Just a normal night.

Maybe he should call Veronica back. Tell her that he hadn't found her.

No. Would Veronica accept failure? She would be kind about it, tell him he'd done his best, and that she understood. But he would know. It would be another tick against him. Last time he tried to help, he got shot. She needed to know she could trust him. No, this wasn't about her. *He* needed to know he could trust himself.

No sign of Moore on Pennsylvania Ave. Unless she sprinted

home every day, she couldn't be so far ahead of him that she'd already turned onto a side street, could she? If so, he'd have to try every single street, a full grid search, block by block. No way to do that quickly.

Independence Avenue, then. The best other option. Maybe she didn't turn.

Stitches be damned. He turned north and sprinted up Fifth Street. He tried to hurdle the leash of a black labrador that he couldn't swerve around quickly enough. *Bad idea.* He came crashing down as what felt like a bolt of lightning hit his side.

"Oh my God, are you okay?" The dog walker asked, his hand over his mouth. "Wait, you're bleeding! Let me help. I'm so sorry, I shouldn't have taken up the whole sidewalk, I wasn't thinking. He's still a puppy, I've never had a dog before. I swear I'm trying, but I don't really know what I'm doing yet. Oh, my goodness, do you need an ambulance?"

Ben looked up at the dark-haired young man in his twenties and sucked in air through his teeth. "I'm okay, please, it's fine," he grunted out. "I have to go."

"No! I need to help!"

"Get away, please." Ben didn't have time to deal with the man's hurt feelings. He pushed himself up off the sidewalk, acutely aware of the pulsing pain in his side. No point looking, he knew the amount of blood that would be pouring out now.

A hand grabbed his. He whirled around to see the dog walker's pleading eyes, less than a foot from his own. "You're hurt. I can't let you do something stupid," the man said.

Ben wrenched his hand back. "Look, I don't know what your deal is," he said. "But I absolve you of all your sins. I was going too fast. It's not your fault. Now please, *for the love of God,* leave me alone."

How much time had he lost? Was that only seconds, minutes? Why did it feel like that was an eternity?

Because every second counts.

Ben huffed as he finally reached Independence Avenue. He better be right.

He had just turned the corner when the sound of a bullet ripped through the air.

CHAPTER 71
ELAINE

Evening, March 23

"Why is everyone and their mother on the road right now?" Veronica seethed as they sat in traffic on the 14th Street Bridge, heading north toward the city on Route 395. "Move!" She honked the horn loudly.

"I think it's just regular commuting traffic." Elaine tried to sound as calm as she could. Her heart felt like it was about to rip out of her chest. She assumed Veronica was the calm one, and she thought she would be able to harness some of that for herself. Help control her own nerves.

She wasn't prepared for this version of Veronica. She couldn't tear her eyes away from Veronica's fingers gripping the steering wheel. They were shaking so fast she could feel the vibration.

She's terrified.

The one other time she had been in a car with Veronica on the way to danger was when she and Detective Brown were driving to World's Edge after Mikaela Alonso was kidnapped by Jacob Jordan. Veronica had been in the back seat, chatting and cracking jokes as if it had been any normal day.

She hesitated, steeling herself for a backlash. "Hey… are you okay?"

"Am I..." Veronica took her eyes off the road. "How could I be?"

"I'm sorry, I just—"

"My husband is trying to stop a potential murder. If we're right, then it's someone who has killed many times before. He was shot ten days ago and has not recovered from that. There's a very real chance that he tries something stupid, out of a chivalrous masculine instinct to prove to me that he can be the protector, and we arrive to find him lying dead in a puddle of his own blood. That's the reality I'm living in right now. We are minutes —" she leaned on the horn again— "away from one of my worst nightmares coming true, just after he finally came back to me."

Elaine gaped at her. She had no idea how to respond to that. What could she possibly say?

"My life is inches away from falling apart," Veronica continued. "I thought that was happening last year. I thought I was staring into the abyss. But I knew nothing about the depth of the darkness. That was a fucking kiddie pool. What happens to my kids? If Ben dies, do you think the state is going to allow them to stay with me? Everything about my life is over if that man tries something heroic. Why do men think they have to be the hero? Thank God, we're finally moving!"

Elaine remained silent as they inched their way forward. She looked out the passenger window, focusing on the riverfront below so she didn't have to meet Veronica's gaze. "I guess that's just how men are taught to be," she finally said, just to have said something.

"It's this macho behavior, and I hate it so much," Veronica seethed. "It's not Ben's fault, I'm not mad at him. But why would he still think he has something to prove to me? Like I care if he can stop a killer? That's literally the one thing that I for sure can do, why does he have to get involved?"

"Because he cares about you. He wants to keep you safe, no matter how equipped you are yourself." Elaine felt her throat begin to constrict. "That's what love is, isn't it? I wouldn't know. No one has ever cared about me that much. My parents might love me, but it's obligatory love and nothing more."

"Life's greatest gift and greatest curse at the same time."

Elaine couldn't argue with that. Parents: keeping therapists in business since the ancient Greeks.

They drove the rest of the way in silence.

"That's Fahey!" Elaine yelled as they drove down Independence Avenue, pointing toward the sidewalk. He was lumbering —Detective Brown had once used that word to describe him and now it lived rent-free in her mind—down the street, taking long strides. She rolled down her window and craned her neck out to watch him. Where was he coming from? She couldn't see his car.

"I don't see anyone else," Veronica said.

Elaine scanned up and down the street, keeping one eye on her temporary partner. "You're right. Where is he going?"

"Help me!" They heard the panicked voice—definitely male—from an alley on their right.

"That answers that question," Veronica said, slamming on the brake and jumping out of the car, leaving it idling in the middle of the road.

Wow is she fast. Elaine watched, helplessly too far away, as Fahey disappeared around the corner. *Who is that yelling?*

Veronica ran ahead, light on her feet as Elaine slipped on a tree grate as she got out of the car. When she finally reached the alley, Elaine couldn't believe her eyes.

A man lay prone at the far end of the alley. Representative Moore was halfway down, holding an obscured object in her right hand.

"Drop it now!" Detective Fahey yelled from his position several yards in front of them.

Elaine watched as Moore turned slowly. *But… that can't be. Is that a gun? It is. Just drop it. Please.*

Slowly. No quick movements.

Moore had almost pivoted around to face Fahey. Elaine allowed herself to take a breath.

The shot rang out. Moore jolted and crumpled to the ground as the bullet hit her lower abdomen, her gun thudding loudly on the cement as it bounced away from her.

"Oh, shit," Veronica said and began running. "Call an ambulance!" Veronica yelled to a bystander, and she raced ahead. "What the fuck do you think you're doing?" She screamed at Fahey as she passed him.

Fahey turned to Elaine, his face ruddy and red. His chest heaved up and down. "She raised her gun," he said plainly.

"She didn't!" Elaine was behind Fahey, but she had been at an angle where she could see Moore fully. She never raised her hand. Elaine would swear her life on that.

"You were too far back, you didn't see," he protested.

"Elaine, come on!" Veronica called from ahead of her. "Help that man while I staunch her bleeding."

"Coming!" Elaine took off running. As she ran past Veronica, she caught a first glimpse of the condition of the fallen representative. She lay supine, her arms splayed out to either side. Her eyes were glazing over as Veronica held steady pressure to a wound in her side, the blood pulsing out despite her best efforts. *Jesus*. She had hoped that Fahey had gone for a non-lethal shot.

Elaine caught Veronica's eyes momentarily and her heart dropped at the despair she saw within them. She ran further to where the man was slowly pushing himself up into a sitting position.

He turned and faced her. She tried to suppress a gasp and failed. Blood poured down his face, obscuring his features entirely. She whipped her rain jacket off and wiped it down his face. Not the most useful article of clothing for the situation. "I got you, you'll be okay," she said, no idea if her words were a lie.

As she wiped the blood away, she realized his wound was just skin deep. A slice on his forehead, the result of a bullet whizzing by but only grazing the surface. A nasty cut, that would require numerous stitches, but nothing life threatening.

She realized one more thing too.

"Senator Thresh? What happened?"

CHAPTER 72
VERONICA

Evening, March 23

I am not going to lose her.

I am not going to lose.

I applied as much force as I physically could to Chamique's side. The only rule of first responding I knew for sure: apply pressure. The simplest of equations. Blood inside equals good. Blood outside equals bad.

I could sense extra movement in my periphery. More police officers had arrived. Where was an EMT? Who was here to spell me? I needed to save her, but I was also needed elsewhere to *save* her. I immediately understood what was at stake. Fahey was already telling his side of the story to anyone who could listen. The truth would die with Chamique Moore.

A police officer came upon a scene where Chamique Moore was holding a gun toward an injured Gary Thresh. At that moment, their titles didn't matter. One was a threat, and Detective Fahey was taught to nullify that threat. Open and shut.

But I knew killers. I knew death. Chamique Moore was not one. Who would believe me, though? How could I describe the intangible, almost unknowable feeling I had?

Finally, after two minutes that felt like a million years, a man knelt down next to me. "How can I help?" he asked, his voice raspy and full of emotion.

"Thank God, you're finally here," I said, turning to see the EMT. My mouth gaped when I realized it was my husband kneeling down next to me. "Ben?"

His face was ghastly pale, his eyes bloodshot. But there was also steel, a resolve that I had rarely seen. He was not the same man as last year. "I'm trained for this. She made sure we all were. Let me help."

I took my hands off her side. As soon as they were away, he pressed his wadded-up suit jacket against the wound. "Do you have a first aid kit?" he asked.

"Where would I… no, I don't," I said. Unless there was a secret one in Nat's car.

"Shit, okay," he turned back to Moore. "Stay with me, boss. Look at me."

If she heard what Ben was saying, Moore couldn't acknowledge it.

"We're losing her," Ben said urgently.

"The ambulance, Ben," I said, pointing over my shoulder to the street. "Look, it's here."

I waved a frantic arm as the responders clambered down. There was no time to waste, even the few seconds we'd lose if they checked on Senator Thresh first might be too many.

Thankfully the pair of them ran straight to me. "Shot in the side, don't see an exit wound, she's barely responsive." I rushed the words out as quickly as humanly possible.

"Got it," the burly one said as he pushed Ben's hands away from the wound and took control.

I stood and backed away, my mind numb. Ben's hand found mine. He didn't attempt to stop the blood dripping down his hands, mingling with the blood on my own before painting the cement. I could tell he wanted to talk, but he couldn't find the words. Sometimes there aren't any.

They hoisted Moore onto the stretcher and began to wheel her to the ambulance. Ben took off in a run and gave her hand a squeeze when he got to her. I watched him take a deep breath before he returned to his place by my side.

Detective Iverson approached us as the ambulance sped away. I gave Ben's palm a squeeze of my own.

She shook her head, disbelieving. "I just don't get it," she said.

"Get what?"

"Senator Thresh." She looked back toward where he was now getting treatment from the EMTs. "He says that Moore cornered him in here. That she was going nuts at him. Bringing up something they've been fighting about in Congress. He says she shot him." She exhaled deeply, her eyes a glaze.

"She would not!" The words burst out of Ben's mouth. "That's a fucking lie."

"They'll check for gunshot residue," I said. "There won't be any on her hands, she can't have shot him."

"What the fuck is he even talking about then? And how did he end up shot?" The adrenaline flowing through Ben was causing him to fidget and twitch madly.

Someone shoots Thresh. Fahey shoots Moore. Thresh says Moore shot him.

How could any of this make sense?

"Maybe Thresh got confused?" Iverson offered. "He didn't see who shot him but then saw Moore and assumed it was her?"

"But that doesn't match." I shook my head. "He said she was yelling at him."

"Ah, you're right." She grimaced.

"Oh, no." The puzzle pieces clicked together in my head. There was only one way Thresh claiming Moore shot him could possibly make sense. He had to know that his version of the story would be accepted. "They planned this all out. To make her look crazy. Think about it." I shook my head. "It's pretty good too."

Iverson and Ben both looked at me, bewildered.

"Think about it. It all fits. This is why Fahey had to be here at exactly the right time. To be the final shooter. How do you concoct a story where someone else is the villain but make sure they can't tell their side of it? You silence her."

CHAPTER 73
ELAINE

Evening, March 23

Elaine listened as Veronica laid out her theory and officers spread crime scene tape around the alley. Flanked only by three-story row houses and not skyscrapers, the scene was still well lit even as the sun began to set. They didn't have all the facts, but she believed the words she was hearing.

Detective Fahey and Senator Thresh were part of this cabal. They hatched a plan to get rid of Representative Moore. But they couldn't just kill her. They couldn't turn her into a martyr. Even a suspicious death would cause too many questions. An accident, maybe. But she'd still be venerated. What they needed was her *and* her support out of the way. She was a lighthouse for those who agreed with her politically.

What they needed was to poison her brand. To make everything she touched fall apart. What better way than making her the perpetrator of the very gun violence she loudly railed against?

"Think about it," Veronica said. "What happens if we're not here? Hell, what might happen anyway? What story gets told?"

"Moore shot Thresh, Fahey then saved him by shooting Moore," Elaine said.

"Exactly. It gets rid of the problem, root and branch."

"But we're missing one piece," Ben said. "What actually happened to Senator Thresh? If not her, then who?"

"Could he have done it to himself?" Elaine wondered aloud.

"You're the only one who saw him up close," Veronica said. "What do you think?"

Elaine shook her head. "It was all too fast. I guess I could've looked for burns but I didn't see."

"It couldn't have been… you know…" Ben looked pointedly at Veronica as he trailed off.

"Not unless you can be in two positions at once," Elaine said to Veronica.

Ben's nostrils flared. "Oh, no. Not her. Umm—" His mouth stayed open, but no sound came out.

"Suffice to say," Veronica cut in, "we know of someone who has the capacity, but let's not go there yet. Anyway, we all know it couldn't have been me."

"Why?" Elaine asked.

"Because I don't miss."

Ben rolled his eyes.

"Wait, you're talking about your friend," Elaine said. "The one that broke out of prison. Do you know where he is?"

Veronica fixed a patronizing stare upon Elaine. "First, we will not speak of any knowledge of Francisco's whereabouts ever again. Second, no, he is not who we're thinking of, and we will drop this for the time being."

"That's not how being a detective works." Elaine felt a rush of confidence. "You have an idea, and now it's in my head. So, tell me who you think could have done this?"

"We don't think he did this, though," Veronica said. "Could he have done this? Sure. But loads of people could. You could. Detective Brown could. We all can enact violence upon others when pushed far enough. But the question is, do we think this man that popped into Ben's head is a member of this cabal? And the answer to that is no, and so what your detecting has discovered is a witness—Ben—who had a tentative lead, but it turns out it doesn't pan out. That is all.

"Anyway, look. Here's the issue. Senator Thresh and Detective Fahey will have had their story straight. My version won't have helped, since I'm not a reliable witness because of," Veronica waved her hand and shrugged, "well, everything. And they'll say you were too far away to see anything different, Detective."

Elaine nodded, biting down on the tip of her tongue.

"How will they explain the lack of GSR on her hands?" Ben asked.

"They'll just say that the gunshot residue came off while the EMTs were administering aid." Veronica shrugged.

"So, what can we do?" Ben asked the question Elaine was about to.

Veronica gave a rueful shake of her head. "Nothing. We can't stop the narrative. There's only one way. Moore needs to survive."

CHAPTER 74
VERONICA

Night, March 23

Ben was still at my side, the two of us sitting together on stiff hospital waiting room chairs. I knew Ben—there was no way he'd feel comfortable going home. His eyes were red and bloodshot, the strain of trying not to cry weighing them down. He was still old school about that sort of thing. He didn't like to cry in front of me. Thought it might make him look weak in my eyes. Like that somehow mattered to me. I imagined it was a deeply ingrained vestige of his upbringing. Something he would eventually get over but no amount of coaxing from me would do it.

I shifted uncomfortably. They really could've splurged a bit on better chairs. To be fair, if they had, then someone would complain and ask why they didn't spend the money on items that could actually save lives. Damned if you do, damned if you don't.

I liked the person I had become. Someone who minds if a chair is uncomfortable. Someone who is used to ease, to peace. Even with everything in my recent past, I knew I could continue to be this person.

But what of Ben? What kind of person would he become? I realized part of my desperation for Chamique Moore to live was for Ben's sake. I needed him not to descend into darkness. He could not become a cynic, walking through life angry with the world. A marriage works best when there are contrasts. I was the one who resided in the darkness. I could handle it. He had to live in the light. Those of us who know darkness only need that little twinkle of light to sustain us. Those who only know light can be brought low by a single dark blow.

Every adult deals with death. We spend a lot of our time thinking about death. Here in America, our thirties are the decade where friends' parents start dying. Once a parent dies, then death lives with you the rest of your life. Barring the obvious, the diseases and accidents, death doesn't visit us often until we're adults.

There's an accepted wisdom that there is a normal amount of death. No one quantifies it because no one wants to think that hard about it, but you know when you've crossed the threshold. Everyone knows when you've seen too much. I traversed that particular Rubicon so long ago I can barely remember which death did it.

Ben had seen too much. Nico and Maria had seen too much. I could feel the resolve in my heart begin to steel. No matter what happened next, this was the end. It had to be. I had to finish this. Not for my sake, but for my husband. For my children.

"Hell of a thing," a man sighed as he settled down into the chair on the opposite side of Ben. Neither of us looked up. Ben acknowledged him with a small nod. What else was there to say?

"Do you know if she's going to make it?"

Ben just shook his head.

"But you think she will?"

I whipped my head around. "Will you leave him—"

I was staring straight into the man's eyes.

Ben looked up, noticing that I'd fallen silent. His brow furrowed as he recognized who was sitting next to him.

"Osmin," I said softly.

He flashed a smile that didn't reach his eyes. "You figured it out."

"What are you doing here?"

"It was Francisco, wasn't it?"

"What are you doing here?"

Osmin sighed. "What do you think?"

"Finishing the job," Ben said. "One word, and the police will descend here on you."

Osmin drew his hand up to his mouth to stifle a laugh. Several others in the waiting room glared over. "Who do you even think I am?"

"Someone who could've been involved in all of this. A murderer who's held a lifelong grudge against my wife."

"There are probably dozens who fit that bill."

"But not you," I said.

"Not me. Never me."

I realized what had felt off in my mind, a subconscious feeling that I couldn't articulate about him since Francisco had told me who he was. Osmin's face when I turned back after killing his brother. The only time I ever saw him in person until days ago. "You were happy," I said.

"When?"

"When you saw me leaving your house those years ago."

He cocked his head, his eyes looking wistful as he remembered the moment. "You saw me there? I never knew."

"I was just past the tree line. I was sure you could see me."

"I never knew. I was just gazing off into the distance, thinking."

"You were glad he was gone."

"Yes. That was the moment," he said. "The first time I finally felt free."

"But weren't you and your brother like a duo?" Ben asked.

"That's what he decided would work publicly," Osmin said, shaking his head. "He thought the two of us together seemed more of a threat. And I think what he also had in mind was that he was safer if there were two figureheads."

"You disappeared after I killed him," I said. "I spent the rest of my life wondering if you were in hiding, waiting to find me."

"I did disappear. But not for the reasons you thought. It was my opportunity for a new life. I snuck into the United States, I changed my name, and I made a life here. I got into photography, nature especially. I'm very good now. I specialize in birds. I submitted a couple for the Audubon Photography Awards this year. I think I have a decent shot. I really didn't think about you anymore at all until everything that happened last year."

"You and everyone else from that part of my life," I muttered.

"I followed you, after you got out of the hospital."

Enough of this. "Okay, I will ask again. Why are you here? What is your game?"

"For the same reason you are."

"Why?"

"Is it not blindingly obvious by now?" Osmin's eyes bore into mine. "I owe you everything. What do you need? Anything I can do to help, please let me."

"You have a weird way of showing it, what with the whole kidnapping my husband thing."

"I saved him," Osmin scoffed.

"A technicality," Ben said. "Keeping me without my permission—I'm pretty sure that is the dictionary definition of kidnapping."

"Fine, I did that."

"You want to help now? Really help us?" I asked.

"Yes, I do."

"And you've been following my husband for quite some time?"

"Yes."

"Why?"

"Originally it was because I was bothered that he had left you alone. Then that warped into keeping him safe, which is what I tried to do in Georgetown."

"Okay, sure. Wild. So, you have some information? Do you know anything we don't about Detective Martin Fahey? Something we can use to prove he was meant to be there to shoot Moore?"

"If we can bring him down, then we don't have to rely on her testimony. Smart." Ben couldn't even bring himself to say her name. The abyss was as close as ever.

"Detective Fahey? The huge one, e*l Gordo*?"

"That's the one."

"He's not the cop on the inside. He can't be."

"What?" I did not like my intuition to be questioned so bluntly.

"It's not Fahey. Think about the timeline. I assume you're thinking that this cabal needed a police influence a decade ago, what with everything at World's Edge? Fahey wasn't there."

"He's been with the police for longer than that," I argued.

"Sure, but how closely did you look?"

"What are you getting at?"

"He was away. That entire year, he was out in Los Angeles with the LAPD."

"So, you're really saying that you don't think Fahey is involved at all? We know that he was looking up Representative Moore's schedule. He found her schedule, and then he went and shot her. That doesn't sound innocent to me," I said.

"If he was looking her up, I would wager it was because he knew she was in danger."

"He. Still. Shot. Her." Ben forced each word out.

"Veronica," Osmin pleaded, "listen to the facts here. You're supposed to be the logical one, right? I don't care what else you might think that you know, Martin Fahey was not present to clean up the mess at World's Edge. You know that there had to be a cop there, someone who was called to divert all other potential emergency services away, *verdad?* It could not have been him."

His words hung in the air, settling into a thick fog that circled my brain. Iverson had come to me with her Fahey theory, and I hadn't had time to flesh it out and check for cracks. Before any vetting, he shot the representative, and I ran with it.

"I believe you," I finally said. "I just don't want to believe the implication."

"If it's not Fahey," Ben said slowly, "there's another cop out there."

CHAPTER 75
ELAINE

Morning, March 24

This was weird now.

How could Detective Brown not have reached out after what happened? No matter whose truth you believed, two members of congress had been shot. It was national, even international, news. So where was Brown?

What kind of family emergency necessitated going completely incommunicado?

She would know what to do. She would know how to handle this. But where could Elaine turn without her? Sure, Veronica Walsh agreed that this was a setup, but as formidable as she was, she wasn't the person who had taken Elaine under her wing and treated her like an equal, albeit begrudgingly. What could Elaine say to the chief? To anyone else?

She drove to her parents' house as if on autopilot, barely conscious of the turns she was making until she reached Chain Bridge Road.

Her mom threw open the front doors and Elaine allowed herself to collapse into her arms. A warmth she couldn't outgrow spread through her. Maybe her parents did only love her out of familial obligation, but it was still love.

"There's some fresh coffee, my dear," her mom said as she led Elaine to the parlor room.

"That awful business yesterday," her mom tutted. "You know, I never thought that that representative could ever do such a thing. I mean, sure, she was always so nasty, but attacking him like that? In an alley?" She placed an exaggerated hand to her forehead.

"I don't think—"

"How lucky are we that that detective was there when he was? Just incredible timing. He should get an award, shouldn't he? I'll have to tell your father. Is there some recommendation process? There probably is. Like the military. A medal of valor or something."

"Mom—"

"How could he have even known? That's what makes some detectives so elite, don't you think? That he worked it out all by himself to put him in exactly the right place at the right time."

"He didn't!" Elaine felt the words explode from her mouth.

Her mother's mouth fell open. "What are you trying to say?"

"I can't believe I thought that by coming here I would find someone I could talk to," Elaine said, standing up abruptly. "How do you not see what happened? It was a setup! Chamique Moore was the actual target, and it happened exactly as they planned except she isn't dead."

Moore was still in surgery, now almost fourteen hours later.

"That's the craziest thing I've ever heard. Who would even think to do something like that?"

"You don't think there are people who want to get rid of her? Who wouldn't set up an elaborate ploy so that not only is she gone, but her legacy is ruined too? In this town?" Elaine grabbed her car keys. "I don't care how I have to do it, I'm going to prove this didn't happen like everyone wants to think. I'll go harass Thresh until he gives it up. He's involved in this cabal. He practically told me as much. He won't be able to hold it in. Maybe I'll even have Veronica Walsh come. I'm sure she knows one or two methods of making bad guys squeal—"

"You'll do no such thing," her father thundered, slamming the study door as he strode out from within. "I forbid it."

"Dad!" Elaine looked at her father incredulously. "He's clearly involved. I know he's your friend, but we have to stop him."

She watched as his eyes flitted back and forth between her and her mother. He pursed his lips and gave an almost imperceptible shake of his head. His gaze finally focused on her mother. "Thresh is a liability." His voice was deadly quiet.

Her mom's eyes flitted over toward Elaine, who caught the nervousness and fear, and then quickly back to her husband. "What do we do?"

"Honey," her father said, turning back to face Elaine. "He doesn't know anything, and I won't have you assaulting him when he's in the hospital."

"He doesn't even need to still be in the hospital! It was just a bunch of stitches. They were done with him last night!"

"Are you trying to talk down an attack on our friend's life? I did not expect that sort of behavior from you." His voice transformed into the scolding tone he would use on her as a child when she got a bad grade or stayed out too late. "That is unbecoming of the law enforcement position you hold. I won't have my daughter going around trying to create a scandal."

"The scandal is happening, dad, whether you like it or not."

Her mom's head whipped up from her position by the coffee bar pretending not to be invested in the conversation. "How dare you talk to your father like that! After all he has done for you. After all *we* have done for you."

Elaine inhaled slowly and turned to face her, feeling her own face turn red. "I don't get it. What's the matter with me running things down? What are you worried I'll find? What, am I going to find out that dad is the mastermind behind it all? That he's been running the scene and it's been under my nose the whole time?"

A split second.

The tiniest gasp.

Curtis Leishear had a great poker face. He would've never given an inch.

But not Belinda. She married into the life. She wasn't as media-trained, as savvy. Her mouth betrayed her before her brain even realized what she was doing.

A gasp.

All it took for Elaine's world to come crumbling down.

"No, please, no, this can't be happening," she breathed out. Short panicky breaths followed, and she felt a rush of blood to her head, as if she were dangling upside down.

Her dad walked over to her mom's side and put a comforting arm on her shoulder. She glanced up at him, a pleading look on her face. He squeezed her arm. "It's okay."

"Dad, how could you?" Elaine felt her legs tremble.

"What do we do, Curtis? She's our daughter! She's not like that other detective."

"Other detective?" Elaine blanched. "What the fuck did you do to her?"

He put up a calming hand. "She's alive and unharmed. And even better, completely ignorant of everything that has happened to her. I think it would be wise to keep it that way, don't you?" he said pointedly.

"Is that a threat?"

"It is whatever you make of it, my daughter. I don't need to threaten. I am simply explaining the lay of the land."

"You… you can't get away with this!"

"Get away with what?" He looked at his wife, an innocent look on his face. "I don't see anything here, do you? All I see is a young girl who never should have been a cop in the first place, thinking she has all the answers and that it's her right to meddle in things she does not, and never will, understand."

"Are you fucking gaslighting me?" White hot rage streaked through every pore in her body. The denial stage didn't last long.

"Gaslighting." He gave a derisive chuckle. "A get-out-of-jail-free card your generation loves to throw around. I am not *gaslighting* you, I am telling you how the world is. I am telling you, once again, that you chose to lead an insignificant life. And those who choose an insignificant life walk a certain path. We who chose power walk an entirely different path. When our paths cross you are the ones who yield, not us."

How could he be talking to her like this? Yes, she'd always known he was power-hungry, but she forever believed that he was a bastion of decency and goodness and doing it the right way. Did she agree with every bit of his politics? No, but what child does agree fully with their parents?

"You won't stop me," Elaine said, attempting to project confidence. "If I walk out that door, you're not going to stop me."

His face was impassive. She'd learned long ago not to try to read it. Inscrutability was one of his defining features.

But she knew she was in trouble. Because he didn't quickly answer in the affirmative. He didn't say, "of course, you can go." She needed backup.

Watching her father closely, Elaine reached her hand down into her pant pocket. She curled her fingers around her phone. Without bringing it out of her pocket, she navigated to the contact she trusted most. The one person who could fix this. She typed out a quick message, silently sending a prayer to the autocorrect gods.

"Be reasonable, dear."

Elaine took her eyes off her father to face her mother. "Reasonable? We are a long way past reasonable."

Her mother closed her eyes momentarily, then looked past her to make eye contact with her father. As Elaine watched, she grimaced and gave a silent nod.

Her father's arms enveloped her in an instant. She inhaled a sweet scent on the hand towel he held over her mouth, and the room began to spin. She caught just a glimpse of her parents standing over her before everything went black.

CHAPTER 76
VERONICA

Morning, March 24

I had gotten used to the Potomac River views. I was going to miss this house. Maybe Natalia would give me a spare key. The kids would love it.

I'd left Ben inside, hovering by his phone waiting to hear an update on his boss.

"I'm sorry about your father," Osmin said, taking a seat next to me on the terrace. "I don't want to pretend he was a good man because you won't believe me, but there is no good way to lose a parent."

"I appreciate that." I hadn't had the mental capacity to reflect on his death yet. That would come in time, I was sure. "Is that why you asked to come over this morning?"

"Maybe partially?" He shook his head and grimaced. "I don't know. I just felt like I needed to see what happens next. Do you know what I mean?"

"I get that," I said, not at all sure of what he meant but unwilling to indulge further.

"That you saved your father's life when you killed my brother meant at least he got a lot more years than he might have."

"Wait, what?" That wasn't what I was expecting.

"He never told you?"

"I have no idea what you're talking about. Told me what?"

Osmin chewed on his lower lip, thinking. "Now I'm wondering if he knew. Okay, let me ask first, what prompted you to go after my brother?"

I didn't have to think very hard. That memory would always be easily accessible. "It was not long after my brother Kelvin had died, and I overheard a conversation about you and your brother. My dad said that you guys were growing a little too fast for his liking."

That elicited a rueful smile from Osmin.

"He said he wouldn't like to see what the mature version of your budding organization looked like," I continued. "And that was all I heard. Someone else came by, and I had to scurry away and pretend I hadn't been eavesdropping through an open window."

"So, at the very least, you didn't know." Osmin nodded slowly.

I shook my head. "All I knew was that you sounded like a problem. And the little thought I couldn't get out of my head was that Kelvin would have fixed it. With my mother and Kelvin both gone, I was the only one left. I told myself I had to stop you. I had no idea what I was doing until I got there, and honestly, you're lucky I didn't find you first."

"You don't think I could've defended myself?"

"Maybe, but Maynor was fiercer than you, and I got to him, so…"

"Fair point. But this is fascinating. I thought all along you'd been sent for a specific purpose. That's why I ran away after. I believed that one of us had snitched to your father, and I couldn't trust anyone anymore."

"Snitched about what?"

"We were going to kill him. The next day."

"Jesus. Really?"

"Every detail of it was planned out. That's why my brother

was in that stupid bathtub in the first place. He liked to spend hours in there doing some sort of contemplation or meditation the day before we made any big move, and this was the biggest we would have ever made. We knew that we were on his radar, and Maynor was adamant that we had to strike before he noticed us further and it turned into a war." Osmin looked me directly in the eye. "We were going to kill him the next morning."

"How?"

"I don't remember all the details, honestly, but it was a guns-blazing, machine-gun-into-the-car-type plan."

"He only rode in an armored car."

"Ah!" He snapped his fingers. "That was it. We had a guy who was the best cat burglar we'd ever seen. We never really knew what to do with him, but then Maynor realized he would be the perfect tool to get your dad out of the car. We were going to have him sneak into your compound and plant a little time-delay smoking device. We'd have it go off while he was out for his morning trip to check on his operation. No one stays in a car when it's filling with smoke. Then whether they rolled the windows down or got out, we'd have our people there ready to start shooting."

I was stunned. It was one thing to logically understand that your father was a target, but even after all these years, hearing the details shook me.

But why did it shake me? He'd been assassinated only days ago in a similar manner. Why did this story make me feel these emotions so deeply?

I quickly realized why. "Everything about my life would've changed," I said. "I would've been an orphan, before my *asesina* days even began. I wouldn't be here."

Osmin inhaled the crisp morning air. "Neither would I. I'd probably be dead by now. Like I said, I assumed someone talked. Someone who wasn't a true believer. Maybe even a cleaner or someone who heard something they shouldn't have."

Someone talked.

The nagging thought I couldn't pin down in my mind clicked into place. Detective Iverson had mentioned that her father implied he knew that I was staying here in Nat's house. Something about how people in his position just know things.

But Governor Leishear couldn't have heard through that grapevine. There was no grapevine. There was no one who could have talked. It wasn't possible. So, how did he know that I was here?

The shooter sent to kill us had found us in this neighborhood. Whoever he reported to must have known we were here.

There was only one answer that made sense in my mind, and it made me jump out of my seat and rush toward Nat's garage.

CHAPTER 77
ELAINE

Morning, March 24

Elaine opened her eyes slowly. In every story she'd ever heard, the victim awoke with a start, and the adrenaline started pumping immediately. They remembered the moments right before everything went black and got to work figuring out how to get themselves out of the jam.

So, why didn't she feel that way? She was groggy and discombobulated. Her left wrist ached as she realized she was handcuffed to the leg of a large wooden table, bolted to the ground. Where was she even? This didn't look like anywhere in her parents' house. What was this place with its large oval conference table and projector screen covering the far wall? The only decorative piece she could see was just a sign that said *Parc de Princes*.

Her hazy mind closed in on one detail that had stuck since she first read it months before. Veronica Walsh had escaped from handcuffs by dislocating her thumb. The key detail that made her remember the story was that it's not the joint you think of. Dislocating the main knuckle on your thumb—the closest to your thumbnail—would just leave you in loads of pain and do you no good. The joint you need to dislocate is down closer to your wrist.

She grabbed her thumb and clenched her teeth as she yanked it away from the other fingers. A stabbing pain shot up her forearm. She squeezed her eyes shut and took a deep breath.

One more time. Another yank, another hiss of breath. More pain, no gain. How did Veronica do this?

After the tenth time, Elaine accepted the mission was futile. Tears streamed down her face, a mixture of pain and frustration.

Holding her throbbing hand, silently cursing Veronica for making human extremes seem like norms, Elaine lay down on her back, her left arm outstretched above her head.

As she lay still, she realized she could hear the muffled sound of footsteps. A glimmer of hope flickered inside her brain. Sound meant the room wasn't soundproof. If it wasn't soundproof, she could call someone. Maybe there was someone out there.

She flinched at the sound of a crisp, ringing doorbell. She looked around the room and saw a small speaker in the upper corner.

"Governor, it's Chief Branaman. Can I come in?"

Elaine's heart thundered powerfully.

She really was still at her parents' house.

But more importantly, salvation was here. The chief had received her message. Her text from her pocket must have gone to the right recipient and been coherent enough that he knew to come here.

"Hi, Andrew."

Elaine inhaled sharply as she heard her father's calm voice. She hadn't realized in the moment the danger she might be bringing the chief into. Surely her parents wouldn't hurt him. Surely, he was wise enough to keep the upper hand. He was a chief, after all.

"What's going on here?"

"Just a nice morning with the wife, what brings you here?"

"I got a distress call from one of my detectives." The chief's voice remained quiet and controlled. "I stopped by to make sure everything was okay. Is it?"

"Of course. Come on in."

No, no, no, Elaine thought. *Don't come in. Don't let your guard down. Bring the cavalry!*

"Can you explain to me why your daughter texted me that she was in trouble here then?" The voices were further away but she could still hear them.

"She's an easily frightened girl. I'm sure you've seen that."

I am not.

"She's all spun up after last night," he continued. "Terrible business really."

"Is she still here?"

Elaine couldn't tell if it was just in her head, but she felt the air get tense. Her own ever-worsening thoughts filled the silence.

"What did you do?" Branaman finally asked.

He knows. He's going to save me.

"I'm in here! I'm here! Help!" Elaine began to scream and pound on the floor with her good hand. "Chief, I'm here!"

"Do I hear something?"

Elaine pounded harder.

But she heard no more voices.

She slid to the floor, exhaustion overcoming her. *Where are they? Can Chief Branaman hear?*

What if her father was upstairs, right now, hurting the chief? What if he killed him? It would be entirely her fault. Just because she was stupid enough to call for help without alerting him.

Wherever she was, whatever this hidden room was for, that speaker in the corner was only for keeping track of movement or sound at the door. Elaine stretched her neck toward the wall, straining to hear anything other than silence. Without knowing where this room was situated, and no windows to guide her, she couldn't tell if that wall was any more likely than any other to be where a sound might come.

This must be where the cabal meets.

A secret room, right there in the middle of her parents' house.

A house she believed she knew every inch of, every nook and cranny.

With a deafening creak, the heavy door swung open, and she scrambled herself upright.

"Get up, get up," her father demanded. He stopped, glancing at her bruised thumb and snorting. "That was never going to work. An impressive attempt, though, I'll give you that."

"Where is the chief?"

"The who?" His mouth curved into a smile while his eyes shot daggers at her.

"Chief Branaman was here. What did you do?"

His smile grew wider. "Oh, did you think your chief was going to save you from big bad dad? That he was going to ride to the rescue, save the day? You'd probably get a promotion off of it, for being the sap who accidentally broke it all wide open? Crowds would cheer, doves would fly, because you were strong enough to turn in your own family? Oh, no." He shook his head. "That's not how it's going to happen."

"What did you do with him?" Elaine's throat felt like it was full of gravel. Her voice was barely a whisper. "And what did you do with Detective Brown?"

"You really don't get it, do you?" He pinched the bridge of his nose, like a frustrated teacher engaging with an unruly pupil. "I didn't do anything. Because I didn't *have* to do anything."

"What do you mean—"

Elaine's voice caught in her throat as the chief entered the room. "Hi, Detective," he said with a smile. "Quite a situation we've found ourselves in, haven't we?"

"What's the containment here?" Branaman and her father sat next to each other at the far end of the table. Elaine was still on the floor, but now with her right leg shackled to the adjacent table leg from her left arm.

"She says Thresh is involved. That's all," her father replied.

"Alright, however you want to handle this, I'll follow the line."

"Who will back her if she gets discredited? Anyone who'd put up enough of a stink that it would give us pause?"

"Emilia Brown will likely listen to her, but she's indisposed at the moment. I hear you handled that."

"I don't like to have to handle things personally."

"I know, Archon, I apologize for that oversight."

Elaine gasped. *Archon. The leader of the Princemakers.*

The realization hit Elaine like an anvil. Her father wasn't just involved in the cabal. He was *in charge*. He was the cabal.

How many times had she asked him for help, for advice? For how many years had she craved his approval, this hard man in a hard city? She figured he was just playing the politician game. Grabbing power at any opportunity and holding it tight. A man she wished would spend more time with his daughter, but not unique in the nation's capital. Sure, he commuted to Annapolis a lot for work, but he was just someone trying to do right for his state and country. He was a Leishear after all—a supporting act in what was now the ruling family of the United States.

Was her uncle the president because of this group? How much influence did they really have? Her mind spun from question to question, with no answers in sight.

"Who else?" he asked.

"Same as ever. I have to assume Veronica Walsh. Francisco Orellana is in the wind, but I believe he's out of the country now, so at least we don't have to think too hard about him."

He bit his upper lip. "Agreed."

"You want us to be able to talk to you. Propose anything," Chief Branaman said hesitantly.

"Of course."

"I think there's only one option here. We can dress it up to be something heroic, give her a legacy, give you another sympathetic vote."

"No! You can't! Dad, please!" Elaine screamed. "Mom!"

His face screwed up, as if trying to process an impossible number of emotions all at once. "You brought this on yourself," he said, his tone weary and somber. He pursed his lips. "What would you have me do? Will you promise to stay quiet?"

"You're murderers!"

"I'm the one who knows your true goal," Branaman said to her father. "Remember, I know the real reason we had to take out Moore. She's the only Democrat worth fretting over. The only one who could possibly challenge you when you run for president after your brother's terms are up."

"What are you saying?"

"You want to take this group global, don't you? You in charge of the country, with a group of acolytes all beholden to you. You've twisted Ulrich's original purpose to be for your own gain." He put his hand up. "Now don't get me wrong, I've got nothing against that. What I'm saying is there's an upside here, a way to make it even more of a lock with voters."

"Sympathy," her father said in a whisper. "Iphigenia."

"What?"

"This is my Aulis moment. I have to make the sacrifice for the wider purpose." He gulped down a breath, hiding a sob. "I'll leave you, Andrew. You take care of it. I can't be here any longer. I'm sorry, Elaine."

CHAPTER 78
VERONICA

Morning, March 24

"What is with that ridiculous scarf?"

Osmin looked down at the pashmina scarf wrapped tightly around his neck. "What? It's light and functional, yet also fashionable. What's not to like?"

Why did I agree to let him come again?

We had pulled over behind several construction workers at the northeast end of Battery Kemble Park. The Leishears' house was on Chain Bridge Road, which ran north-south along the west side of the park. New properties were being built on both sides, and signs lined the street saying parallel parking was for workers only.

I never was one for following rules that got in my way.

We clambered through the trees and underbrush until we got to the main trail, the only one in the north section of the park.

"I know you have that knife of yours, and you're pretty damn handy with it, but take this too." Osmin handed me a small black handgun.

I nodded a tacit acknowledgment and tucked it into my waistband. "Can I trust you here? Really and truly, with my life as needed?"

"You can. We'll take them down. What's the Alessandra special here? I know it's not guns blazing."

"Stealth. We don't know what we're approaching, so we go cautiously. It's not rocket science. We get down to the parking lot in the middle of the park, then walk along Chain Bridge Road. We keep an eye out at all times."

"Okay, but what's the actual plan when we get there?"

"There is no plan." No one ever understood this. Plans only work if you know the layout. When the fog of war is so thick you can't even see in front of you, what good is a pre-packaged plan? "We adjust and react as we go."

"Hmm." Osmin didn't say more but I could see the wheels spinning inside his head. I let it go and continued walking.

"That's a mansion," Osmin helpfully stated as the house came into view. "Wow."

"Nine beds, eleven baths. Exterior limestone facade with a triple-arched portico. The slate roof is somehow important too, but I forget the details."

Osmin shot me a quizzical look.

"I know how to use Google." I shrugged.

We ducked down behind the arched row of shrubs beside the crushed shell driveway.

"Curtis Leishear, we know you're there! Now come out slow-ly!" Osmin yelled.

The fuck? So much for the 'wait and see' approach.

Looking at my aghast face he smirked. "Maybe it was rocket science. I never was much of a rule follower anyway."

"You told him there was more than one of us!" I hissed. "He wouldn't have known."

"Guess I just like a challenge." He smiled infuriatingly.

Not for the first time, I wished Francisco was with me instead of Osmin. I would have implicitly trusted him.

We waited. No apparent movement from inside the house. "What now?" I asked.

"You're asking me?"

"You seem to have a problem listening anyway, so you tell me."

"We could try the doorbell."

"Are you trying to get us killed?"

"If I didn't know better, I'd say you didn't trust yourself here. The Alessandra I always knew about could do anything."

"And if I didn't know any better, I'd say you were having fun."

"Oh, I am." Osmin smiled wide. "This is exhilarating. Do you know how many times I imagined I was you?"

"It's a bit weird hearing an adult man talk about his child-like fantasies."

"Ah, get over it. It's 2024."

"Doesn't make this less weird," I muttered under my breath. He was right, though. I felt uncomfortable because he was a variable I couldn't control. It took all the strength I had to keep Ben from jumping in the car with me, so when Osmin said he was coming I just let it happen. But this is why you work alone.

"Look!"

I whipped my head toward the direction his finger was pointing. There was movement in the thick trees to the east, back in the park across the street.

"What is that?" Osmin asked.

"Nothing good. Let's go." We ran across the street and shuffled along the tree line, though our presence wasn't exactly secret at this point.

"Looks like someone dragging another person along," Osmin whispered. "A man and a woman."

They must have snuck out the side door. It wasn't like we could have covered all exits. This wasn't that organized an operation.

They weren't trying to be quiet. The plan must have been to outrun us. But where to?

"They're moving along the upper path," I whispered to Osmin.

South of the parking lot, Battery Kemble Park turned into Palisades Park, although I wasn't sure exactly where the border was. That wasn't important to me. What was important was that there were two parallel trails. The westernmost was at the top of a steep hill, covered in shrubs and leafless trees this time of year. Invisible from the lower, eastern path, it was the perfect escape route. It would meet back up with the other trail at the south end, where I was sure they would have a getaway car parked down on MacArthur Boulevard.

We hustled onto the trail after them, staying one curve behind so we were out of sight.

I had never seen Curtis Leishear in person, but from the back, it seemed highly unlikely that was him. But the woman was definitely Detective Iverson. I needed him to turn his head. I needed to know who we were up against.

I snagged a heavy branch and, before I could rethink my plan, chucked it hard at a tree several feet to the left of them. It struck dead center *(still got it!)* and the crack resounded. He spun his head around.

"Holy shit," I whispered. "Chief Branaman."

"Woah," Osmin breathed out next to me.

"Chief! Stop!" I called. Time to end this. "Keep an eye out, the Leishears could be nearby," I mouthed.

Branaman slowly turned. He held Iverson's collar in his right hand and had a gleaming silver gun trained on her temple with the other. "You move, she dies. It's that simple, Veronica," he said.

I ducked behind a tree, twenty feet away from the pair. I saw Osmin take up a similar position to my left. I raised a calming hand to him. *Don't move,* I mouthed.

"Alright, you don't show yourself, she dies too," Branaman said.

Never assume a foe is bluffing. A lesson I learned as a child. From Francisco's father, if I remembered correctly. Always assume deadly intent and religious fervor.

I raised my hands and stepped out from behind the tree and

onto the path. I held out my gun, then tossed it ahead of me, into a thicket. Throwing it toward Osmin would be too obvious a move. He knew there was someone else with me, that would be the first thing he would think. "I'm right here."

"Who else is with you?"

There you go. "Someone was with me back at the house," I said truthfully. "But does everything you know about me tell you that I'd work with a partner?" Another true statement. The easiest way to lie was, simply, not to lie. Answer a question with truths, just not the truths they want to hear.

"Who did you toss your gun to?"

He was diligent. Probably wouldn't have become chief if not. "No one."

"Okay, slowly walk to your left, off the path, while I go pick it up."

I followed his command as we each shuffled through the underbrush. There was enough space between the trees that movement was not hindered, but roots and shrubs spread on the ground slowed us down.

I ended up in front of the tree Osmin was hiding behind. I saw him pull his gun out and I glared a silent no at him. Nothing rash.

I turned to face Branaman. "What happened? You wanted a more lavish lifestyle than the police could give you? Some faux feeling of power you could never achieve in your day job?"

He laughed mirthlessly. "You still don't understand us. I was hand-picked. You think I stumbled into this? I was chosen by Ulrich Belle specifically. Then when Iverson's father here took over as the new Archon, he put his daughter under my command so we could eventually use her too. Look how that turned out, though. First wrong move he's ever made."

"What even is the point of your organization?" I asked. Always keep them talking. The ubiquitous first rule of hostage negotiating.

"Power, obviously."

"Okay, sure, but what exactly do you do?"

"We place our hand-picked people in positions of power around the city."

"Cool. Great plan."

"This city is full of people who crave power like a man in the desert craves water."

"Solid simile." I couldn't help myself. "All that practice in front of the mirror paid off. You nailed the delivery."

"We don't attract attention. We set people up below the surface, in the weeds. We plant them there and let them bloom naturally so that when they're in power there's no scrutiny."

"My God, you're so boring." Time to get a rise out of him and force the mistake. There's always a mistake. The painfully obvious key is not to be the one who makes it. "Wow, your plan is just so novel. My father did that for years. We had people everywhere."

"Not enough people to stop his own assassination, though."

"Assassination implies power. If you get killed no one will call your death an assassination," I replied calmly. He was attempting the same ploy. "You couldn't ever dream of the power he had. It makes me a little sad for you. Like you've played all of life in kiddie mode, never having a chance to see the real thing."

"Keep your hands up!" He barked suddenly.

I hadn't moved. He just wanted me to second guess a future move.

He had no idea.

His hand was on the trigger, but it was pointed at Iverson, who remained silent, her eyes flitting fearfully between us. In the time it took him to swing his gun toward me and fire, I could reach down and, in one motion, flick my knife at his throat. A faster move, with much better precision. I'd have to trust he would miss his first shot. Highly likely, even for him, who I imagined had plenty of practice over the years. Shots in anger rarely hit their target. But not a risk I was fully ready to take.

I wanted to see how it played out. Iverson could handle herself, she might make a move. She could—

"Stop!" Branaman yelled past me and whirled his gun up. I

felt the crackle of air as two bullets whizzed past me in quick succession.

But by the time he fired, my knife was already flying through the air. I watched it hit the target, and lodge into Branaman's neck. He dropped the gun and fell to the ground. Released from his grip, Elaine ran towards me.

After making up half of the ground between us, she had a change of heart. She slowed and turned back around. She strode carefully back toward Branaman, stepping past him, gurgling in the dirt, and grabbed his gun. She stood a yard away, drawing down on him.

"I got him!" Elaine called. "Look at that blood, chief. Don't move. I'm calling an ambulance."

I took a long deep breath. We got him.

A groan from behind me made my heart drop. A pit opened up in my stomach and I would rather the world had swallowed me up than turn around.

But the world had other ideas.

I turned and saw Osmin, lying in the dirt and moss, his hands clutching his stomach. Blood pulsed through his fingers at a rate that could only mean one thing.

His eyes caught mine. "Help," he pleaded, his voice soft as a pillow. "I don't want to die. Please."

I couldn't get any words out, but my eyes told him everything he needed to know. He squeezed his own shut and I watched tears spill out.

I knelt down and pressed a hand over his. A futile gesture, only there to comfort. I pulled him toward me, allowed him to rest his head on my shoulder.

"I'm sorry," he gargled. "I tried. You needed a distraction, so I provided it."

"Shh." I stroked his head. "You saved her. You did it."

He smiled weakly. "You know," he took a deep breath, "I did everything I ever wanted. I got a chance that I never should have. But I always thought the one thing I'd never get to do was thank the woman who made it possible. But here I am. Thank you, Alessandra. Thank you, Veronica. Thank you for this beautiful life."

He closed his eyes. My throat constricted and I clutched his hand as I felt his breathing go still.

CHAPTER 79
ELAINE

Morning, March 24

"I'm sorry," Elaine said, patting Veronica on the back. She didn't know what else to say. She didn't know who this other man was, except that he had clearly meant something to her. The feeling must have been mutual for him to risk everything like he had.

She looked down at her boss as she now held both guns over him. She was doing her best to grip Veronica's with her hurt—*but not dislocated*—thumb. When the other man died, Veronica laid him down on the grass, grabbed his scarf, and wordlessly walked over to the chief. She roughly yanked her knife from his throat and watched with a practiced disinterest as blood poured out. Then she wrapped the scarf around his neck and pulled it tight. "That'll keep him alive until the ambulance comes," she said. "Or it won't. Either way, I'm not letting him keep my knife."

Elaine gaped and involuntarily put her hand to her throat.

"Unless an ambulance takes ages to get here, he'll live," Veronica said. "Anyway, it's over."

"What do you mean?"

"Everything. The Princemakers. It's all over."

"But, how?"

Veronica held her phone up. "Ben texted. Chamique Moore woke up. The cover-up is over. Senator Thresh, Chief Branaman, your parents. It'll all come out now."

"That's not true. That's not how my dad works. And remember, my uncle is the president. He's not going to let this happen to his brother."

"That's where I think you're wrong," Veronica said. "That's exactly why he will. Because he needs to make a strong point about his own legitimacy. He needs distance."

"They'll all just deny it. You don't understand these people."

"I don't think our fathers are too dissimilar if you stop and think about it," Veronica pointed out.

She was right, in a sense. But the power she knew was also completely different from a political dynasty. Dennis Leishear still needed the people on his side. A powerful leader without a following is neither powerful nor a leader. The will of the voters could be tweaked, swayed, made to fall in line, but the country was too vast to overcome a groundswell. If his own party turned on him, the Leishears would be finished as a political force. "I just —I don't know what to do now."

"What do you mean?"

"Well, my entire life has been a lie, hasn't it? At the very least, my adult life. I thought I always wanted to be a detective, and it turns out that even that part might have been preordained by my parents. Now that I say it out loud, they were probably trying some reverse psychology bullshit on me. They set me up to be where I was, all the while telling me they didn't believe in what I was doing. Just to make sure I kept doing it out of spite."

"You surprised him."

"What?"

"Your father. He didn't expect you to turn against him."

"Yeah, well… I just don't know. Do you really believe that he planned for me to be another asset inside the DC Police?"

"That's exactly what his plan was. Once he realized that was what you wanted, he turned it around for his own benefit. You were there, ready to be called into action as needed, probably sometime in the future. But what I'm guessing happened is that he didn't realize until it was too late that you aren't built like them. You didn't get a whiff of power and immediately come back for me. That's often the Waterloo of power-hungry people: they don't realize not everyone thinks like them."

"The chief said that my father wanted to be president."

"What?" Veronica's eyebrows shot up. "Really?"

"Yeah, and that Moore was the only one who could stop him, or something." Elaine rubbed her eyes. "I don't know. I don't want to be him. But who am I if I'm not my parents' daughter?"

"You know my story well, I think," Veronica said. When Elaine nodded, she continued, "climbing out of your parents' shadow is never easy. I left the country, and it followed me. But it's an opportunity. Take some time, think about your life and what you want it to be."

"I thought I was going to die."

"Do you think that was his plan?"

"Yes. My dad called me Iphigenia. He told the chief to deal with me, and he was bringing me out here to kill me."

"Iphigenia?"

"A Greek myth. Agamemnon is forced to kill his eldest daughter in order to get what he wanted. I think it was necessary to get to Troy, maybe? He had wronged one of those goddesses and she retaliated. I don't remember all the details."

"His Troy was the presidency." Veronica looked around as they heard incoming sirens. "Not a bad place to kill someone. Easy getaway down at the end of the park. Low chance of any witnesses. Easy to explain why you were in the area."

Elaine couldn't stop the tears that burst out and ran down her face. Heavy sobs racked her chest as she let all the fear and adrenaline rush out of her body.

"I got you. Breathe," Veronica said as she made up the space between the two of them. She took Elaine's hand. "Let it all out."

The sound of sirens closed in. "Stay right here," Veronica said, giving her hand a quick squeeze before letting go. "Your only job is to sit quietly and feel the emotions you're feeling."

Through blurry vision she saw Veronica run off and direct a paramedic to Chief Branaman.

Elaine sat in the dirt, contemplating digging a hole and retreating into it. Maybe she could be one of those people who went and lived off the grid. A friend of hers kept posting on social media about her 'detox' trip to Central Asia and spending a month in a yurt camp. Maybe that was what she needed right now. Just to disappear and leave all of this behind.

But she knew she couldn't. She knew she had to get up, dust herself off—*figuratively and literally*—and keep fighting.

Because Emilia Brown was out there somewhere, and Elaine had to save her.

CHAPTER 80
EMILIA

Afternoon, March 24

What does dying of starvation feel like?

The only hunger-related effect Emilia Brown had ever considered was the intense mood-altering pangs. What does true need elicit?

Emilia had spent the entire day contemplating a slow death from thirst and hunger. She had played the board game Outdoor Survival as a child, loving the realism of getting lost in the woods, or stuck in the desert with no water because you thought you were on the verge of finding the missing person. The game involved so many characters perishing that her grandfather had given it the moniker "Death in the Woods." It had burned into her brain that the intrepid explorer could last twenty-three days without food, but only seven without water. Twenty-three days. How long had it been since she'd last eaten? Just last night?

So, why did it feel like her stomach had been empty for days?

She'd gotten a meal each morning and night since she was shoved into her jail cell. A pittance, some white rice and chicken in a tiny plastic bowl and no utensils, but enough to sustain her. When no food came this morning, she immediately went on high alert.

Something was different. Something was wrong.

The shouting, yelling, and banging that followed left Emilia on tenterhooks. Schrödinger's saviors outside her room. Were they dead or alive? Was that a rescue crew come to save her? Iverson, leading the band of heroes, stepping up to the plate? Veronica Walsh, dispatching enemies without hesitation or remorse?

Or was the silence that followed because things had gone wrong? Because there was no one to save her? Whatever threat to The Princemakers that had come through the door was sent back out, either with their tail between their legs or in a body bag?

Where was Archon? Or, more accurately, where was Curtis Leishear?

Her gut had never led her astray before. But this was what happened when the stakes were life or death. A single mistake, the wrong word spoken in haste to the wrong person, and the punishment could end up being the ultimate.

When Emilia realized that Curtis Leishear might be Archon, she knew she could not tell her partner until she was absolutely certain. That sort of news is only broken with one-hundred-percent certainty. But the governor of Maryland is not someone you just show up to talk to on a whim, even if he spent considerably more time in Washington, DC, than he did in his own state.

It hadn't even been incredible detective work, or some stroke of genius, that led her to him. There were loads of power players in this city, but members of Congress had their own constituents to answer to, and they came and went as they forayed back home every so often. She felt certain at least one other politician besides Senator Billingsley was involved, and the list of politicians whose home bases were in the DMV area was much more manageable. The person who held the ultimate power must be reasonably local, she had determined.

It must be a politician who had connections to Senator Billingsley and the Belle family. Well, Curtis Leishear jumped off the page at that point. She knew that Iverson had concerns about Senator Thresh, but he wasn't charismatic enough to be in charge of anything. A damp squib of a man, who continued to get elected solely because he hated the same people his constituents did.

What did Emilia do with her hunch? What any good employee would do with an idea. She ran it up the chain.

Rather than asking permission, she just made a note in passing to the chief that she thought she might have a breakthrough and that she needed to talk to Curtis Leishear. A quick passing comment in the hallway, safety in the assurance that someone else knew what she was up to.

The buzz in her stomach and brain, a feeling akin to being pleasantly tipsy—a familiar force that she always felt when she was on the verge of something big, breaking a case, or catching the bad guy. The positive feeling was only tempered by the knowledge of what it would do to Iverson when she found out.

To that point, Emilia almost hoped she was wrong. As she walked up to the imposing French doors, she knew there were two possibilities. Either she was right, and her partner's life would be irrevocably changed, or she was wrong, and they were back at square one, no closer to stopping the violence beset upon the community by the Princemakers.

Three possibilities, actually, counting the unforeseen one where Curtis Leishear opens the door with his gun drawn and raises it just in front of Emilia's temple.

"Get inside," he said, pointing with a flick of his head.

What could Emilia have done? Barring unholstering her own gun before she knocked, which Leishear would've easily been able to see on his security camera, she could not stop what happened next. All the synapses in her brain were firing as she tried to determine her best move.

That was when he swung the butt of his gun against the side of her head, and she crumpled to the floor.

Thirty seconds. Half a minute that could decide the fate of the rest of her life.

Then hours and hours to sit in the dark and think about it.

What went wrong? There was only one answer, and it hurt her brain more than the blow had.

Chief Branaman had told Curtis Leishear she was on the way. It had to be. Branaman was the only one who could've forewarned him. Her fatal mistake was trusting the man she believed in the most. How could anyone win against that?

You couldn't. You could do everything right and it didn't matter if by happenstance, a coincidence, or the vicissitudes of fate, you could end up in front of an oncoming freight train. That was life.

The thought calmed her more than she'd expected. She didn't need to fret about past decisions, because she made the correct ones. That they led her to this dark abyss didn't matter, because they were the decisions she would make over and over again if put in the same position.

The noises of footsteps had grown louder and more frequent. There were people up there. More than just the two Leishears.

Salvation? Or doom? The time to wait was over. Whatever the result, she needed to make it happen now. If they killed her, they killed her. That surely was the plan anyway.

She took a deep breath and screamed as loud as she could.

CHAPTER 81
ELAINE

Afternoon, March 24

"I swear, there is a secret room in this house." Elaine could hear the frustration creeping into her voice. "I heard the doorbell ring, and the chief came in here. He then dragged me back outside."

"I don't know what to tell you, Detective." The bald officer rubbed his shiny head and offered a conciliatory look. "There's no room in here like you are describing. Where did he take you?"

"I don't know! I'm sorry. All I can see in my mind is the foyer and the front door." Elaine watched as he shrugged and walked off, joining the horde of officers collecting and cataloging anything in her parents' house that could be considered evidence.

Representative Moore had come to and, despite the considerable difficulty, made a full statement about what happened in that alley. Senator Thresh came clean, unable to keep the lie going that Moore had been the aggressor. Not after everything Elaine had gone through. Chief Branaman was out of surgery, but still in critical condition. The speculation was that he would live, but no one was willing to hypothesize further.

News anchors were almost giddy in their reporting, such was the size of the story and scandal. Thresh had hid in the alley, waiting for Moore to pass by along her daily route home. When she did, he called out to her, and she walked down the alley toward him. When she was far enough inside the alley that no other pedestrians might see her, the shot that sliced Thresh's forehead was fired by the Princemakers' go-to assassin. Moore pulled her gun as Thresh lay stricken on the ground.

What they hadn't planned for was Detective Fahey, who realized that Moore's public outspokenness against the cabal made her a target. He found her schedule and was following her. In the end, his misunderstanding that she was a threat to Senator Thresh, that he had it backward, was what saved her life. His shooting of the representative preempted the assassin, who would have fired the kill shot into Moore.

The good guy with a gun. That's what the story was supposed to be. If Thresh had shot Moore, they'd have to wade through all the self-defense arguments—was it really necessary or not?

But not this way. Veronica had mentioned it first to Elaine and it rang true as soon as she heard the theory. Thresh wasn't supposed to shoot Moore. He was meant to play the innocent victim, complete with a superficial head wound with gushing blood that would look perfect for the front page of The Washington Post. A story of how a passerby heard the cries and ran into the alley and his quick thinking saved Thresh's life. They would have had someone in place who had no criminal record, Elaine was sure of it. Someone who they could credibly claim was just a regular old citizen, who had leapt into action and heroically saved the day, at the cost of Chamique Moore's life.

Instead, as Veronica put it, Fahey accidentally backed into being the hero. If the shot he fired had killed her, the outcome might have been the same.

Thresh had thought giving up the assassin's moniker was a small matter. Little did he know that his action would bring down the entire house of cards.

When the FBI connected the name Bedrock to a safety deposit box in a local bank with the same last name, they found a detailed docket, describing years of payments. Who paid, who died, everything. A treasure trove of information.

Everything but the identity of the assassin.

With Elaine's statement corroborating, the national headline was that Maryland Governor Curtis Leishear, the brother of the president, was in charge of a syndicate that had committed dozens of murders. The talking heads immediately began to speculate, just as Veronica had suggested, as to the president's involvement. He was expected to make a statement later tonight. Reports were that he and his Cabinet were scrambling. Citing lack of evidence as proof of lack of involvement rarely worked in this town.

No one had found Curtis and Belinda Leishear yet. Their house was now swarming with police, and their vacation homes were empty.

Elaine couldn't bring herself to care about them right now. Not when she could hear the words of Chief Branaman to her father ringing in her head. *"I heard you handled that."* Detective Brown wasn't away for a family emergency. She had been handled. But how, and what did that mean? Was she dead? Was she locked away? He had said she wasn't dead, hadn't he?

Her father hadn't had any unscheduled trips away, so unless he had driven off in the middle of the night—*possible*—then however he handled the situation was likely done at the house.

She couldn't allow herself to believe her partner was dead. The hope that her partner was locked in a secret room was what drove her energy. If she was hidden away, she could be found. Elaine needed to find the secret room where they had kept her. If she could find that, she could find any other secrets this house might have been keeping from her. Was Detective Brown here, tied up just a floor beneath her, waiting to either be found or starve to death?

Which direction inside the house had she come from? After her father had left her to die at the chief's hands, what happened next? She thought hard. He had pulled her up roughly, taken the handcuffs off, and then held his gun to her forehead.

"I don't want to do this here, but I will. I will not hesitate if you make this at all tricky for me," Branaman had said.

Elaine had just stared at him, her brain not working properly. She couldn't bring herself to comprehend what was happening. She could feel her mind telling her she had to do something, to fight, but she couldn't make her muscles work. What kind of police detective was she? A coward, in the end. Not a hero. Not Veronica. Not Detective Brown.

Where had he dragged her? A spiral staircase formed in her mind. Yes, she went up one step in front of him, but to what? A door.

"Open it or I shoot," he had said.

There it was. The memory clicked back into place. She had come out in the laundry room. He'd hustled her quickly through as they hurried through the house and out the side door.

"The laundry room!" She yelled as she took off across the foyer. "There's a secret door inside!"

To his credit, Shiny Head—*she'd have to learn his name soon*—came running.

"It's somewhere in here," she said as she watched them break the locked door open. The laundry room was unremarkable, given the luxury of the rest of the house. Just a small room, with two washing machines and two dryers lined up next to each other on the back wall. Several drying racks stood haphazard throughout the room, and a single table held a pile of her parents' dirty clothes.

"It looks like just a room."

"It obviously isn't! Why would they keep it locked?" Elaine didn't have time for trial and error. "Does anyone have a stud finder, or something that can see through walls?"

When the responses all came back negative, she said, "Okay, someone go run out and get me one ASAP." She let the other officers decide who drew the short straw for this errand.

After a twenty-minute wait that felt like hours, an officer returned and handed Elaine the stud finder. "Couldn't have bought a few to speed up the process," she grumbled.

She ignored the wall behind the washer and dryer. The wires and hoses would be too much to deal with for the door to be there. She painstakingly dragged the stud finder across the remaining walls until she found what she was looking for. "Check this, there are no studs for almost two yards here. Why else would that be?"

"I mean, it could be—" one of the officers started.

"Come on, man," Elaine interjected. "We're finding a secret room, do you really want to bore me with whatever architectural curiosity you were about to say?"

He didn't respond.

"Okay, everyone, start pushing, pressing, whatever you can think to do. There's a switch or a button or a knob on this wall and we need to find it."

Elaine didn't know who actually found it. But after a couple of minutes, a portion of the wall lurched backward and slid away, revealing a dark cylindrical space filled by a spiral staircase.

"I'm going first," Elaine said resolutely. "Anyone want to try to stop me?" She looked daringly at the selection of officers assembled behind her. No one spoke.

She fought to keep her breathing regular as she descended, the walls claustrophobically close. She let out the breath she didn't realize she was holding when she took the first step into the room.

The sturdy oval table took up almost the entire space. Elaine stepped aside and let her fellow officers hustle in, and they began to comb through every inch of space.

It didn't take long. There wasn't much to the room. Sighs of discontent rippled through as they checked the bare walls, tore down the Parc de Princes sign, and crawled under the table.

"Nothing." The nearest officer shrugged. "I'm sorry. What you see is what you get, I'm afraid. This is just a hidden meeting room."

Elaine despaired. "Did you hear something?" She glanced behind her, toward the exit.

The officer paused, looking around. "Nope, did you?"

"I just thought… never mind." Elaine closed her mouth. What did she think she heard? Muffled screams? It wasn't possible. It must just be her mind trying to force it. She was already standing in the secret room. "I just thought if I found this room again, we could find Detective Brown," she said softly, feeling a single tear form in her right eye and squeezing it tightly closed.

What had her father said? He'd taken care of her? The doomer part of her brain rose up, and she couldn't quash the overwhelming finality of that phrasing.

Could she be gone? Elaine didn't know how she would manage if Brown had been killed by her own father. There would be no one left. No heroes, no role models. Her father, her boss who got her this job, and then her senior partner. All out of her life for one reason or another. How did it come to this? She had a nice life, the easy childhood and adolescence that only privilege begot. All the American Dream truisms that rang false for so many others had been hers.

Who could she turn to now? She wasn't emotionally ready to be on her own. Living in your own space, making dinner for one each night, that was one thing. But having nowhere to go, no one to ask for advice when a day got too hard?

The one name that sprang to her mind revealed just how desperate things had become. Veronica Walsh. The only person she could think of who could help her was the woman who she until very recently had believed should spend the rest of her life rotting in a forgotten prison cell.

She continued to pour over every inch of the room. The three officers with her tore down the projector screen, ripped all the wires out of the wall, and took down the speaker connected to the front door.

Nothing.

Eventually they all stopped, standing still and looking to Elaine for guidance.

"I think we're all done here," she finally said, shaking her head sadly. "Thanks for your help."

EMILIA

She held the scream for as long as humanly possible, then inhaled and screamed again. She continued until her throat felt like it was lined with daggers.

Nothing. No one ran to pry open the door brandishing either a gun or a flashlight.

Were twenty-three and seven even the correct number of days to last without food and water? She'd never bothered to look, just taken them as gospel from that board game.

Maybe now she'd learn.

CHAPTER 82
VERONICA

Evening, March 24

Ben hung up the phone and sighed, closing his eyes. "This is agony. I need to see them, V."

I looked up from the romance novel I was reading, a doomed attempt to take my mind off of everything that had transpired. "My parents sided with me, didn't they?"

"They did. Ricardo said he knew I would call and try to persuade them, and he seemed pleased about that."

"They know you'll do anything to see your kids. They love that about you. Easiest way to grandparents' hearts."

"But."

"But. This isn't over. Archon is still out there, and he's a danger to us even if he has no more allies." I grimaced with the realization. "Actually, he's likely even more dangerous to us now. I helped take the Princemakers down, what does he have to lose anymore?"

"Why would he still be here, though?"

"This is the governor of a state," I said. "He's a white-collar criminal who ordered some violence but never got his hands dirty. He's lived a privileged life."

"What do you mean?"

"He's got money, sure, and that means you can escape plenty of justice. But he's lost all that power, so he needs to be on the run like a petty criminal. Like someone who has just robbed a bank on a whim and needs to lie low."

"You're saying he's not off on a private jet to some island forever?"

"I don't see how. Any legitimate use of his money is going to get tagged immediately. POTUS is going to disavow him. This ends in a confrontation, it can't be anything else. So, until then, I don't want Nico and Maria anywhere near here."

I knew Ben understood and the logical part of his brain agreed with me. The emotional part of my brain agreed with him. But when you're talking danger, logic has to win.

"We do whatever we need to do together, then," Ben finally said.

"Together," I agreed.

It was another one of those senses I couldn't explain. I'd felt it the entire afternoon. So, when the phone rang just as I was cleaning up from our white bean, quinoa, and cauliflower bowls—the kind of dinner you don't cook with kids around—I wasn't surprised.

"Ben!" I called into the living room. "Detective Iverson on the phone."

He came running in and I answered and put her on speaker. "What's up, Detective?"

"Veronica, look, I need your help."

"You need help finding Archon," I said, a certainty bordering on haughtiness in my tone.

"Actually, no," she hesitated for a split-second. "You know, if you do know something about my father, I need to hear it."

Huh. Maybe my Spidey senses didn't always work.

"No, I don't have anything to go on right now," I admitted. Now I was curious what this call was about. Ever since I left the scene this morning, I had been waiting to be asked back. Eventually someone in power would decide that I was an asset, give me a little spiel about how they don't care about anything that happened before, that the most important thing for the country was that we put an end to this entire Princemakers thing, yada yada yada. I'd say, "of course," and we'd go back to that merry equilibrium of the past several months. Me, the hero to so many, the villain to the rest, but legally untouchable for the time being.

"We need to find Detective Brown, and I don't know where to turn."

"She's missing?"

"Yes, I'm sorry. I didn't mention it before, but there was just so much going on, and all the adrenaline and everything..."

"I understand," I said, realizing Iverson wasn't going to finish that sentence. "Talk to me, then."

"My father." She stopped and took a deep breath. "He said he had taken care of her. That's the line he used when telling the chief."

"Shit. Tell me everything you know."

I listened as Iverson detailed how she had heard from Chief Branaman that Detective Brown was unexpectedly away for family reasons, and how it got more confusing the longer she went without checking in at all.

"She didn't give you any hint where she was headed? She just took off?"

"No, and I can't understand why she left her own partner out of it."

"Can't you, though? What could she have found out that she didn't want to include you in?"

I listened to the silence. She had to get to the realization herself. "Oh. Of course. She figured out something about my father but decided to go alone."

"Or she might've told the chief, for all the good that would have done," I added. "Did he sound like he had any idea of where she might be?"

"No," Iverson answered without hesitation. "I thought about that, but it seems unlikely."

"Okay, then where are we? You have to think of your father as a criminal now, okay? If she is alive, where would he hide her? If she is dead, where would he dump her?" I knew that sounded callous, but subtly tiptoeing around it wouldn't help us find her.

"There's that war room in our house where he kept me, but we were just there and searched the entire place and didn't find anything. I don't even want to think about the other option..."

"You found a secret room? What does it look like?"

"Well," Iverson paused for a second. "Like an office meeting room, really. A big, long table with chairs all around it. That was basically it."

"The secret lair of the Princemakers." So that was where they all would meet. It made sense that the ringleader would have a place they couldn't be seen meeting. None of them would have aroused suspicion being around each other anyway, but taking risks was not how people like that stayed in the shadows. If World's Edge was searched more thoroughly, I had no doubt they would find an extra room there too. "But that's not a place to hide someone. That's not a safe room. So why did he put you in there?"

"Well, it was probably the best place in that house."

"I don't like it. Look, whatever we think about your father, he's a smart man and a careful planner. You're telling me that he really dumped his daughter in a meeting room just because it could lock? Why not just any other room? He could easily lock you in any other. Was that really the best room possible?"

"Oh, I see what you're saying. He couldn't have locked me in a better room." Iverson's voice was deadly soft. "Because there was already someone in that room."

CHAPTER 83
ARCHON

Evening, March 24

Archon puffed out his cheeks and laid his head back against the lumpy pillow. He knew that a Comfort Inn was the last place someone would look for them, but as he tried to make himself comfortable on the bed, he wondered if maybe prison beds could provide better sleep.

He looked over at his wife, scrolling through her social media as if she didn't have a care in the world. She always had that way about her. He had clocked it immediately. It was infectious, her ability to be completely present and yet seem so above it all. Like she knew we were all living in a simulation, and nothing actually mattered.

The Princemakers were over. No matter what happened next, he knew that to be true. Ulrich and Yvonne Belle, Andrew Billingsley, Dan Flint, Gregory McAllister, and Xavier Henry were all dead. This was supposed to be the sort of group that had their hand on the scales but never got themselves into real danger. They propped up decision-makers, and their influence ran deep, but they were always a small group. Now all that was left of them was Branaman, Thresh, and himself.

Ulrich's pitch to join the Princemakers had been that no one besides the president had more power than his group. When Ulrich died and he assumed the role of Archon, he thought back to that line. Maybe Ulrich's problem was that his ambition was too small. Why not have the Princemakers power *and* the presidency? Behind the scenes and center stage at the same time.

Living in the shadows was fun. Knowing you have secret power that others could only dream of. But every day he watched the world venerate his brother. How could he not be jealous?

A subtle shift of focus over the first few months of his tenure as Archon, and he had been happy with the progress. He had a machine behind him that would make his presidency far more effective and long-reaching than his brother's ever was. He just needed to win. No one out there was a threat until Representative Moore burst onto the national scene. She turned her new name recognition as Ben Walsh's boss into a profile as a tough truth-teller who wouldn't back down.

She would be a problem. Especially after she began speaking out against him, not that she knew he was the leader of the cabal she was decrying. But then she and Thresh got into a public war of words and he realized the opportunity that presented itself.

The Princemakers would believe it was for their benefit as a whole. She needed to go and be turned into a pariah as she went. If that allowed him a clear run at the presidency? Well, what a coincidence that would turn out to be.

He couldn't help himself—he turned the television on to watch his friends and colleagues fall over themselves to turn on him. As soon as he got wind that Representative Moore was alive and telling her side of the story, Thresh had crumpled. He gave them all up. There was no reason for Branaman not to jump in headfirst as well, assuming he recovered. Get the nice cushy deals they each were no doubt being offered. Deliver the Big Bad. Everyone loved to watch that guy fall.

That Bedrock had detailed everything going back years had surprised him. He should have known, since they had the same documents. Archon knew his identity, but what good would that do? *Here's the hitman I hired for years, take him rather than me?*

Curious that he'd written in detail about how he'd been hired by the Princemakers to kill Gregory McAllister. Archon didn't know where to begin with that bit of news.

The high wire act they played for years necessitated that they didn't have ammo for a mutually assured destruction situation if it came to it. They propelled key individuals into the correct roles, but with their own time and money. The single motivating factor was fear. Everyone they placed received a visit from a masked individual who explained that if they ever spoke up about where the money and influence came from, they—or their families—would end up in the bottom of the ever-shallowing Chesapeake Bay. There was no conspiracy, barely even criminality in this day and age associated with taking shady money. A little campaign finance fraud? Who really cared?

What it meant was there wasn't a contingent of mercenaries ready to spring to Archon's defense and tell all manner of tales of his good deeds and how he must have been set up. No, there were only the two of them left.

The reporter pivoted finally, ending the inane time-filling she was doing. The camera changed, and the man that Archon knew would cast the final nail filled the screen.

His own brother.

The president of the United States. Dennis Leishear.

Archon listened as Dennis began with an anecdote from their youth, a story of love and companionship, a first trophy won in youth baseball together, when young Curtis was so good he played with the older boys. A heartwarming tale, meant to show the president's capacity to care, and just how much denouncing his brother and calling for his arrest meant to him.

"It's all circumstantial, nothing is corroborated," Belinda said, glancing up at the TV. "They've got nothing on you that would actually stick."

A bit myopic, Archon thought, but she wasn't entirely wrong.

No evidence, just hearsay and an unsourced journal. Branaman and Thresh could talk all they wanted, but all he had to do was come out and say "no." His own daughter might be a problem, but he could spin that. He was under duress—he knew that Branaman was planning to kill his daughter, so he couldn't be expected to have thought rationally. How lucky he was that Veronica Walsh showed up when she did, how he would've tried to stop the chief but had to get his wife to safety first before coming back to save his daughter. He was innocent, a patsy clearly set up to be the fall guy. Just the sort of corruption he was fighting to stop.

It could work. A truism of politics was that your supporters tended to blindly follow whatever makes them feel better. Easier to accept the obvious lie than to tell yourself you were duped.

There was only one problem.

That detective that was still locked inside his house right now. He had planned to just come back later, dispose of the body in whatever state it was in, and move on. But now, she was the final bomb he had to diffuse.

Get rid of Emilia Brown, once and for all.

Once she was gone, his money and his lawyers would do the rest. He hadn't achieved all he had in life to give it up so easily. There was still hope. The only thing the public liked more than dragging someone down was raising them back up.

"What are you doing?" Belinda groaned as he rose from the bed.

"Don't worry, my love. One last thing I need to take care of. I'll be back soon." He blew her a kiss and went out into the night. One final deed, and then the name Archon would be gone forever.

CHAPTER 84
ELAINE

Night, March 24

She wasn't wrong. She couldn't have been wrong.

Elaine spent the rest of the afternoon racking her brain, trying to figure out how she had messed up. Detective Brown had to be in her parents' house.

The only other possibility was unthinkable.

She had a key. They wouldn't have changed the locks, that would be crazy. Her parents were in the wind, a situation she could not wrap her mind around. But that meant the house was now empty, save for the single officer who would be standing guard. She could return. Explain the situation.

She didn't want to drive in case there was someone else nearby—it would call too much attention—and it was too dark and chilly to run. So, the bike it would be. She threw on her police windbreaker and hustled outside to the communal bike stand. She bought the bike assuming it would be useful in a city with bad traffic, but she ended up rarely using it, specifically because the traffic made her too uncomfortable. Too many cars that could easily send her flying if their drivers were distracted and didn't check a blind spot. But tonight, the evening roads were quiet as she zoomed down toward her parents' house, letting gravity do much of the work as she headed south.

With the all-hands-on-deck call coming from up on high—maybe even from her own uncle?—they had combed through almost the entire house and grounds already.

The house was dark, and the grounds had an eerie quality in the moonlight that she had never noticed before. Elaine shivered as she dismounted and laid her bike down in the gravel in front of the house. Why did she suddenly wish she had brought a flashlight? As soon as she got inside, she could just turn the lights on, no different than thousands of other nights she had spent here. And where was the officer who was supposed to be here? She felt the chill continue down her spine.

She slipped her key into the lock and hurried inside as quickly as she could. With a quick slam of the door, she turned on the foyer light and took a deep breath. *This is normal. This is my house.*

Just a few hundred extra yards of crime scene tape strung around it, plus a million or so evidence tags, showing where every piece was collected.

She tried not to dwell on where the officer was. She had a job to do here. But where could that extra room be?

It didn't make sense for it to be upstairs. She had mapped it out in her head as she cycled over. There were five bedrooms on this floor, each with its own bathroom and walk-in closet, and then a single hall bathroom and a hall closet. They were like a set of locked puzzle pieces. There was no space between. This wasn't some old house with a crawl space leading to a secret room under the stair that had been used in the Underground Railroad. This was a recently built mansion designed for the modern elite.

Which is why the basement level was the only space that made sense. The hidden door to where her parents had kept her was in the laundry room. That was on the main floor, but the spiral staircase was long enough that the meeting room was likely below the basement level. What else could be down there?

She walked further into the house and switched on the light

illuminating the cavernous family room. That they called it the family room always felt a little forced, considering it was only ever used for hosting. Why spend time in such a big room when it was only the three of them? The family room had floor-to-ceiling windows on the front. No possibilities there. But the fireplace on the far wall could hide something. Flanked by built-in bookshelves painted a blinding white, the imposing wood-burning brick fireplace was fully operational, but Elaine could never remember them using it. "Why heat a house like a caveman would when we've evolved in every other way?" her dad once said.

Detectives in movies always made it look so easy. They just grab a book and pull, and no one asks how they knew it was that specific one. Or they push down on the fireplace poker as if it was the most obvious move in the world. Elaine focused her eyes, willing something to jump out at her. Something out of the ordinary. Where was the clue that would mean that she didn't have to try to pull every single book out one by one?

She heard the noise first.

A sharp creak, evolving into a long slow whine. She stared, disbelieving, as the bookcase just to the right of the fireplace swung open.

What did I do?

CHAPTER 85
EMILIA

Night, March 24

The footsteps slowed, from the incessant march, the purest sound of hope, to a trickle, and then eventually silence. There was no hope to be found in silence. Silence could only mean despair.

But despair was an emotion Emilia had no interest entertaining. If something had happened upstairs, and there was no chance of escape, or even just continued captivity but with sustenance, then she would face that outcome head on. If she was to die down here, she would die with hope in her heart. Until she took her final breath, she would believe that there was another one coming. Why live your life any other way?

Nothing good in life came from pessimism. It wouldn't be overegging it to say that her life had irrevocably changed when she realized that truth in college. Pessimism's only selling point was that it softened a later blow. So what? Life wasn't about making sure any blows were soft. Life was about reaching for the highs and experiencing them to the fullest. Enjoying the anticipation of something about to go right, even if it also could go wrong. Sports fans that followed perennially successful teams were the only group who she thought truly got it. There was always something more to be excited about. Another chance to make things right, even if this play, game, or season went wrong.

Was she about to die in this dark, cold room? Possibly. But maybe, just maybe, she was about to escape. The thought was so rich, so full, that she could practically taste it on her tongue. It nourished her the way the doom never could.

She felt her eyelids begin to sag. A little sleep wouldn't hurt, would it? After all, what else was she up to locked in here?

Her dreams would be nice. Wide open spaces, fresh air. Maybe the dream would go on forever. Wouldn't that be a lovely way to go?

The door flew open. Emilia instinctively threw her hands up in front of her face, palms outward, squinting as her eyes tried to adapt to the burst of light.

"Get up!" a gruff voice said. "We're getting you out of here."

CHAPTER 86
ELAINE

Night, March 24

The gun swung up out of the darkness first. Elaine dove to her right, landing with a thud next to the low glass coffee table. She scrambled further, putting the bookcase/door between her and whomever was emerging.

What am I doing?

"Police, stop where you are!" She yelled, drawing her gun. Her breath went in and out in short bursts, and the words sounded like they came out of a panicky pre-teen's mouth.

"Stand back!" A voice said. A familiar voice.

"Fahey?"

"Iverson?"

"What are you doing here?" she asked as he came into view. "Where did you even come from?"

Detective Fahey didn't respond. He simply stepped aside and let another person pass.

Elaine felt her heart soar as she saw her. "Oh, my goodness, Brown! You're okay!" She rushed over and enveloped her partner in an ill-fitting hug. "I was so worried."

"Thank you, Iverson." Brown grinned, looking back and forth

between her two most recent partners. "You two didn't come together? You're each here on your own? Incredible."

"I knew you had to be here! I'm so sorry we couldn't find you earlier. I was sure you were being hidden here, I knew you must have come to confront my father, but I couldn't find you and the other officers all tried helping too but we weren't able to and I'm so so sorry about everything."

Brown put up a calming hand. "Breathe, Iverson. It's okay. I'm sorry for you, too. This must have come as a shock."

Elaine felt tears begin to well up. *No, I will not cry here.*

"Look, this is touching, but we have to move," Fahey said to Brown. "We need to get you to a hospital to get checked up."

They walked back toward the front doors together. The burly and ornery stereotype, the purple-mohawked rebel, and the young unsure protégé, an unlikely trio. Elaine allowed herself her first true smile for days.

Brown glanced around. "Wait, where is the officer who was supposed to be here? Surely you didn't just leave this place unguarded?"

Fahey barked a laugh. "Howson? He was so desperate to get out of here that he was halfway down the driveway by the time I finished telling him I'd cover his shift."

"I can't believe it… how did you find her?" Elaine asked Fahey as they reached the foyer. "How did you know where to look?"

"How, indeed?"

All three detectives whipped their heads up in unison to see where the voice had come from. Elaine stifled a gasp when she saw her own father, standing just inside the doorway, both arms up, a gun in each hand.

CHAPTER 87
ELAINE

Night, March 24

"Why don't you tell them, Detective Fahey?"

"Tell us what?" Elaine asked her father. She watched his eyes as he calmly flitted his gaze back and forth, resting for a split-second on each of them. His guns weren't trained on her, she realized. One was aimed at Fahey's head, and the other at Brown.

"Why should I tell the story when it's his to tell?"

Elaine had never heard this falsely saccharine, mocking tone from her dad.

"It's over, Archon," Brown said. "You're outnumbered."

He chuckled. "If you say so."

"You've never fired a weapon before," Brown said. "You can't possibly think you can take us all down."

"It's not about what I think. It's about what are acceptable losses to you. I'll grant you, you might have the upper hand. But I'm not willing to go, ah, what's the word… peaceably, if you will. So, which of you is okay being killed while you try to stop me? Would you like to die? You're probably closest to death as it is, Brown. What is it, a full day without food and water by now?" He turned to Fahey. "Or you, Martin, maybe you're the unlucky one today. After all, you're the one least liked by your peers, so it wouldn't dampen the celebrations too much. They'd pause for a second, mourn your loss, and then carry on with their joy. Or maybe my own daughter."

Elaine heard Brown intake a sharp breath. "You wouldn't," she said.

"Not on purpose, no," he admitted.

"You just left me to die with Chief Branaman! You didn't care if he killed me then." The words flew out of Elaine's mouth.

"Of course I cared. That's why I couldn't have done it myself. But if bullets start to fly, who can fully control where they go? Are you prepared for that?"

"Scant consolation," Brown muttered.

"We're prepared for you to step down, dad," Elaine said. "Don't make us hurt you. Don't make me hurt you."

"My darling, you can't anyway. Guns down now. I will only make this request once. Place them on the floor slowly, then kick them toward me."

Elaine waited, taking her cue from the others. Brown didn't have her gun on her, but Fahey began pulling his out with the speed of molasses. "Good, good," her father said as Elaine followed suit.

She and Fahey prodded their guns forward toward her father, the weapons bridging half of the distance between them before they lay still.

"Thank you." Her father offered a tight smile.

"Why do you think I can't hurt you?" Elaine asked.

"Because you fail to see the situation right in front of your eyes. Ask the question again."

"What question?"

"The question you were asking before you realized I was here."

What were they discussing? She had been so happy to find them, to see Brown, and then they were hustling to get her out to get checked on. What had she just asked?

"No, that can't be," Brown whispered.

"Can't be what?" Elaine asked.

"Ask the question again," her father repeated. "You know what. How about I ask it myself? Detective Fahey, would you please enlighten us? How did you know about a secret room installed behind those bookshelves?"

Elaine had never seen the look on Fahey's face. Shame. An emotion she didn't think had ever crossed his mind before.

Fahey opened his mouth, and then closed it again.

He sighed. "Alright, if he's not going to tell you, I will. This is taking up too much of my time. You two young ladies should know that the man you're standing next to is the Princemakers' hitman."

"I don't believe you," Elaine said, her tone defiant. "You're just trying to mess with us. That's the only way you can gain the upper hand."

"Bedrock. Come on now, the clues are all right in front of your faces."

Bedrock. The name the news reported. No one had yet determined his or her given name. "Some hitman named Bedrock. What of it?"

"Do none of you know anything about the etymology of Irish names?"

"Fuck," Detective Brown whispered after a second of silence.

Of course she would know something like that.

"There's a clever girl," her father grinned wide. "Fahey, derived from the Gaelic 'fothadh', meaning what, Martin?"

"Foundation," Brown said when Fahey didn't respond. She whirled her head around to face him. "Explain," she hissed.

"I..." The words failed him. He looked into Detective Brown's eyes and then turned back to face Archon. His beady pupils dilated and bulged out, as if straining against an invisible forcefield. "How dare you go after my partner?"

He laughed. "Detective Brown? That's your red line? You murdered loads of people for us for years. You shot Chamique

Moore days ago, exactly as we planned, and now this is your breaking point? Give me a break. What a joke."

"Exactly as we planned?" Elaine glared at Fahey. "You meant to shoot her the entire time. What the hell?"

"A smart idea, if I do say so myself." He turned both of his guns on Brown. "This is your biggest fear, is it, Martin? That your one meaningful connection in life is going to be taken away from you? That the person you think of as your best friend is about to die?"

"Don't you dare!" Fahey thundered as he lunged forward, grabbing and raising his own gun.

Elaine could swear she saw her father roll his eyes.

"You stupid, stupid man," he said as he nonchalantly pulled both triggers.

The two bullets ripped through Fahey's chest, a one-two punch of devastating consequence.

"No!" Elaine cried as Fahey fell, the floor reverberating under their feet as he crashed forward. His eyes were wide, and unfocused. She jumped toward him and hot blood poured out over her hands as she tried in vain to stem the flow. "What the fuck, dad?"

"Your partner is next!" he roared.

She looked at Brown, unarmed. Her partner, who took a chance on her. *Sure, Chief Branaman had saddled her with you, but she'd taken you on. She nurtured you, even if only for a very short time.*

No one was riding to the rescue now. Veronica Walsh wasn't about to break down the door. There wasn't time to negotiate. It was all happening way too fast.

Her gun was on the floor near Fahey's head, where she had kicked it. Inches away, she could grab in a flash. As long as her father didn't notice how close she was.

BANG.

Later, Elaine would tell everyone that she'd done it on instinct. She would say it to fellow officers, family members, even reporters. *My mind went blank. I just had to act.*

They would all laud her for her bravery, her selflessness. A hero, they'd call her.

Her story would become international news. The kind of story that would become a Netflix special a decade down the line. Hell, it was probably in the works already.

The woman who shot and killed her own father. The woman who brought down DC's latest underground cabal. The police detective who watched her colleague get killed right in front of her and had the wherewithal to do what was needed in the most extraordinary of circumstances.

But in the quiet of her own home, when she turned off the lights at night, she allowed the truth to have its moment.

That it wasn't an unthinking act. That she knew exactly what she was doing.

When given the life-or-death choice, she decided, with a clear mind, to grab her gun and aim for the head. To trust her skill with a firearm and take the shot that would put her father down permanently. To look at his body so dispassionately that Detective Brown assumed she must have been in shock.

She could have aimed for his torso. That would have been the logical play. Make sure she hit him. He was a moving target, ten yards away, it could've gone wrong.

But his guns were raised.

The man who cried tears of joy when he first held her after she was born. Who held her hand and told her she was brave when she got her first haircut, sure that the scissors would inflict unimaginable pain. Who brushed the single loose strand out of her eye when she walked down the stairs in her junior year prom dress, nervous as anything about what the other kids would say when she turned up with a girl as her date.

Archon. Curtis Leishear. Governor. Dad.

Gone.

CHAPTER 88
ELAINE

Morning, March 25

Elaine didn't want to get out of bed. She didn't want to do anything anymore. She killed her father last night. Patricide. One of the murders so egregious that they have their own word for it.

But Detective Brown was knocking on her door, calling out for her to open up or else she'd break it down herself.

"Fine, I'm coming, I'm coming!" Elaine called, as she blearily forced her legs over to the side of the bed and pushed herself upright into a sitting position.

The knocking continued. How did she have energy for this? She'd sat in a pitch-black cell for the last few days. Elaine threw on a ratty t-shirt and her closest pair of sweatpants and made her way out to the front door.

Detective Brown nodded when she got a look at Elaine as the door swung open. "Just as I figured. Come on, Ivy, we're getting you out of the house."

An hour later, Elaine was sitting at a table in an Aussie-style cafe on Massachusetts Avenue. "This is the weirdest girls' brunch I've ever been a part of," she said, looking around at the three women gathered with her.

"We want you to know you've got people here who care about you," Veronica Walsh said, seated directly across from Elaine as she sipped on what the menu called an "Aussie Iced Latte," which looked to be a regular iced latte but with a scoop of vanilla ice cream plunked into the glass on top.

"I get that, and it makes sense that you and Detective Brown are here—"

"Call me Emilia," Detective Brown cut in. "We went through too much shit in the last few weeks not to be on a first-name basis now."

"I... I didn't actually know your first name," Elaine said, cracking her first smile of the day. "Your name plate just says 'Detective' on it, and I've been too nervous to ask."

"Emilia and Elaine, crime-fighting duo. Put it on a billboard." Veronica smiled with her tongue between her front teeth.

"Okay, but why exactly are you here again?" Elaine looked at the amber-skinned woman with her hand on her stomach next to Veronica.

"You remember Mikaela, my—" Veronica paused and glanced left "—I think we just say sisters now, right? Half-sister-in-law is a mouthful."

Mikaela offered a self-deprecating chuckle. "I don't really know what I'm doing here either, Veronica just asked me if I wanted brunch, and I said yes."

Veronica slurped her drink and smiled innocently.

"All four of us have gone through trauma, and while we should never have to compare ours, I thought it would be a good idea to get you out of bed and get you talking," Emilia said. "If it were me on admin leave, I'd go crazy because I'd want to throw myself into the next case to take my mind off things."

Veronica raised her hand. "Emilia said we shouldn't compare, but let's be very clear about which one of us has had to dish out the most violence here."

"Recently?" Mikaela asked, in a harsher tone than Elaine expected.

"Don't." Veronica's side-eye silenced her sister. "The reason I bring that up is to validate your feelings right now, Iverson. Or, Elaine, if we're all just going to lean in on the first names thing. You're probably hurtling back and forth, wanting to throw up, feeling relief, possibly even a disturbing amount of joy, intense self-loathing, all the hits. Lurching from one emotion to the other."

"I'm angry," Elaine said softly. "I'm really angry at him. He made me do it. One last little fuck you to his own daughter."

"You saved my life," Emilia said, reaching over to grip Elaine's hand.

"I think I owe you an apology, Veronica," Elaine said.

"Oh, yeah?"

"I believed you were a bad, irredeemable person. I thought there was no way anyone could do what you did and still have a soul left. I thought taking a life, any life, meant there was something deeply wrong with you. That's been an overarching feeling of mine my entire life. It's part of why I felt strongly about being a detective." The words were all spilling out now. "Right and wrong. You killed someone, you were in the wrong. No matter what the situation was, no matter whether you had the best possible excuse. I looked at you and saw a monster. A heartless killing machine. But now I know different…" her voice lost out to the lump in her throat as tears formed in her eyes.

"Elaine," Veronica said. "You're right, though. That is how it's supposed to be. Most of us shouldn't ever have to know what it takes to pull a trigger. That's not our life anymore."

"I just, when he shot Fahey, something snapped in my mind. And when he turned his guns on Emilia…" Elaine swallowed the lump forming in her throat.

"It's okay, we get it," Veronica said.

"I think that's why Veronica brought me here," Mikaela said, and all eyes turned toward her. "Because I also understand that deep-in-the-bones hatred of your own father. I don't want to say I wish I had done what you did, but I know that if you hadn't—and you'd survived—you might be sitting right here with the exact same anger and angst over what you didn't do."

"Thanks, Mikaela. But I don't want to talk about my father anymore," Elaine said. She looked at Emilia. "Do you think he really was telling the truth about Fahey?"

Emilia hesitated, shooting a quick glance at Veronica and Mikaela.

"I already know." Veronica shrugged. "And she's a vault."

"I poked around a bit this morning," Emilia said. "Obviously there's a ton to get through, and we have to reopen everything Branaman ever touched. But it does seem likely that he was telling the truth. That journal the FBI found where the hitman gives all the details of every murder committed for the Princemakers for the past decade, it's Fahey's. We don't officially know for sure, but I know."

"But, why?"

"I don't think we'll ever truly know, but I can hazard what I think is a pretty decent guess," Emilia said. "He got paid well for it and it made him feel powerful. In the end, money and power are all that ninety-nine percent of men want anyway. What did it get him except an early death?"

"What do we do about him?"

Emilia looked off at a random spot on the wall. Without turning back, she spoke. "I think we don't do anything." She shook her head. "The only two members of the Princemakers left are taking pleas and telling all. There are some things the public doesn't need to know. That Fahey was the hitman only muddies all our waters. It's not entirely clear he was, by the way—we'd still have to comb through all his old crap. Only the three—*four*—of us know and I think it's entirely fine to keep it that way. If it comes out, it comes out. But we don't need to drag it into the light. Especially because of what he wrote about him being the one who killed the Georgetown president."

"Why would he take the rap for killing McAllister?" Elaine didn't make eye contact with Veronica.

"I don't know," Emilia answered. She looked back and forth between Veronica and Elaine. "Look, he was no angel, we all know that, but I think we also all know that he has let a particular someone we care about off the hook, and for that reason above all else we'll leave his legacy unsullied. Is that fair to everyone?"

CHAPTER 89
MARTIN

2018

"Fahey, do you like your job?"

Martin frowned. That wasn't the question he expected when Chief Branaman had called him into his office. "What do you mean?"

"I mean, is this the sort of thing you want to be doing forever, or is this just a job you'll do for a few years and then move on? Are you a lifer?"

"I'm a lifer, sir, of course." Martin wasn't sure of the veracity of that statement. He wasn't sure of much, truth be told, but he enjoyed stopping crimes and solving clues and, despite being of a similar size, he couldn't just go out and be Jack Reacher. So, police it was. But when your boss asks how much you value your job, there is only ever one answer.

"Glad to hear it." Branaman leaned back in his chair. "I've been watching you, Fahey, and I think you're the perfect guy for a situation I need help with. Can you help me?"

Only one answer to that question too.

Which is how Martin ended up in a small, wooded area in Arlington two nights later, joined by the Chief and a man he didn't recognize but whose suit looked like it cost more than

Martin's yearly salary. The man dragged a hooded figure in front of him and threw him down at their feet.

"What is this?" Martin asked.

"This is you if things don't go right," Branaman said calmly, pointing to the grunting man on the ground.

The suit spoke. "This man used to work for us, doing an important job of ridding the world of people who do not belong in it. People who would hurt the country. But he decided that he wanted to make his own decisions. He wanted to have a say in who gets hurt and who doesn't. Shut up!" he yelled and kicked the man, whose muffled noises had gotten steadily louder, in the chest.

He fell silent.

"I don't—what is it you want me to do?" Martin looked pleadingly at his boss.

"You're a man who believes in justice, don't you? You think you understand righteousness better than others, and I've seen how upset you get when courts don't hold up your arrests."

The chief had a point.

"But..."

"Look." Suit had a baritone voice, and he spoke softly and deliberately. "My name is Ulrich Belle. I am possibly the most important person in this town. I have more power than you could possibly know. I am looking for a man to join me, to be paid more money than you could ever dream, and be on call to help... *ahem,* eliminate certain problems for me. The chief and I have worked together splendidly for years, and he personally recommended you. Haven't you always felt you were destined for more than just your job? This is an opportunity. You can be part of something greater than all of us. Now, take my gun and shoot that man. I will not ask twice."

2020

Martin wrote with his left hand, a skill he'd perfected while bored in school. No one would be able to trace his handwriting back when nothing he wrote in this journal would match any of his recorded right-handed writing. He flipped through the pages. Eleven deaths now. Every time he needed to add another name, he took a trip to the bank and retrieved his special notebook. He couldn't remember where he'd seen it, but some book or movie from his childhood had given him the idea to use a deposit box. As long as no one ever had a reason to search it, there were few safer places. He disguised himself and never looked directly at any of the cameras, just to be sure.

He understood what he was. He didn't try to hide himself from it, convincing himself that he was on the side of the angels, that the men and women he had killed for the Princemakers were all bad people. They weren't. They were just people who got in the way. That's how Ulrich talked. Other people were simply pawns to be removed as needed so a more important piece could move forward.

But the rush. The feeling of being more than what he was. Exactly as Ulrich had described. He had no one to talk to about it, knew that he never could speak to anyone. But he had to get the stories out, so he wrote every detail—except anything that could incriminate himself—down in a journal. In his mind, he knew it could act as a get-out-of-jail-free card later as needed, but that wasn't its purpose.

He found himself using his spare time looking up other assassins and learning as much as he could. He tried to imagine all the others who didn't have Wikipedia pages because they stayed hidden their entire lives. What must that be like? He wasn't interested in serial killers. Some madman gets off on killing as many prostitutes as he can until he eventually gets caught? That's not legendary; that's just sick. The men and women who were living, breathing bullets, death incarnate—those were the ones he obsessed over.

None more so than Alessandra Portillo. He'd audibly gasped

when he first read about her. The long-missing, presumed-dead, *asesina* for the Portillo crime family. An anonymous henchman, with a calling card of cutting off a pinky finger, who terrorized El Salvador's criminal underworld before being outed as a teenage girl. He devoured every piece of content about her, read all the theories about what might've happened to her. Where she might be now. He couldn't let himself agree with those theories that she must be dead. He liked to imagine she was out there, somewhere, back amongst the shadows. He and Alessandra, two peas in a pod, killers for a cause.

2022

He waited for the call. It had to come, and when it did, it would either change nothing or everything. Ulrich Belle and his wife and one of his daughters were dead. There would be a new Archon. Curtis Leishear seemed the most obvious candidate. Once he—or whomever—took the throne, he would decide what to do with their hitman. Did he have a guy of his own? Did he want to keep Martin on the payroll?

When it came, he was in the car with Brown. He wondered if somehow Leishear knew, like it was a test. Could he maintain his composure when having this conversation in public?

"I have to get this, sorry," Martin grimaced as she snatched his phone, disconnecting the speaker from the car. "Hello?"

"Is this Detective Martin Fahey?"

"Speaking."

"I believe you know who I am. Or, you know my public-facing moniker."

Martin could feel his heart thumping and did his best to steady his breath. Brown had already affixed him with a concerned look. "What do you want from me, sir?" He said, attempting a calm devil-may-care tone that he knew he could not pull off.

"Nothing at all. Just keep doing what you're doing, and we will be in touch as needed."

"Thank you, sir. Talk soon." He dropped the phone as if it were on fire.

Breathe. In, then out.

"What was that about?" Brown asked.

"Nothing, just a family friend asking for a favor," Martin ad-libbed on the fly.

"Some favor that must be," Brown muttered. "Seeing as you've gone white, and I can see the beads of sweat dripping down your face."

"Do I ask about your personal life?"

"No."

"Then butt out of mine!"

He knew he would now have to keep up the temper that he'd established here. Before all of this he had been an easy-going guy. A co-worker you'd enjoy being around and then one day realize had seamlessly crossed the line and become a friend. But no more. No personal questions, a closed book. It pained him, since he liked his partner and hoped they'd have a lengthy and fruitful relationship. But the walls had to stay up now. He had thought maybe he could have it all, but he was mistaken.

October, 2023

When they were told that the water bottle pulled from Rock Creek had DNA that was a family match to Yancey Portillo, Martin had told Zeke that he hadn't seen anything yet. That Yancey Portillo was like a combo of Omar and Marlo from *The Wire*, a ferocious figure the likes of which had no parallel.

But that wasn't who he was thinking about. A family match to Yancey Portillo? His white whale had been living in the same city as him the entire time. There was no doubt in his mind. Veronica Walsh was Alessandra Portillo. The elation he felt was akin to watching your favorite team win the Super Bowl, or so he assumed, since as a New York Jets fan he hadn't ever seen that happen in his lifetime. He wanted to jump for joy, punch the sky in celebration.

But who could he tell? Again, he was stuck inside his own secret. He had already talked enough about Yancey Portillo that others in the police station knew of his obsession. At least he'd managed to steer the conversation to him just being an odd duck, someone who thought that much power was impressive. That it wasn't his hitman daughter who was the true object of his many thoughts.

He never had a problem with Ben Walsh. The best way not to show your angle was to over embellish another one. So, he decided that while he and Brown searched for Veronica Walsh, he would pester Ben Walsh, making him think that he believed he was the true villain, or maybe that both of them together were. The truth was that Martin was desperate to ask Ben real questions. He didn't care about where they met, or whether Veronica had ever shown any murderous tendencies on their honeymoon. He needed to know what made her click. He needed to understand her. But there was no way to ask that type of question without drawing ire, or worse, too much attention.

Alessandra Portillo, in the flesh. He doubted even her husband was wishing for her safe return as much as he was.

November, 2023

She woke up. Any lingering doubts he might've had, fears that this was all a big ruse, were swept away when Veronica Walsh woke up.

Your random suburban mom doesn't recover from being shot in the neck. She sure as hell doesn't bury a kitchen knife deep into the wall in a last-ditch attempt to stop her attacker.

He had sat there, enthralled, while her adoptive parents told them what they knew about her childhood, and explained how she had entered their lives. Now, once she was able to, he would get to finally interview his idol. It consumed his every waking moment. The chance, any day now, to sit down across from Alessandra Portillo. He had his list of questions on a folded piece of white paper that he kept with him at all times. Detective Brown would add her own, of course, but that didn't matter. Because he didn't care at all about the case. That would all fall out in whatever manner made most sense. That's how much of life happened, anyway.

Even after Ben Walsh ensnared Jeremy Wiles—*who saw that coming?* —and the whole conspiracy was laid bare, they would still have to interview Veronica. Her involvement was key, and no lawyer worth their salt would rest their case solely on a confession.

"Did you hear?" Brown asked as Martin took his seat the morning after Jeremy Wiles was arrested.

"Hear what?"

"There's talk of giving Veronica Walsh complete immunity."

"The fuck? For real?"

"It's way above our pay grades but sounds like the public support is going to get her off the hook." Brown shrugged. "She probably deserves it. It's not our business what goes on outside our borders, so I'm not interested in speculating about how this affects Salvadoran relations."

"What of our case here?"

"What case? We got Jeremy Wiles. All we have on her in this country is the immigration issue. Frankly, it sounds like they want it all to go away. Close it up, move on to the next thing. No need to drag on an American scandal."

Martin barely heard a word she was saying. Immunity. He

wouldn't have another chance to sit down with her on the record. How could they have dangled this right in front of his face and then yanked it away? How was he supposed to just go on, living life like everything was normal, when Alessandra Portillo was just across the river, seemingly going back to her own normal life?

March 18, 2024

It was time. Every conversation he had previously had with his contact ended the same way. *Not yet.* He was always worried he would hear that his words finally had been ignored. But Archon had laid it out precisely: Yancey Portillo needed to be vulnerable, but only to make the move when the timing was right.

"Diego, I understand your passion, and your cause is just," Martin said for what felt like the millionth time when they had last talked. "You have every right to do it. Everything is in place. I'm just telling you, if you wait for my signal, you will be rewarded handsomely. If you don't, I can't stop the people above me from coming after you."

And they would do just that, Martin was sure of it. If an asset stepped out of line, they were snuffed out. That was partially what kept Martin employed by the Princemakers. His obsession with Yancey Portillo had led him to find and develop relationships with friend and foe alike in San Salvador.

But now the moment was here.

He could hear the giddiness in Diego's voice, and he relished the feeling that he was the one who could give him the ultimate gift: a green light. "I've been waiting for this ever since Yancey killed my brother," Diego said, beginning the same story Martin listened patiently to every time they spoke.

You need to keep your assets happy. Fear is a strong motivator, but loyalty wins out every time. He had been the one to track down Diego and offer him the initial financial resources to plan his revenge.

Diego's older brother, Angel, had been on track to rise inside the Portillo organization, and all the money he earned came straight back to Diego and his other brother Pedro, both over a decade younger than Angel. When things turned dire, and they needed more, Angel had begun sneaking small extra amounts out. He told them not to worry, that Yancey would never know, and even if he eventually did, he would understand. Family was everything to him, that's what Yancey always said.

It turned out Yancey only meant his own family. He didn't think twice about Angel's family, about the poor children he had stolen for, when he shot Angel to death.

Martin didn't want to hear the details. He didn't need them, and any words spoken out loud can be heard by prying ears. He said go, and then waited like everyone else to hear how it happened.

March 20, 2024

Of course Veronica Walsh had killed Gregory McAllister. But it was too obvious. Her first mistake since she allowed herself to be kidnapped all those years ago.

Martin didn't expect the level of anger that rose to the surface. It wasn't just anger, though. That anger was propped up by something deeper. Disappointment. This wasn't how her story was supposed to end. Her legend was supposed to last forever. He would rant to anyone who'd listen about how she should be locked up and the key thrown away, but that was all an act. Was she just not up to it anymore? Years of domestic bliss had taken her edge just enough that she was imperceptibly worse at this? Maybe she should never have been found. What was the quotation from that British ex-soccer player? *Leave the football before the football leaves you*. No one likes to see a former superstar struggling.

Like a lightbulb popping on in his head, the idea appeared in Martin's head fully formed. He knew how he would get her out of this one. It would require his journal to become public, which would mean the Princemakers' time had come to an end. But that would be okay. A fair trade. Their end would mean Veronica's acquittal, if it went that far.

He grabbed his pen and wrote with a fervor he had rarely ever felt. He read the police report over and over, making sure that his version would ring true.

The Princemakers' hitman had killed the president of Georgetown, because he was planning to rat out the organization. That would be the truth.

It was the least he could do.

March 22, 2024

Refusing the Veronica Walsh hit had been the most nerve-wracking moment of his life. When Archon called him, he knew what was coming and had prepared his answer. It wasn't that it wouldn't be a fitting end for the *asesina*, being taken down by a fellow assassin. It was a trait that he possessed that he rarely showed publicly that caused him to say no. His humility kept him from the task.

Maybe also because he didn't have a death wish. What kind of person would say yes to that? An inflated ego and sense of self-worth never ended well.

He clocked the disappointment in Archon's voice when he turned him down. He'd have to turn to a backup, someone they surely had in mind, but that wasn't information Martin needed to know. The only thing Martin did know was that it wouldn't be another police officer. That was the one question about the Princemakers that he asked when he joined. How many other cops? He trusted the answer, that it was only him and the chief.

Then this other wannabe fucked it up. He allowed himself to be seen by her, following her out of a residential neighborhood? Did they get this guy by putting up a flyer by the side of the road? Call here, if you have experience in clandestine murder, competitive rate offered!

He was relieved, though. He hadn't realized that he would feel that emotion so strongly. But why shouldn't he? In every line of work, the employers can empathize more with those on their own level. Should he really care about his boss' happiness over someone whom he felt he had a connection to?

March 22, 2024

"Fahey!" Chief Branaman barked as Martin walked by.

Martin stopped on a dime. "What's up, chief?" he asked as he entered the office.

"Brown is out of commission for a while. Family issue. I need you with Iverson. And I need you to put your best foot forward on this." The pointed tone told Martin everything that words hadn't said.

"So, success would be..." he trailed off.

"Exactly what you think it would be. I am trusting you on this."

"Got it." Martin left without another word.

He and the chief never shared more than necessary in the police station. Only the most cursory of conversations, which led all of their co-workers to wonder what caused the frosty relationship. Most assumed it was Martin's demeanor. In any other case, they'd be correct.

Every instinct he had was screaming at him that something was wrong.

Emilia Brown did not let family issues get between her and policing. Not least when she and Iverson were bearing down on the rest of the Princemakers. Martin had understood why the chief had split up his partnership with Brown. There was only so much he could do alongside her, knowing full well that he didn't want the investigation to lead down the right path. Martin wasn't a fully-fledged member of the Princemakers, he was more like a contractor. Branaman wasn't ready to test his loyalty. Well, more likely that missive came from Archon anyway. Branaman let Brown and Iverson continue to investigate, letting them come to any conclusions naturally, and positioned himself to intercept anything major.

Martin always figured there would be a line. Somewhere down the road, he'd come to it, and he'd understand that he could not cross it. He hoped he would catch it before he crossed, rather than looking back with regrets.

The line stretched out just in front of him. He didn't care that he had an important role in the plan to kill a United States representative in the next few days. His conscience for that sort of thing was long gone. But Branaman had served up Detective Brown to Archon on a silver platter. And he must have done so behind Martin's back because he knew, deep down, that Martin wouldn't have the stomach to kill his former partner.

He would do what needed doing with Moore, including leaving a trail of clues as to why he had a legitimate reason to be there at the perfect time. He would set up early, as expected, across the street on the top of an apartment building and take the shot that would superficially wound Thresh. He'd decide in the moment where he'd hit him. Moore would pull her gun out, and then he'd race downstairs and across the street and turn up toward the alley to fire the shot that would kill Moore.

But this was it. He didn't show it outwardly, but he was very fond of Emilia Brown. If he tried to find her now, before the plan was enacted, he'd put her in even more danger. If she was already dead, there was nothing he could do anyway. But if not, he had to trust they were keeping her alive for a reason.

He knew exactly where they would be keeping her. The secret room in Archon's house. Not the Princemakers' war room. That wasn't the real secret. As much as it pained him to wait, he had to stay patient until the rest of the police left the scene. That he even knew there was a secret room to look for was already too much knowledge to wave away. Once everyone was gone, he'd sneak back at night, and rescue Detective Brown. No witnesses, no one to catch him if he slipped up and made it too obvious that he knew where to look. Just heroic behavior.

The only thing standing in his way was time.

CHAPTER 90
VERONICA

Morning, April 1 (One week later)

"Hey, V, there's a letter on the table for you!" Ben called from downstairs. We were finally back in our own home, complete with a new window and alarm system. The kids were readjusting, in that calm and scary way children always seem to. As if nothing had happened. They would either grow up to be supremely well-adjusted adults or require loads of therapy. Maybe both.

In the end, Ben had been right. What we needed most as a family was stability, peace, and quiet. Something I could never be sure to give us if I were a private investigator. He didn't drag me kicking and screaming to this conclusion, and I was grateful to him for that, but this venture would end before it had barely gotten off the ground.

What would be next for me? I didn't know.

What a freeing and terrifying thought.

I finished unpacking my hodgepodge of hastily strewn-together clothes from a couple weeks ago when I left this house. I went down the stairs, feeling like George Bailey with his loose banister knob when I stepped on the creakiest step. The smile that spread across my face matched any I had done in the previous several months.

The number of stamps. This was from outside the United States. I felt my heart begin to race as I tore open the standard white envelope. Two pieces of paper fell out. I picked up the smaller one.

Alex,
A parting gift for you. Be well.

It was unsigned, but there was no question it was from Francisco. The gift must be the other sheet of paper. I put that one down and unfolded the second.

My hand shot to my mouth as I recognized the distinctive, flowy handwriting.

My Dear Alessandra,

I have never given up on you. I believe in you, and I know you're out there somewhere, doing your best. Because that's what you've always been, ever since you were a baby. Your mother and I were so proud that our daughter—I could scarcely say the word out loud for how powerful a feeling it was—made it to every milestone faster than every other child. You smiled at just four weeks rather than the usual eight. The most joyous moment of my life—up to that point—was when you gave me a smile for the first time. That moment was surpassed with every smile I got from you, for the next fourteen years. You slept through the night at eight weeks, you crawled by four months. You were determined to be the best, the fastest, at whatever you set your mind to, and I couldn't have been prouder.

I never knew how to parent a girl. That's why you're reading this. If so, it means you are still out there somewhere, and my time has come.

In my world, strength is king. I could teach that to my son. Kelvin got the best version of me. But to you? My beautiful flower, all I knew how to do was give you thorns. I couldn't raise you, water you and nourish you the way you deserved. I know I let you down when I allowed you to take up Kelvin's mantle. I should have been stronger. I should have been able to tell you no. In truth, I think that the true problem was years earlier, when I killed Angel in front of you. I think that's the moment your life truly changed. You realized that life was cruel and violent, and you should not have had to learn that lesson at that age, and especially not from a parent. I was supposed to protect you from the cruel world, not thrust you headfirst into it.

But what a light you brought into it. A beacon of joy that even my hardest men couldn't resist a smile over. You lived life to the fullest every single day, and that is all any parent can ask for. The greatest part of my life was watching you and Kelvin grow. Every day, every year, you became more interesting. More confident.

I am sorry. For everything you were put through.

But most of all, thank you. Thank you, Alessandra, for blessing my life with your presence. If somehow, somewhere, you are reading this, then I hope we have reconnected. It will be the happiest moment of my life. But if I have gone to my grave, then just know it was with a smile, because of you.

With more love than I could possibly say,

Papa

I felt the lump grow in my throat, and I allowed it to take up residence there. Nothing he wrote was news to me. I was an adult woman, I already understood all of this. But to see it in writing, to see what he wrote when he thought he'd lost me…. my cheeks flushed and I took a deep, heavy breath.

I had never felt as far away from my childhood as I did now. Even through all the years that my past was secret, it felt like it was right there behind me, ready to extend a spiny hand out of the darkness and tap me on the shoulder. Ready to drag me back.

But now what was there? My father was gone. My mother. My brother. Francisco was back where he belonged, sitting on the throne that should have always been prepared for him. But that was it.

I had thought that Alessandra Portillo had been reborn. That the dormant part of me that came roaring awake would be a constant companion from now on. This time I'd control it, use it for good.

But that was a fool's dream. What I thought was a rebirth turned out to be death's last gasp.

"V, are you okay?"

Ben stared at me, his face full of concern. I hadn't noticed the tears streaming down my face. I glanced at the note and gave him a small nod. He crossed the room and read it through, grasping my hand as he did so. "Jesus, that's heavy," he breathed out as he folded it back up.

I grabbed his arm and spun him toward me. I wrapped my arms around him tightly, and he enveloped me in a ferocious embrace. I cried heavy racking sobs into his shoulder.

Yancey Portillo was my lighthouse. He guided every move I made for fourteen years. He sent me out to sea and always made sure I made it back to harbor safely. If I were being truthful to myself, I had to admit he was the reason I turned out the way I was after I left him, too.

Death is a parasite. It eats away at your insides, little by little, piece by piece. You don't even know what it has done to you until one day you look inside and realize your soul is but a husk. A shell of what it once was, before your life turned. Kelvin, Miranda, those poor college kids that Jeremy Wiles shot, Dan Flint, everyone who lost their life due to the actions of the Prince-makers. Osmin, a friend to the last, even if I only learned it just before his death. My own father. It was too much. It was all too much.

When the tears exhausted themselves, I picked my head up and looked into my husband's eyes. "No more of this," I said. "Never again will our family be in danger."

CHAPTER 91
VERONICA

Morning, April 22 (Three weeks later)

"I need to tell you both something," I said, wording it as carefully as I could. "There's going to be a big change ahead, and we're going to have to be brave."

Nico and Maria, recognizing the seriousness of my tone, stopped listening to their Toniebox and faced me. I came into their bedroom and squeezed myself down between them on Nico's bed, the mattress squeaking a vain protest.

"Mom!" Maria squealed, lunging to retrieve the Ghost Spider figurine that I accidentally dislodged.

I waited until she hopped back onto the bed. "Do you remember the night dad didn't come home?"

Of course they did.

They nodded apprehensively. These poor souls had already gone through more than any kindergarteners should have. They were strong and fierce and battle-hardened—all qualities I loved but wished they never had to learn. Parents are supposed to make life easier for their kids than they had had it. That's the entire point.

I never understood those complaints about how previous generations of eighteen-year-olds went to war and now current generations just did dances on TikTok. Wasn't that exactly the sign of society moving forward? We had all gotten too comfortable. Things had gone so well for so many people that now they were pining for olden times when life was tricky because hard times provide opportunities to prove yourself.

As someone who had proven myself over and over, it wasn't worth it. It never is worth it.

I realized I was just procrastinating talking to the kids. Letting my mind wander to anything but the next discussion. Two pairs of expectant eyes looked up at me.

I took a deep breath and grasped one of each of their hands. They say kids grow up too quickly, but these little hands, they were still so small in mine.

"Look…"

"Are we moving?" Maria asked

I let out a little laugh of surprise. "How…?"

"Dad told us when he woke us up," Nico said happily. "We're going to have a big house and new friends and lots of room to play!"

"And we'll be right next to one of those dunking donut stores!"

I couldn't help but smile, and I corralled my two loves into my arms. "I see what your father has emphasized," I said, squeezing them tightly.

To think, I had planned the entire speech about how we had such turmoil and that now they'd dealt with each parent being gone and it being scary. That the truest versions of ourselves were when we were with them, and nothing in the world could ever stand in the way of that. Home wasn't a specific house, a specific place, but home was wherever the four of us would be. Shared experiences, shared love, that was a true home.

All of that out the window, because Ben had snuck up here first. The small, often funny, joys of parenting. This was what life was all about. Little moments every day that made all the hardship worth it. It was time to maximize these.

We merged through traffic, crossing the Potomac on the Woodrow Wilson bridge for the final time as Virginia residents. I glanced back over my shoulder, gazing down at the Old Town Alexandria Waterfront. The only place I ever wanted to call home as an adult. A place I would hold in my heart forever.

But now it was time for a new era, a new adventure. We needed to start afresh. And where better to do so than in the city we met?

A city of universities, steeped in the early history of the country I adopted as my own. Ben was to head up the exploratory committee for a gubernatorial campaign for Representative Moore. If she didn't go through with it, he would switch over into some state or local politics. With his CV, he would be snapped up fast. In the meantime, I already had a couple of leads. There were some who thought maybe Georgetown was too hasty in firing me. And what place would be better for my rehabilitation than Boston, a progressive city with a history and passion for righteous violence?

Ben and I planned it all out over a bottle of Montepulciano red. The twins would eventually get into Boston Latin School, the oldest school in the United States. We'd make a new life together, taking weekend trips to Concord, Newport, and the Cape.

Mikaela would stay in DC, for now at least. But she would be welcome anytime, and Ben and I would take turns traveling back down and helping when her new baby arrived. She and Elaine Iverson would stay in touch, and I had high hopes for their budding friendship.

I didn't know if I would ever see Francisco again. Maybe that was for the best. Our lives—our adult lives, anyway—should not overlap. For a short time, he had a chance here in the United States to stay, to once and for all leave the violence behind. But that was his world, and the throne my father left was exactly where he now belonged.

I glanced over my shoulder, looking into the past one last time. I locked that door in my mind. No longer would the specter of Alessandra Portillo hang over our heads.

With visions of clam chowder and a Dunkin on every corner, I grasped Ben's hand and looked forward toward the horizon.

Only forward.

Make sure to join our Discord
(https://discord.gg/aethon)
so you never miss a release!

THANK YOU FOR READING FACE THE STORM

We hope you enjoyed it as much as we enjoyed bringing it to you. We just wanted to take a moment to encourage you to review the book. Follow this link: **Face The Storm** to be directed to the book's Amazon product page to leave your review.

Every review helps further the author's reach and, ultimately, helps them continue writing fantastic books for us all to enjoy.

For more information on Matthew Becker's books, check out his website: www.matthewbeckerbooks.com.

ALSO BY MATTHEW:
RUN
DON'T LOOK DOWN
FACE THE STORM

Calling all thriller fans: be the first to discover groundbreaking new releases, access incredible deals, and participate in thrilling giveaways by subscribing to our exclusive Thriller Newsletter. https://aethonbooks.com/thriller-newsletter/

Want to discuss our books with other readers and even the authors?
JOIN THE AETHON DISCORD!

Facebook | Instagram | Twitter | Website

For all our Thrillers, visit our website at www.aethonbooks.com/thriller

ACKNOWLEDGMENTS

There are loads of people to thank for all their (structured or unstructured) help and guidance throughout, but I want to use this opportunity to thank you readers. If you're reading this, not only did you take a chance on a debut author's novel in the past year, but you stuck with me all the way to here as we told the entire story. Thank you from the bottom of my heart.

ABOUT THE AUTHOR

MATTHEW BECKER is a mathematician, and formerly worked as part of the national Covid-19 response. He has a doctorate in applied mathematics from the University of Maryland, College Park, and is published in the Bulletin of Mathematical Biology. Matthew currently lives with his wife, a U.S. diplomat, and their two children in Tashkent, Uzbekistan. Run is his first novel.

Made in the USA
Columbia, SC
25 June 2025

59857509R00250